His eyes were soft and his lips slightly parted.

He stroked her cheek with his thumb as his fingers slipped behind her head, drawing her towards him. He was going to kiss her. And she intended to let him.

Roger's mouth sought hers. Lucy tilted her head until it was within reach. His kiss was eager, his lips hungry for hers. The scent of him flooded her limbs...the taste of him made her grow weak. She gave herself over to the pleasure, allowing him to guide her in pace and pressure until her head spun.

Roger broke away first. He held her gaze in a moment of stillness. The world contained only them.

'After I won I started thinking about my future—and yours. You don't have to live the way you do. There is another way.'

He pushed a lock of hair behind Lucy's ear in a gesture that was at once intimate yet proprietorial. He smiled.

'I want you to become my mistress.'

D0611032

Author Note

We first met Roger Danby in *The Blacksmith's Wife*, which ended with the disreputable knight heading to York for one last tournament and then planning to go abroad, determined to make his fortune after realising too late the value of the woman he had spurned. His story was going to end there, but readers kept telling me that they wanted to know what had happened to him. I too became curious to see how this knight who had jousting 'groupies'—to use a slightly anachronistic term—dropping at his feet coped when he didn't have his flashy armour, his fine horse and his noble connections to tempt them.

Brewing was once a female task, with many women making a living as ale-wives, selling from their houses. When I wrote my undergraduate dissertation on 'The Changing Role of Inns and Ale houses in English Rural Society' I never suspected I would get to use the information for writing a book!

Lucy brews so frequently because back then beer and ale—there is a difference—did not last. An anonymous source from Saxon times wrote: 'After two days only the bravest or silliest men of the village would drink the ale, but usually it was only fit for pigs.' I planned to brew some myself, but decided against it—partly because I suspected I'd end up very drunk or very ill, and partly because an acquaintance told me I'd need a much bigger bucket!

As always, this story has a theme song. Roger chose 'I Would Do Anything for Love (But I Won't Do That)' by Meat Loaf.

REDEEMING THE ROGUE KNIGHT

Elisabeth Hobbes

Published in Great Britain 2017
by Mills & Boon, an imprint of HarperCollins*Publishers*
1 London Bridge Street, London, SE1 9GF

© 2017 Claire Lackford

ISBN: 978-0-263-92603-3

Printed and bound in Spain
by CPI, Barcelona

Elisabeth Hobbes grew up in York, where she spent most of her teenage years wandering around the city looking for a handsome Roman or Viking to sweep her off her feet. Elisabeth's hobbies include skiing, Arabic dance and fencing—none of which has made it into a story yet. When she isn't writing she spends her time reading, and is a pro at cooking while holding a book! Elisabeth lives in Cheshire with her husband, two children, and three cats with ridiculous names.

Books by Elisabeth Hobbes

Mills & Boon Historical Romance

Falling for Her Captor
A Wager for the Widow
The Saxon Outlaw's Revenge

Linked by character

The Blacksmith's Wife
Redeeming the Rogue Knight

Visit the Author Profile page at millsandboon.co.uk.

To Mark, housebreaker and hacksaw wielder
for damsels in distress!
I owe you a pint!

Chapter One

'Wake up, my lord! We have to leave!'

Urgent shouts infiltrated Roger Danby's dreams, whirling him from the home of his childhood on the heather-covered moors to the battlefields of France. The carnage there came almost as a relief.

He'd been dreaming of Yorkshire again, as he had done nightly since returning to England: the endless, purple moors and deep valleys that he had not seen for almost four years. The people from his past were present, too, which invariably caused Roger's dreams to darken. Even though he was somehow aware he was dreaming, his stomach twisted with loss. He wondered if they thought of him as often as he had thought of them and if his name was ever mentioned within the pink stone walls of his father's house.

Someone was still calling his name and a

dying archer was tugging at the neck of his cloak. He waved his arms to fend off the man, but the tugging continued. The shouts were not part of the dream and when he opened his eyes it was his squire, Thomas, looming over him, hands on Roger's bare shoulder.

The young man's eyes were wide and his hair was unkempt. Thomas had fought beside Roger in France so his presence on the battlefield in Roger's dream was unsurprising, but it took a moment for Roger to shake his dream completely and return to the comfy bed in the manor house of a Derbyshire nobleman, so strange after months of straw pallets or bare ground.

'My lord, please. We need to leave,' Thomas repeated.

Dreaming of home always left Roger's nerves as tightly strung as a bow. He glared up at Thomas in confusion and irritation from the feather mattress. Soft light peered around the edge of the tapestries covering the window. His breath made a cloud in the cold room.

'Did I oversleep?'

'No, it's early.'

Roger threw himself back with a groan. They had stayed three nights with Lord Harpur at Bukestone and had planned to leave in the morning, but Roger had not intended to start so early. The maidservant who had been his companion the previous night rolled on to her side, still fast asleep. Her bare buttocks rubbed against Roger's hip as she shifted her position and sent small throbs of pleasure through him. He reached for the wine flagon by his side, but found it empty.

'It's barely daybreak,' he growled. 'What's the hurry?'

Thomas was already lurching around the small chamber, gathering possessions and stuffing them into his saddlebag. He threw Roger's boots and cloak at the foot of the bed.

'Lady Harpur decided to pay her daughter a visit early this morning,' Thomas muttered. His face took on a pinched expression, his cheeks turning pale beneath his wispy beard. 'She discovered Katherine was not alone in her room and hadn't been all night.'

Roger swore. Katherine Harpur was a maid of sixteen with her mother's fine, pale skin and her father's dark curly hair. She was a fruit ripe for picking, but Roger had put the flirtation he'd seen pass between her and Thomas as nothing to concern himself about. Apparently he was wrong. He pushed himself from beneath the covers. The cold blast of air served to wake him fully, but even if the room had been comfortably warm his

soldier's instincts made him alert to the sudden
danger they were both in.

'You bloody young fool! Lord Harpur has
every right to cut you down where you stand and
I've half a mind to let him get on with it.'

Thomas's round face twisted in panic and
Roger was reminded of how young his companion
was. Despite having survived the battlefields of
Europe, the thought of death clearly terrified him.
Thomas had not yet reached his nineteenth year
and if he continued to act so recklessly would be
unlikely to do so, Roger thought with the disdain
that ten years' seniority granted him. If Thomas
was old enough to stick his staff into a willing
woman, he was old enough to bear the consequences of unwise decisions.

'How long ago were you discovered?'

'I ran straight back here,' Thomas said miser-
ably. 'Katherine was entreating her mother not
to go straight to Lord Harpur, but I do not know
how successful she will be.'

That bought them some time. If luck were on
their side they would be gone from the house before the incensed father came searching for them.

'I hid behind the door and slipped out before
my face was seen. Lady Harpur might not know
it was me.'

Thomas sounded hopeful. Roger turned away

so Thomas did not see the irritation on his face. How many dark-haired visitors were staying in Lord Harpur's house?

Two, he reminded himself, scratching at the beard that covered his own face. With luck, Katherine Harpur would confirm with which of the two men she had been indiscreet and Roger would not be put forward as a culprit. The urge to knock some sense into Thomas filled him, but recriminations and reprimands could wait for later. A quick departure was paramount. Their mission could not be jeopardised by something so trivial, not when it was Roger's chance to make the fortune he craved.

He pulled on his linen braies, woollen breeches and tunic, casting a regretful glance at his own bed companion. He'd hoped for another tumble with her before they parted. Thomas deserved a clout around the head for that, if nothing else. Ah well, there would be another bed before long, and no doubt someone else to warm it. This way had the advantage of no tearful farewells from a girl who had hoped he would stay longer than he intended. Roger tossed a farthing on to the pillow where the girl would see it on waking. He tied his scrip with his last farthing and penny to his belt.

Thomas had gathered the leather bags containing all their possessions, including the fuller bag of money Roger had hidden rolled in his spare linens. Roger finished dressing rapidly in his thickly padded jerkin and travelling cloak and reached for his sword. He cast a final look around the room in case they had forgotten anything before leading the way to the kitchens where he knew there was a door that would be unguarded. Making friends with the maidservant was proving to have a benefit he had not anticipated and they were able to creep out without being spotted and make their way to the stables.

In silence, they wrapped sacking around their horses' hooves and shouldered their saddles. The animals snickered in protest at the early start and Roger paused to run his hand across the rough winter coat of the chestnut courser. They led their mounts around the edge of the courtyard. Fortune was on their side as they passed through the gateway without notice.

They saddled the horses, stowed their bags and mounted. Their breath hung in the frosty morning air, but gathering clouds promised the day would be warmer and wet. The horses were not warmed through and to push them beyond a canter would do no good.

When they came to the fork in the road, Roger turned right.

'This is the wrong direction, my lord. We came this way when we arrived.'

Suppressing his annoyance, Roger nodded. 'Lord Harpur knows we are heading into Cheshire. If he decides to pursue us that's where he will go, so we are going in the other direction. Now ride!'

They stopped when Roger's stomach began to growl, dismounted and led their horses into the shelter of the trees. The rain had begun in earnest and the two men pulled their oiled wool cloaks around themselves for warmth.

As soon as they were settled Roger cuffed Thomas around the ear. The younger man yelped.

'What did you think you were playing at?' Roger demanded. 'I know we've been out of civilised company for months—and perhaps in your case you have never been in it—but the general rule is if you're going to bed one of the household, don't pick the finest jewel of the lord's treasure chest.'

'We didn't…make love.' Thomas flushed scarlet. 'We did nothing wrong. We only lay beside each other and talked through the night.'

Roger laughed. 'You wasted your time and caused trouble for nothing! What's a woman for besides swiving? If you're going to risk getting your throat slit or your bollocks hacked off by an angry father, at least make sure you get your end away first.'

Thomas stuck his lower lip out sullenly. 'Katherine and I are in love.'

Roger guffawed.

'After three days in her company! Don't fool yourself, lad. You may tell yourself—or better still the wench—that it's love, but don't confuse the twitch in your braies for the thump of your heart.'

Thomas flushed red. Roger leaned back against a tree and chewed his thumbnail, his anger subsiding now they were clear of Lord Harpur's lands. He knew well the hot fire that riddled a man's limbs and refused to be ignored, so his next words were spoken more gently.

'Balance the pleasure gained with the trouble caused. I don't blame you for responding to your pole, but you can't let it rule you.'

Hypocrite, a small voice in his mind shouted. His own had led him into trouble often enough.

'Not at the moment, when we've got work to do,' he clarified. 'Once we've delivered our message you can sard as many women as you like. You'll be rich enough to pay for the best.'

'And what if I don't want to pay?' Thomas mumbled. 'What if I want to marry?'

Roger felt his jaw tighten. 'Then hope the girl's

father thinks you've got enough in your pockets to warrant handing over his treasure and don't leave it too long to decide she's the one you want.'

'Is that what you plan to do?' Thomas asked.

Roger thought of Jane de Monsort, the woman he had briefly been betrothed to before her father decided Roger's pockets were not full enough. Thanks to a stint in the newly formed Northern Company fighting as a mercenary, they were fuller now.

'I have to marry eventually. I'll find a dutiful, dull girl with good connections and a little wealth who can give me an heir to appease my father.' He scratched his belly. 'I can't say it appeals.'

Thomas was silent, perhaps thinking of Katherine Harpur. Another face filled Roger's memory, one that caused deeper pangs of regret even years after he had last seen her. He had been fond of Joanna, his brother's wife, but had not realised quite how deeply until it had been too late. He concentrated on the pattern of raindrops falling into the puddles that were forming rather than let his mind drift back to the mistakes he had buried in his past.

'Much better to stick to tavern wenches who will give you what you want in return for a ribbon or a kind word,' he commented, to no one in particular.

'Do you think Lord Harpur will send men to fight in France?' Thomas asked.

Roger stretched out his legs, glad of something fresh to think of. He uncorked a wine flask and drank deeply.

'We don't get our bounty otherwise, but I don't see why not. Leaving aside you seducing his daughter, he was interested in the thought of increasing his fortune. The peace won't last forever, and a man prepared to fight is a man who will become rich.'

A man such as himself.

Roger drew his cloak tighter around him.

'We're going to stay here until the sun has passed overhead. Then we'll head back the way we came.'

'Past Lord Harpur's house instead of the higher road to Mattonfield?'

The roads that bordered Lord Harpur's estate gave it the shape of a triangle with sides of uneven length. To take the route Thomas suggested would mean they travelled on the longest side and over the steepest edge of the hill.

'Yes. It would add more than a day to the journey if we took the other side of the hill.'

'We'd be close to my home!' Thomas said wistfully. 'It's a fine inn, the grandest on the road to

Mattonfield, and my father would welcome us gladly.'

Roger considered the possible routes. There was hope in the lad's voice, but Roger was damned if he was going to detour to allow Thomas to pay a call, however tempting a night at an inn sounded.

'No. I want to be done here as quickly as possible.' He stared moodily at the ground, Thomas's mention of home raising an unwelcome thought. 'I should visit my father before I return to France.'

Thomas looked startled by the dark tone his voice had taken on.

'Don't you want to see your family?'

Roger took another drink to delay answering the question that had troubled him since he stepped back on to English soil. Finally he spoke.

'It's been a long time. I parted angrily with my brother and I vowed not to return until I was rich and had proved myself. At least that is within my reach now. Let's get some rest.'

He closed his eyes and settled back. The day had started far too rudely.

The weather had worsened into driving rain by afternoon. Iron clouds rolled across a steel sky as they climbed the hills into Cheshire. Early spring in England was truly appalling and Thomas looked more miserable with every twist of the road, glancing behind him and pulling his cloak forward to envelop him.

'Of all the reasons that compel me to return to France, this weather might be the greatest,' Roger called.

Thomas merely shivered and glanced around moodily. They passed the turning for Lord Harpur's manor without encountering any hindrance and as they skirted round the far side of the densely forested hills Roger began to believe his plan had worked. Tension he had not known he was carrying began to melt from his shoulders and he slowed his horse to a walk, rolling his head around to ease the knots.

It was probably this slowing that saved their lives, because as they reached the brow of the hill Thomas gave a cry of alarm. The road ahead curved downward, then sharply snaked left around a pool. Just beyond the bend three riders were waiting. If Roger and Thomas had ridden a few paces further the men would have been hidden from view until they rode straight into them.

The men could have been ordinary travellers, but they lingered at the edge of the road in a manner suggesting they were planning trouble.

'I think we've been found,' Roger muttered.

Thomas let out a moan. 'Lord Harpur's men?'

'Probably,' Roger muttered. That was the simplest answer and the most welcome. The suspicion they might have been followed from France by men intent on preventing him completing his commission for the King had crossed his mind once or twice since setting foot back in England. Roger felt for his sword, wishing he had a lance to hand. He'd ended more lives with his preferred weapon than he cared to count.

'We can't fight them,' Thomas whimpered.

He was right. Three men against two was not good odds. Roger stared around him. The road was crossing the highest point as it circumnavigated the forest and night would soon be upon them. Taking the easier road had been a mistake after all. In the distance beyond the forest, Roger could see lights coming from different villages and a large cluster that must be the town where both roads joined.

'We'll cut through the forest and try to reach the other road,' Roger decided, wishing he had taken that route in the first place. Cross-country in the near darkness was risky, but better than riding straight into trouble. 'If we can reach one of those settlements, we may be able to hide.'

A shout echoed in the silence of the hills. One of the prospective ambushers pointed towards them. Roger cursed his stupidity. He'd been so intent on watching the men ahead he had given no thought to their own visibility; on the hilltop they would have been in clear view. Already the horsemen were riding towards them.

Roger plunged through the trees away from the path. Thomas followed. They rode fast into the darkness, pushing their horses as hard as the forest would allow. For the first time since returning to England, Roger was thankful it was early spring. A few months more and the undergrowth would have grown up, making it impossible to ride quickly.

A quick glance behind reassured Roger they had not been followed, but he had not accounted for being intercepted ahead. One horseman appeared seemingly from nowhere to their right. His head was down and he rode directly at them, his cloak obscuring his face.

Roger swung around in the saddle, reaching for his sword, but before he could draw it something punched him in the back of his right shoulder, sharp and cold and forcing the breath from him. He had been stabbed in the leg once during a brawl over a whore in a French inn and the sensation was familiar. There was no real pain yet, but he knew from experience that would follow shortly. He looked down to discover the barb of an arrow protruding from below his collarbone close to his armpit.

Arrows! Roger hadn't anticipated that! He gave a laugh that ended as a grunt as pain began to spread through him like ripples across a pond when a rock was hurled into the depths.

They were in real danger now. The bowman was fumbling behind in his quiver, but on horseback and amongst trees he was struggling.

'Give me your sword,' Roger barked at Thomas.

The boy passed his weapon, but the strength was already going from Roger's arm. He took the sword in his left hand and wheeled around, slashing behind him blindly. He felt the sword make contact. The bowman gave an unearthly, wordless gurgle. Roger looked and saw to his disgust that he had caught the rider full in the throat. The man fell forward over the horse's neck. Roger retched and leaned across to slap the horse with the flat of the blade. It whinnied in fear and pain and galloped away with its rider still in the saddle. He dug his heels into his own mount's flanks.

'Come on,' he grunted at Thomas, riding in the opposite direction the horse had taken. There was no time to think where they were heading now, but he rode towards what he hoped was the smaller of the villages. The other two men would not be far behind, but he hoped they would follow their comrade in confusion.

Roger's head was spinning and his arm felt like ice by the time they reached the depths of the woods. His fingers refused to grip the reins and he knew he was becoming drowsy. He bit his lip, the small pain sharpening his senses as the greater one dulled it. Instinctively Roger reached for the arrow, but stopped. Without examining the shape of the tip he did not know whether to pull back or forward. At the moment there was little blood, but he had seen what happened when such wounds were treated. Now was not the time to deal with his injury. He did not think they had been followed so finding refuge was the priority.

He heard splashing and realised they had reached a shallow river and were halfway into the water. On the furthest bank, the trees began to thin. A single light flickered in the darkness, so briefly that he thought he had imagined it.

'Can you find your home? Will it be safe refuge?'

'I think so. I hope so,' Thomas answered.

'Get me there,' Roger ordered. They were his last words as he slumped forward in the saddle. He dimly saw Thomas dismount and take both reins. Roger closed his eyes. His last thought was that if he died tonight he would at least be spared from making the decision to return to Yorkshire and face his family.

The chickens were safely shut away for the night. Any fox that hoped to help himself would find he was out of luck. Lucy Carew picked up the lantern from the ground and made her way round the side of the brewing shed towards the door of the inn, swinging the light back and forth to light the path.

She dropped the bar across the door. Shivering as a draught blew through the rip in the linen window covering, Lucy hung her cloak beside the door. The fire was almost spent. She gave the solitary log a vigorous prod with the poker and sank on to the stool beside the hearth. The rain had eased, but the earlier downpour had meant no passing customers had called since mid-afternoon. Lucy took her cap off and let her hair fall loose from its plait.

A hammering on the door made her jump. She was halfway to her feet when she caught herself and sat back down. She badly needed the money that customers would pay for their drinks, but her head ached and several tasks remained before she could retire to bed.

Apart from the lantern and the glow from the fire, the inn was in darkness. If she sat quietly they would leave. She felt a pang of sympathy for whoever was about in the bad weather, but not enough to rouse herself and let them in.

The hammering grew louder and more insistent. It was not going to cease.

A male voice bellowed, 'I know someone is there. I saw your light.'

Lucy pushed herself from the stool. Clutching the poker behind her, she eased up the latch and pulled the door open a crack. It was pushed open with unexpected violence from outside, causing her to spring out of the way with a gasp of alarm.

Two men pushed their way inside. One had his arm slung around the other's shoulder and was being supported. He staggered as he walked, moaning softly, and his tangled black hair obscured his face. The second man's head was bowed under the strain of bearing his companion who was taller and broader.

Lucy gritted her teeth.

'I don't want drunks at this time of night.'

'He isn't drunk, he's hurt,' the supporting man wheezed. He raised his head and Lucy gave a cry of surprise at the face she had not seen since he declared his intention to fight with King Edward's army in France.

'Thomas? Is it really you?'

Lucy started forward, but her brother drew a short sword from beneath his cloak and brandished it. Lucy gave a squeak of alarm at the sight of her younger brother with such a fierce expression which ill suited his kind face. Thomas was an amiable dolt and to see him acting so fiercely was disconcerting. She clutched the poker firmly in her hand and retreated to the bottom of the staircase.

The man she had taken for a drunk now raised his head, which had been lolling to one side. He gave a wolfish grin beneath his thick beard, but it was his eyes that transfixed Lucy. Brown as walnuts and studying her with such intensity that a sensation stirred inside her she had not felt in longer than she could remember. She felt a blush begin deep between her breasts that was only prevented from spreading by the dawning realisation that her admirer's gaze was so intense because he was struggling to focus.

'What happened?'

'Ambush,' the injured man slurred. 'Don't fear, little dove. We won't hurt you. *If* you do what we ask.'

'Are you alone?' Thomas raised his sword again and stepped towards Lucy, dragging his companion with him. 'Has anyone else come this evening?'

'No one,' Lucy answered, sweat pooling in her lower back at the sight of the weapon. 'I'm the only one here.'

Except for Robbie. A throb of anxiety welled inside her as she thought of her son lying peacefully in his cot in the room above. A son whose uncle did not know of his existence.

'Thomas, what is happening?' she hissed. 'You

left four years ago. Why are you here and who is this?'

'I've been in France, fighting with the Northern Company.'

Lucy gaped. 'A mercenary? You?'

'Why are you here?' Thomas asked. 'Where is Father and why is the inn in darkness so early?'

Lucy dropped her head. When Thomas had lived here the inn was always busy and open late. Now was not the time to explain why it had changed so greatly. 'I came back…to nurse Father. Thomas, Father died almost a year ago,' she whispered. 'I didn't know how to contact you.'

Thomas shook his head, his eyes filling with grief.

'No! Oh, bad tidings, Sister.'

Lucy's heart twisted. This was not the way a son should learn such news. Thomas would regret their father's passing more than she did. But then Thomas had never suffered the consequences of having disappointed him as greatly as Lucy had.

The man groaned. Thomas glanced at him. 'Tell me more later, but now we need to take him upstairs to a bed.'

Lucy took a step back, shaking her head. Not to the floor where Robbie slept in peace, blissfully unaware of the drama happening beneath him.

She barred the way, finally revealing her poker and brandishing it like a sword.

'Come, little dove,' the injured man slurred, grinning crookedly. 'Be sensible and we all might live.'

Lurching forward unexpectedly, he raised his left arm and knocked it out of her hand. He staggered, as if this had taken the last of his strength, and fell forward towards her. Instinctively Lucy reached her arms out to catch him, her hands sliding beneath his armpits. She stepped backwards and found herself wedged between him and the wall, his weight crushing her. She yelped in pain as something sharp scratched her left shoulder through her thick wool dress. She looked down to see the head of an arrow protruding from the man's right shoulder.

'He's really hurt!' she exclaimed.

'Don't let me die unmourned, dove,' the man slurred, his voice deep and husky.

Before Lucy could think how to reply he had reached his left arm to the back of her head, tilted it back and covered her lips with his.

Chapter Two

The kiss took Lucy by surprise, the rough beard scratching at her cheek and lips teasingly, sending shivers through her. His mouth enclosed hers, his lips firm and his tongue seeking hers with a fierceness that left her weak. Her mind emptied as desire lurched in her belly and without intending to she was kissing him back. If he could kiss like this when close to death, what would his touch be like when at full strength?

She came to her senses almost immediately and jerked her head away. His mouth followed, greedily seeking her out again, and his good hand slid from her neck down her body, fumbling at her breast.

A kiss she could tolerate, but the groping was too much. Outrage surged inside Lucy and now she had her wits about her. He was not the first of her customers who had tried to force attentions on her and was likely not to be the last. Injured or not made no difference. She twisted her leg until it was between his and brought her knee sharply upward.

The man gave a whimper of pain and crumpled on to her, his eyes rolling back in his head. He went limp and Lucy realised, aghast, that he was close to passing out. Her hand shifted against his back and touched feathers. The fletch of the arrow was sticking out. Guilt swept over her that she had done such a thing to a wounded man. She bit her remorse down. She had not asked for her home to be invaded, or to be kissed. He had brought it on himself.

She supported him as best as she could, but he was a tall man and broad with it, and was crushing the breath from her as she leaned against the wall. Even by the feeble light of the fire, the man looked as pale as a wraith with a waxy sheen to his brow. His hair was matted to his cheeks. He must have bled from his wound, but against the darkness of his cloak it was impossible to tell.

'I'm sorry,' she murmured, reaching to brush the hair from his face. His forehead was cold to the touch and her fingers came away damp with his sweat. He opened his eyes.

'Do you have wine? Anything stronger?' he moaned.

'Enough of this!' Thomas cried. He wrinkled his nose in disgust, reminding Lucy he had always been as prudish as a monk when it came to shows of physical affection. 'Get him upstairs before you do him any more harm. We may not have much time.'

He pulled the injured man off Lucy. Lucy ran to get the lantern, thrusting the poker back into the fire where she could find it later if needed.

'Bring wine,' the injured man growled.

Lucy ran to the counter where the flagons and cups were stored and found what he had requested. Carrying a bottle in each hand and the lantern hooked over her arm, she followed as her brother half dragged the injured man up the narrow staircase.

The first floor was low ceilinged and dark. Lucy's room took one half of the space, though it was filled with all manner of boxes and piles of unused or unusable objects she could not bear to throw away. The second room contained pallets for travellers who wished to spend the night, but until the better weather arrived the frames were piled up and the straw mattresses wrapped in oilcloth as prevention against vermin. It was this room that Lucy intended to take the two men into, but Thomas entered the bedroom that had once been their father's and where Lucy now slept.

She opened her mouth to protest, but decided it was better to make no arguments and hope that Thomas would explain before long.

Robbie's cradle was pushed into the far corner and he slept silently, mercifully not stirring as they entered. Lucy did not dare look directly at him, fearing she would alert the men to his existence, but they were more intent on reaching Lucy's bed beneath the small window.

'Lay me down and give me a drink,' the injured man mumbled. He appeared to be drifting in and out of consciousness. Lucy wondered how much blood he had lost.

They lowered him on to the bed, pushing the blankets to one side and edging him over so that his shoulder was hanging over the furthest edge of the frame with the fletch of the arrow free from the mattress. Thomas pulled the injured man's boots off and placed them at the side of the bed. Lucy held out the bottle of wine and he tipped it back, drinking deeply until it was half-empty. He put it on the floor and fumbled with his left hand to unclasp the buckle of his cloak. His fingers were clumsy and he let loose a string of expletives.

'Help me get this off,' he commanded.

Thomas began to fumble at his neck, but the man pushed his hand aside.

'Not you, Thomas. You go tend to the horses.
Dove, you can do it.'

Lucy knelt by the bed and tried to do as he
asked, but when she attempted to ease the cloak
from his back, it stuck fast around the shaft of the
arrow. The man gave a gasp of pain as she tugged.
Lucy let go, realising the arrow had gone through
all the layers of clothing. Something moved in the
corner of her eye. Thomas was pointing a dagger
at her face. His hand shook and the expression of
fear in his eyes made him almost unrecognisable.

'Cut it free,' Thomas said, pushing the dagger
into her hand. 'Remove all the clothing you can.
When I return, we remove the arrow.'

'Where are you going?' she asked, alarmed
at the prospect of being left alone with the man
who had earlier appeared intent on violating her.
The word *we* did not give her any comfort, either.

'You heard what he said. I must hide our horses.
We are being hunted. I'll explain properly later.'
Thomas gazed around frantically as if expecting
assailants to appear from the wooden chest at the
foot of the bed or behind the open door. He lumbered out, pulling the door shut.

'What is this place called?'

The man on the bed had spoken, his voice
rough and rasping. Lucy jumped in surprise.
She looked at him more closely. His cheeks had

a touch of colour beneath the mass of beard and his eyes were brighter. Lying down and filling himself with wine seemed to have rallied his spirits and returned some of his vitality.

'It has no name,' Lucy answered.

The man gave a wheezing laugh. 'A nameless inn. Perfect for a nameless man such as me. Does its mistress have one or are you equally anonymous, dove?'

'Lucy Carew is my name,' she answered reluctantly.

'Carew! Sister of Thomas, or wife?'

'Sister,' Lucy answered, wondering what sort of man would kiss a woman who might be his friend's wife.

'Give me more wine, Lucy Carew,' the injured man demanded, reaching for the bottle. Lucy picked it up, then paused before handing it over and took a sip herself. It did little to calm her nerves. The man drained the bottle, spilling a good measure down his face and neck. Lucy wrinkled her nose in disgust. Her mattress would reek of wine—though if it survived without blood being spilled on it that would be a wonder in itself. Gripping the dagger, she bent over the bed to do as she had been bidden. Her hands trembled and she hesitated, drawing her hand back from the cloth.

'Have you never undressed a man before?' the man asked with a leer.

'Never with a knife,' Lucy answered curtly.

He laughed.

'I thought a pretty dove who can kiss like you did must know her way around a bed.'

His voice was mocking and Lucy flushed with anger. Voices of condemnation pressed down on her, whispering names that set her cheeks aflame with shame. The voices were right though, weren't they? Otherwise why would her body have responded in the basest way possible to the uninvited touch of his lips?

She held his gaze, noticing his eyes were increasingly unfocused and the colour was leaving his cheeks once more. He would most likely pass out again, if not from his injury then from the wine he had drunk. She bent over to widen the hole around the arrow at the front and back. The evil-looking tip was crusted with blood, as was his clothing, and her stomach heaved.

The cloak was thick, but the dagger blade was sharp and it came away without too much work. She dropped it down between the bed and wall. Beneath the cloak the man wore a sleeveless padded jerkin, laced at the front. By some fortune the arrow had missed this, piercing his flesh where arm joined body, and the garment was intact. The jerkin was the colour of oak and the cloak was of good quality. Lucy wondered for the first time who he was. She unlaced the jerkin, aware all the time of the man's eyes upon her.

'You'll have to sit up to take this off.'

'You'll have to help me, Lucy Carew,' he slurred, raising an eyebrow.

He gave her the same grin that had made her stomach curl. Now alone on her bed with him she felt a stirring of anxiety. It had been a long time since a man had shared her bed and, even though he was not there for that purpose, the sight of him made her stomach twist. She weighed up the likelihood of him repeating what he had done downstairs and decided he looked incapable of much harm.

She sat on the edge of the bed and eased her hands beneath his armpits, pulling him forward until he sat upright with his face close to hers. He eased his left arm about her waist, holding tightly to support himself and tried to do the same with his right arm, but there was no strength in it. Lucy slipped her hands inside the front of the jerkin, acutely aware that her hands were running across the contours of his chest. He drew a breath as her fingers slipped across the bare flesh at his neck. He looked at her with an expression of hunger, tilting his head to one side and parting his lips as if he was preparing to kiss her once more. She hastily bent her head to better look at what she was doing, conscious of the heat rising to her face.

'You haven't asked my name, Lucy Carew,' he breathed as she pushed the jerkin over his shoulder.

'I don't care to know it,' she answered.

Together they contrived to remove the jerkin, easing one arm out, then twisting the fabric until it slid over the arrow. Once or twice it caught, jerking the shaft slightly. Each time it happened the man gave a guttural growl deep in his throat, the fingers of his left hand tightening on Lucy's waist. Now he was left with only a wool tunic.

'Cut it off,' he whispered, closing his eyes. 'I have others and I fear I cannot sit any longer.'

His grip on Lucy's waist slackened and she eased him back on the bed. Lucy made a long cut from the neck past the arrow and down to the hem of the tunic. She did the same along both sleeves and hacked away at the fabric until he lay naked to the waist. Lucy concentrated her gaze on his blood-encrusted wound. She didn't want to think what would happen when Thomas tried to remove the arrow. The idea of her own involvement made her stomach heave.

The man was sweating yet shivering violently, his chest rising with each uneven breath he drew. Removing the jerkin must have caused him agony, but beyond the growling he had made no complaint throughout. Gently Lucy pulled the blanket up to his neck, easing it over the arrow. His eyelids flickered, but did not open. He smiled and for the first time it was neither leering nor mocking and Lucy's lips curved in response. She reached for the second bottle—the one containing the spirits he had demanded—and lifted it to his lips.

His eyes opened and he frowned, blinking to focus on her.

'When Thomas returns…' He sighed and fell silent. He appeared to have lapsed once more into unconsciousness, or perhaps the amount of wine he had consumed had sent him into a stupor.

Lucy stood anxiously by the bed, waiting for the footfall on the stairs. Where would Thomas have concealed two horses? The barn where she brewed her ale would be too small, but she hoped he had not tried to force the door.

The room was silent so when Robbie stirred in his cot and gave a whimper it sounded as loud as a cockcrow at dawn. She glanced at the man in the bed to see if he had heard, but he showed no signs that he was aware of anything.

She crept to the cradle and patted her son's

head, smoothing down the dark curls and pressing a cool finger against the red spot on his cheek where his latest tooth was growing through. He opened one eye, yawned and closed it again, rolling on to his front with his mouth drooping open. Lucy knelt by his side and watched as he settled back into sleep, overwhelmed by the love that consumed her. Robbie would never know the crisis that had played out while he slept.

An intense annoyance at Thomas filled Lucy's entire being. He had left four years before with no plans beyond intending to seek his fortune as a soldier. There had been no word and no way of contacting him. Now he had returned with no explanation, bringing chaos with him. With luck he would leave again as soon as possible.

Thomas burst into the room, slamming the door back against the wall.

'Sir Roger, I am back.'

Slowly Lucy turned and stared at the man on the bed, recalling the fine clothing she had cut from him and the imperious manner in which he had commanded her, as if he was used to giving orders. Her stomach tightened with dread as she remembered the assault she had made on him. Cold sweat crept down her spine at the thought of what his retribution might be against the commoner who had dared oppose his attentions.

She had no time to dwell further on the revelation because the door slamming and Thomas's voice had woken Robbie, who gave a high-pitched, wordless wail. He pushed himself up, his tiny hands gripping the edge of the cradle as he attempted his recently discovered trick of climbing out and making his way to Lucy's bed half-asleep.

'A child?' Sir Roger roused himself, craning his head to follow the sound.

'My son.'

'You have a son? Where is his father?' Thomas looked at Lucy, his eyes wide with astonishment and outrage. 'You said you were alone here.'

Lucy lifted her chin and glared at the men. She had done enough explaining and apologising since Robbie's birth almost two years previously and the shame that had once weighed heavy on her shoulders had dulled into a low throb in her belly. Nobleman or not, she had no intention of justifying her son's existence to a stranger. Come to that, Thomas could wait for his explanation, too.

'He doesn't have a father,' she replied curtly. 'I *am* alone.'

'Good, I want no disturbance,' Sir Roger grunted from the bed. Thomas merely glared at her, scandalised.

Lucy picked up Robbie from the cradle and hugged him tightly to her breast, making soothing noises.

'Put the brat down and come over here,' Sir Roger instructed loudly. 'You're going to help Thomas before I become fully sober.'

Lucy kissed Robbie's forehead. He beat his fists against her shoulder and screamed louder, making his displeasure at being awoken known.

'Let me soothe him first,' Lucy said, jiggling up and down rhythmically.

'This is more important than his temper,' Sir Roger growled. 'I'm stuck through with an arrow and every moment wasted puts me one step closer to the grave!'

Arguably he was right, but Lucy bridled at his tone when the child was distressed.

'He isn't in a temper. He's been woken from sleep and his room is full of strangers who are shouting. He's confused and probably scared. On top of that he's cutting teeth.' She hugged him tighter and realised her hands were trembling. Robbie might be scared, but he was not alone in that. Now that something familiar from her life had intruded on the evening's dreamlike events, she was most definitely frightened.

'The quicker you put him back, the quieter he'll be,' Sir Roger insisted.

Lucy walked to the bed, still rocking Robbie against her chest, and stared down at him.

'You clearly know nothing about children.'

'Nor do I want to,' he retorted with distaste, eyeing Robbie's red face.

'It will be easier to lay him down if he's sleepy and calm,' Lucy insisted. 'Otherwise he'll scream for hours and be clambering half-asleep into your bed a dozen times during the night.'

Sir Roger looked horrified at the prospect. Lucy glared back until he grimaced.

'The dove has become a crow! Or perhaps an eagle defending her young. Do what you need to, but be speedy. And give me that bottle back. I need to dull the pain. Thomas, are you ready?'

Lucy gave Sir Roger the bottle, but instead of drinking it he splashed it on to his shoulder. He paled and swore, his chest lurching upward as the sharp liquor bathed the wound. Lucy winced in sympathy. The man was rude and crude, and whatever circumstance had led to him being shot was probably well deserved, but Lucy could not help but feel sorry at seeing him in such pain.

Thomas had been searching inside a large leather bag that he had brought inside with him. He crossed to Sir Roger and pushed a small bottle into his hand. Sir Roger took a swig. Thomas picked up the dagger Lucy had used and bent over the bed. He rolled Sir Roger on to his left side, straddled him and began to carve away at the shaft sticking through Sir Roger's back to pare the feathers away.

'Isn't that child asleep yet?' Sir Roger grumbled.

Lucy moved into the darkness to better settle Robbie. In a low voice she sang the song that usually settled him when she put him to bed and he yawned. She was surprised to hear the same tune whistled from across the room and stopped. Sir Roger was waving his left arm over the edge of the bed, his lips pursed.

'You can sing me to sleep, if you wish, dove.' He slapped his naked chest. 'Right here against my heart. Or anywhere else you wish to lay your lips.'

Lucy ignored him, but blushed. Half insensible and wounded, the man was still fixated on lovemaking. In full health she dreaded to think what he would be like. She hoped he would be gone before she had to discover it. She lowered Robbie into his cot with trembling arms.

Thomas dropped the fletch of the arrow to the floor.

'We will remove the arrow now,' Thomas muttered. He mimed pulling the head towards him. 'There will be blood that needs stemming. Fetch your poker from the fire.'

Sir Roger groaned and his left hand curled into a fist. For the first time he looked genuinely fearful rather than in pain or intent on seduction. 'Do what he says. And bring more wine while you're about it.'

Lucy glanced towards Robbie's cot. He was sleeping and would be no bother to the men. She ran down the stairs, heart in her mouth, hoping the poker would be heated enough for the purpose that turned her stomach to think of it.

Roger closed his eyes and listened to the rapid footsteps. The girl would be quick. She had already proven to be biddable when it came to doing what needed to be done. He clenched his fists. His left was strong, but his right curled limply and seemed reluctant to obey his commands. He lifted his hand to the wound and probed gingerly with his fingers. The blood had congealed and a crust had formed across his breast where it had trickled. He had lost less than he feared, but that would change when Thomas pulled the arrow free. He explored further, relieved to discover the arrow had missed bones, passing through the muscle between his arm and collarbone.

Roger's head swam with weariness and cold. He reached for the blanket, pulling it up to his neck once more. There was something important he needed to do. He could not lie here waiting for the girl to come back to his bed, however appealing she was with her hungry lips and wide blue-grey eyes, so like another pair and with an equally familiar expression.

'She looks on me with fear,' he murmured.

'Did you speak, Sir Roger?'

Roger opened one eye. Thomas was peering down at him, Thomas who had started the day with his ill-considered swiving. Curse him for bringing Lord Harpur's men upon them.

'This is your fault.' Was he speaking? His voice was deep and bold, not a husky whisper. 'It was you they wanted.'

Thomas fell to his knees. 'Forgive me. It was weakness. Madness! But I will make amends. I'll pay their due. Tell me what to do to right the wrong I have done.'

What had the lad done? Roger was finding it hard to think. He licked his lips. They tasted strangely bitter. He'd drunk something to ease his pain, but it had dulled his thoughts. Ah, yes. A woman was the cause of it all. They always were. Was it the wide-eyed girl in grey; the dove whose fingers had been cool against his aching muscles? No, she was someone else. Someone here.

'She's taking too long.'

He'd seen on the fields of France what lay

ahead for him once she returned with the heated iron and the longer she delayed the less his nerves would bear it.

'I'll go see,' Thomas replied.

'Can we trust her?' Roger reached for his arm.

'I think so. She won't betray her brother. My only family now!' Thomas sighed. 'Poor Lucy, she looked half out of her mind with terror.'

Clarity broke through the clouds surrounding Roger's mind. He clutched Thomas's arm. 'Is the message from King Edward safe?'

'In your saddlebag, still on your horse,' Thomas answered.

'Good. Hugh Calveley must receive the summons from His Majesty and send troops to France,' Roger cautioned Thomas.

If he did—and if he lived to claim his fee—Roger would be rich. He could return to Wharram and pour coins into his father's hands. Finally he would have the means to show he was a success.

He listened to the hammering of the blood in his veins. Through the fog of the wine and Thomas's drugs he understood the noise was not within his head. Someone was beating at the door of the inn and there was nothing to stop the girl admitting whoever was knocking.

'Go,' he instructed Thomas. He let go his grip, his mind struggling to remain clear. 'Take your sword. Leave without me if you must. King Edward's message must be delivered, without me if necessary.'

He tried to keep his eyes open as Thomas left the room, but he found it impossible. Unable to fight the demands of his body, he slipped into unconsciousness.

Chapter Three

The embers of the fire glowed a dull red and gave off little heat. It did not seem possible it would be fierce enough to heat the poker to the required temperature to seal the wound. Though she really could not spare the wood, Lucy added a little kindling along with a handful of old rush stalks from the floor to wake the flames a little. She buried the poker deep, causing sparks to fly on to the floor. She stamped them out urgently before they caused the rushes to catch, letting the floor bear the brunt of her anxiety.

Lucy put two knives on the countertop, thinking they might be useful. She slid on to the stool beside the hearth and closed her eyes, her legs feeling hollow as straw as she imagined the additional pain the poker would cause when the iron tip seared Sir Roger's flesh. The sooner she returned with the poker, the sooner the deed would be done and the men would be on their way.

She knew it was a comforting lie. Even assuming Thomas was not home to stay, the injured man would not be going anywhere until morning. He must be close to reaching the limits of endurance now and a wave of sympathy rippled through Lucy. Leaving aside his continual innuendo, she decided on balance she would rather he lived than leave her with his corpse and an agitated brother.

She pushed herself from the stool and began to hunt in the cupboard beneath the counter for the bottle of eye-wateringly strong spirit her father had kept for when the canker in his gut ached him beyond endurance. She also found a clay pot of powdered pain-killing draught that she had bought from the surgeon in Mattonfield.

Bought! Her nose wrinkled at the description of the transaction. No money had exchanged hands, but she had paid for it dearly, indeed. Mixed together, the brew always sent her father into a deep sleep in which he would experience much less pain and from which Lucy could gain an afternoon of peace from his continual censure of her for producing a baseborn child. Sir Roger would no doubt benefit from the same remedy and Lucy would appreciate the silence.

She had her head beneath the counter, feeling her way in the near blackness when three loud thumps on the door made her jump in alarm and she banged her temple sharply on the edge of the counter. Dazed, she sat on the floor and was hidden from view when Thomas appeared from the floor above.

'Where are you, Lucy?' he muttered, his voice low and urgent, and laden with anxiety. He raised his sword before him. 'Show yourself quickly.'

His voice was unexpectedly vicious. Whatever he had done in four years had given him a tough attitude, but Lucy could see the desperation in his eyes. She raised a hand to her forehead, which felt tender from the bump. She stood and placed the bottle on top of the counter alongside her two knives.

'I was finding…' she began, but Thomas silenced her with a hiss and a wave of his hand. He held his finger to his lips. Lucy gestured at the bottle and he relaxed his stance. The beating on the door started again. Lucy started towards it, but Thomas stepped in front of her, seizing her upper arm.

'They must not come in,' Thomas muttered. 'Keep silent. Perhaps they'll go of their own accord.'

'Who are they?' Lucy whispered, her blood chilling at his words. 'Why are they looking for you?'

Thomas looked shiftily from side to side.

'I have done everything you asked,' Lucy reminded him. She folded her arms and gave him the look she used on Robbie when she caught him pulling the kitchen cat's tail. 'You appear here with no explanation or warning and throw me into something I don't understand. Why has my home been invaded?'

'It's my home, too,' Thomas muttered.

Lucy placed her hands on her hips and glared. 'A home I've been keeping while you were off doing goodness knows what!' A thought occurred to her. 'Is this to do with your Northern Company?'

'No!' Thomas protested. He bowed his head. 'We were staying with a nobleman not far from here. It was Sir Roger's fault. He offended our host.'

'What did he do? Tell me or I will call out right now.'

'He seduced Lord Harpur's daughter,' Thomas admitted with an odd expression on his face.

Lucy folded her arms tighter as surprise coursed through her. To hear that hated name from Thomas's lips! He couldn't know her connection to the nobleman.

At the same time, her worries eased a little. They were not thieves evading capture. They had not murdered or committed treason, or any of the other crimes she had been imagining. From the little she had seen of Sir Roger's behaviour towards a woman, a seduction did not seem unsurprising and the tale had the ring of truth to it. Sir Roger was guilty of doing what any nobleman assumed was his right, but to trespass against John Harpur, then take refuge in Lucy's house was a cruel twist of fate. It struck her as far too funny and made her want to laugh: a deep eruption bubbling beneath her brittle surface that would most likely never cease if she allowed it to the surface.

The thumping on the door stopped abruptly. Perhaps the men had assumed the inn was deserted and gone. Lucy was uncertain whether or not to be relieved. She felt a pang of sympathy for cold, pinch-faced Katherine Harpur who would no doubt be suffering her father's cruel temper. She was mildly surprised that Sir Roger had found the mouse-like woman worth risking his neck over. The kiss he had pressed on Lucy—unwelcome though it had been—felt oddly diminished by the knowledge.

Nevertheless, she felt a delicious sense of spite that Lord Harpur had been shamed in such a way. If Katherine had been left with a child, would she, too, be cast out to starve?

She smiled at Thomas and reached for the bottle.

'Let's take this back to your friend. I think they're gone, but I promise I won't open the door. Lord Harpur is no friend to me.'

'Why?'

Thomas looked puzzled at her abrupt, and what must seem confusing, change of attitude, but she had no intention of revealing the reason behind it. That was her secret alone.

'That is no concern of yours.'

Thomas was not completely dull-witted; perhaps he would work the reason out for himself. Eventually.

Thomas lowered his sword. They were halfway to the stairs when a thump louder than before thundered around the room. The previous noises had sounded like fists on wood, but this had a more sinister tone. There was a second thump and the door hinges creaked, light bursting round the frame. Lord Harpur's men had found the means to try to force entry and the old door would not withstand them for long. She glared at Thomas in desperation.

'They'll break in. I can't refuse to answer it.'

Thomas glanced from the door to the stairs. He crossed the room, drawing his sword once more, and slipped into the shadows, crouching at the end of the counter where the door would conceal him once open. Lucy ran her hands through her hair, tangling it and pulling some of the fine, brown strands forward across her cheek. She unlaced the front of her kirtle and pulled at the neck, easing it low until more of her linen shift could be seen than was decent. She eased the neck of her shift down, too, dragging the cloth to one side. She rubbed her eyes to redden them. Taking a deep breath, she crossed to the door.

'Who is it?' she asked, pressing her hands on the wood and putting her lips close to the gap at the side of the frame. The door thumped once more, sending tremors running through her palms and up into her arms. She cried out in shock.

'Open up!' came a harsh voice. 'We mean you no harm. We are searching for fugitives.'

Thomas paled.

'That voice! Open it. But please, do not betray us,' he whispered.

He sounded terrified and Lucy ignored the unfair insinuation. She nodded.

Thomas hid beside the door, disguised amid the folds of Lucy's cloak. For the second time that night, she slowly drew the latch back, her hands trembling. She opened the door slightly and peered through the gap. Two men tried to look past her, one large enough he had to stoop to look at her. She wedged her foot against the door.

'I have seen no one all night.' She yawned and

brushed the hair from her eyes, frowning at them in confusion. 'You woke me from my bed.'

'It took long enough to rouse you,' the smaller man remarked. 'Let us in. One of them might be hurt. Perhaps both. They're dangerous men and we need to find them.'

'On whose authority?' Lucy asked.

'On our own,' rumbled the giant from deep within his hood. 'Let us in or we'll flay the skin from your back.'

Lucy opened the door wide, careful to conceal Thomas without hitting him and making the door bounce back. Still holding the door to prevent the men closing it, she beckoned them in. Her heart was in her throat as she watched them take in the sight of her inn, gazing all around the small room. Lucy stood silently, glad the only light was from the dying fire.

The men finally turned their attention to Lucy. One man, dark haired and swarthy, could not take his eyes from her. She smiled nervously, hoping he would treat her kindly. His companion, hulking, equally dark but beardless, was not so easily distracted.

'What's in there?' he asked, jerking his thumb towards the storeroom.

'It's where I keep the ale.' She tried to keep her voice level. 'Who are you searching for?'

The giant walked into the storeroom. His companion stayed with Lucy. She could hear the sound of boxes being moved and the lid lifted and dropped on the ale cask.

'We're hunting a pair of thieves and rogues,' the dark man answered, his black eyebrows coming together.

Neither man looked like someone in Lord Harpur's employ. Lucy wondered if Thomas had told the truth about why they were being hunted.

'They took something that they should not have,' the large man called from inside the storeroom. He emerged with a hunk of bread in his hand, chewing loudly. Lucy's eyes narrowed in anger that the man could talk of theft while helping himself to her bread.

'What did they take?'

'What it was doesn't concern you. They're thieves and killers.'

'Killers?' Lucy's scalp prickled. For all his new-found ferocity, she could not imagine Thomas cutting down anyone in cold blood. Sir Roger she knew nothing of, but her brief impression was that his mind seemed to focus entirely on seducing women and not on fighting, stealing or killing.

'No better than a dog in a bear pit. When we find them, the misbegotten curs are dead men.'

He made a slitting motion across his throat, then tossed the bread to his friend who snatched it from the air and tucked it into the front of his tunic, eyes still on Lucy.

'What's upstairs?'

'My bedchamber,' Lucy answered. She swallowed. If they asked outright if the men they were looking for were there she could not lie, but the mention of death set her legs trembling with terror. The men began to move to the stairs. Unless she prevented them, they would discover Sir Roger.

'Stop! You can't go up there!'

'Why not? What are you hiding?'

Lucy faltered, desperately trying to think of a reason. Perhaps it was the talk of Lord Harpur and his wife that put the idea into her head and she blurted out the first thing she could think of.

'My husband is up there asleep.'

The men paused and looked back suspiciously. Lucy hoped she had been the only one to hear Thomas's sharp intake of breath from behind the door. The men exchanged a glance, then looked back at Lucy, eyes raking over her. She drew her kirtle high to her neck as if ashamed of what they might see, whilst at the same time contriving to push her breasts together with her wrists so that the full mounds were visible where the fabric dipped. The smaller man was leering openly, his eyes following and lingering on the shadow between her breasts. Good. If he was looking there, he was forgetting to search the inn, or examine the space behind Lucy too closely.

'So it wasn't sleep that kept you from answering straight away.' The dark man laughed, finally raising his eyes to meet her face. 'Why was it you who came down rather than him?'

'My husband has a fearsome temper,' Lucy whispered. Tears sprang to her eyes as the composure she had somehow maintained throughout the evening began to crumble. She edged around the room to the bottom of the stairs so that the men had to turn to keep her in view, their backs to Thomas's hiding place.

'Please don't disturb him,' she entreated.

The large man loomed over at her. 'If I find you're lying...'

He raised a fist and Lucy flinched. He lowered it again and peered at her face closely, his thick fingers lifting the hair at her temple. She recalled the bump on her head and lifted her fingers to it. The mark must be red and the man's assumption was clear. Lucy looked at the floor, caring nothing that she had in one instant branded Sir Roger as the basest of husbands.

'We're going up anyway. You first.'

Almost in tears and unable to think of another way of preventing them, Lucy led them up the stairs. The men followed close behind her. She would be unable to warn Sir Roger, even if he had been in a position to defend himself. She stopped in the doorway. The oil in the lamp had burned almost to nothing and the room was in near darkness. Lucy hoped it would be enough to prevent the men recognising the occupant.

Sir Roger was lying where she had left him, the blanket tucked high beneath his chin and covering the arrow. He was unmoving and appeared asleep with his head lolling towards the window, though Lucy suspected he was unconscious. His right arm had dropped down the side of the bed and his left was tangled in his dark curls that spread across the pillow. Just in case he was conscious and pretending to be asleep, she spoke loudly, filling her voice with fear that she did not have to act.

'See, my husband is sleeping. Please, kind sirs, don't wake him. It will be the worse for me if you do.'

The smaller man sniffed deeply.

'Sleeping? I think not.'

Lucy's legs threatened to give way, but instead of pulling a sword and running them both through, the man gave a guffaw of laughter.

'I can smell the wine on him from this far away!'

Drunk. Of course! Why had she not thought of that? The blanket was sodden with wine, as was the occupant. Lucy slipped across the room and knelt by the bed, blocking Sir Roger from view. She gathered the empty bottles in her arms. Bowing her head over them as if ashamed at least gave her the opportunity to collect her thoughts. It was possible this might just work.

'You could be tricking us.' The giant sounded less certain now he was confronted with the scene before him. 'How do I know this is your husband?'

Lucy raised her head imploringly.

'Who else would he be? Please, leave us alone,' she begged. 'I cannot bear the shame if this becomes known. My husband is a good man, but he cannot help himself.'

She began to cry in earnest, the tears falling freely down her face as her fear and exhaustion threatened to overwhelm her. As she wept she leaned slightly forward, knowing that it would give the men a perfect view of her full breasts and hoping that would draw their attention from examining Sir Roger too closely.

'Lucy?' Sir Roger mumbled, lifting his left arm. He attempted to fumble for her, but merely succeeded in clouting her across the shoulder. It did not hurt, but Lucy sensed the opportunity for further proof of his abuse and gave a small cry.

'Just bring me my wine like the sweet, obedient dove you are. I need warming,' Sir Roger crooned. His voice was thick with the effects of the painkilling draught. She looked round at him. Shadows played over his face giving him a demonic—and hopefully unrecognisable—demeanour. A lustful grin spread across his lips, making his face glow with life despite the sweat beading on his forehead and the pallor of his flesh. 'Sweet one, my dove. I'll never hurt you.'

His words sent her stomach tumbling, until she recalled he had most likely said something similar to seduce Katherine Harpur into bed. Lucy clambered to her feet, deciding a change of tone was needed. Still standing in front of Sir Roger, she wiped her hands violently across her eyes and stared coldly at the two intruders.

'Are you satisfied?' she asked angrily. 'You see I am harbouring no rogues here. Is it enough I must parade my shame before strangers, or would you further question my integrity?'

The giant nodded slowly.

'I still don't like this,' muttered his companion. 'What is your husband called, mistress?'

Lucy opened her mouth. She could not call

him Roger and reveal his identity, but an alternate name had not occurred to her. It would be too cruel for the deception to be uncovered when it was so close to success.

'Henry,' Roger slurred from behind her. 'Leave my woman be!'

He dropped his head back and began to snore. Before she could wonder how Sir Roger had pulled the name from the air, or if his shout had been a coincidence or intentional, Robbie gave a shrill wail of alarm. He had been slumbering in his cradle, but for the second time in the night his home had been invaded and his sleep interrupted by strangers.

Nailed to the spot, Lucy watched her son clamber from his bed. Red-faced but half-asleep, he tottered across the wooden floorboards towards the bed. Pulling at his dark hair with his podgy fists, he looked around with unfocused eyes then, in a manner that Lucy would ever be grateful for, he did what he always did when he half-awoke in the night.

He tumbled on to the bed, tugging at the blanket until there was space to climb beneath and pulled himself up beside Sir Roger. The two men in the doorway looked at the bed where two dark heads now lay. Seeing her salvation Lucy exclaimed, 'See! My son knows his father!'

That might have been the end of the matter in any case, but at that moment there was a commotion from outside. A voice shouted. Then another answered. The sound of hooves—two sets—grew louder as they neared the inn and diminished as they went past. Lucy had forgotten Thomas in her desperation to prevent the men discovering Sir Roger's identity, but he had clearly been active while she had been engaged upstairs. He must have led the horses on foot along the road before mounting to give the impression they were riding past.

The two men lunged for the stairs in unison. Lucy raced after them, close on their heels, and slipped her way between them. For a moment the three bodies stuck at the top of the narrow stairs. She succeeded in tangling their feet between hers and wedging the giant back into the door frame, delaying them all reaching the bottom of the stairs. The door was closed and by the time they pulled it open and ran outside, the two horses were the size of Robbie's toy cow, climbing the hill towards Mattonfield. Both horses were close together and heavily laden. One rider appeared oddly hunched over until Lucy spotted that the old sacking she had wrapped around the small apple tree had been removed. Thomas had cunningly contrived to give the impression there were two riders.

The pursuers ran to where their own horses were tethered to the fence alongside the house and attempted to pull the reins free. Upon discovering they were knotted and tangled together, the giant swore loudly. Lucy hid a smile and backed into the shadows as the men fumbled to disentangle their animals. Thomas had been hard at work while they had been distracted upstairs. As the men swung themselves into the saddle the smaller one shifted round to look at Lucy. His expression was not unkind.

'You had a lucky escape, mistress. Keep your door barred until daylight. Your life will be worth nothing if you stand in the way of these rogues. Liars, thieves, and one is a killer. He's killed tonight already.'

He dug his heels into the horse's belly and galloped off to join his companion who was already ahead, leaving Lucy alone in the dark.

Chapter Four

Lucy watched until the figures began their climb up the hill. They rode fast, but Thomas was far enough ahead by now that once he reached the town his pursuers would have too many roads to choose from to catch their quarry for certain. Even if they did not catch him they were very unlikely to come back to her again now they had proof that she was not harbouring the fugitives.

He's dangerous. A liar, thief and killer.

The warning echoed in Lucy's ears and she clutched weakly at the door frame, willing herself to not faint. Relief coursed through her that the men had gone. Dread followed it close behind. She had felt so clever at hiding Sir Roger from their sight but now she was left with a dangerous man in her bed. She could not hope Thomas would return that night; it would be far too risky. He would surely find a way to double back as soon as it was light, but until he did, Lucy was alone in the inn with Sir Roger.

Except she wasn't alone.

The blood drained from her limbs, leaving her cold as the grave as she thought of her child upstairs with Sir Roger. How could she have let Robbie slip from her mind so easily? She spun on her heel, racing back inside, and only paused long enough to bar the door as advised. Her hands shook as she lowered the latch. Was it worse to be trapped inside with a murderer or leave the door open for other intruders to enter? She looked around frantically for anything she could defend herself with should Sir Roger take it in his mind to harm her or her child.

The better of her two knives had gone. Thomas, of course!

'Oh, Thomas! You horrible thief!' Lucy exclaimed.

He had always had a tendency to help himself to anything he liked, even as a child. She took the poker from the fire and clutched it tightly, focusing on the now-glowing tip as though it was a beacon. If he had hurt Robbie, Sir Roger would not live to see the sun rise.

Lucy crept back up the stairs, torn between the need to hurry and the desire to remain unnoticed. She pushed the door open, heart in her throat pounding painfully. She stopped in the doorway and lowered the poker, taken aback by what she saw.

In the darkness she could make out the bundled shape of the two figures still lying together. Robbie was curled up in the crook of Sir Roger's arm, his small face buried deep against the man's neck, his tiny fist clutching the edge of the sheet. The blanket had slipped and the child's linen night-dress contrasted with the dark hair and tanned flesh of Sir Roger's bare torso. Sir Roger's broad arm was draped across the child's back in what looked like a caress. He had his eyes closed and lay unmoving. He looked as if the grave had already stamped a claim on him and for a brief, unkind moment, Lucy's heart soared in hope that this was the case and the problem was solved. She drew closer, still holding the poker. He had already surprised her by revealing himself to be half-conscious before and she could not trust he would remain asleep for long.

They looked serene, the two dark, curly heads together, so close in colouring it was no wonder they had passed for father and son. Robbie had never slept in the arms of the father who refused to admit his existence and never would. At the sight, an odd pang of sadness clutched at Lucy's stomach that the boy had found comfort so quickly. What instinct had told him he was safe with the man who had forced his way in and apparently killed a man tonight? It felt almost cruel to move him when he was sleeping so peacefully after a night of chaos and disruption.

She shook her head forcefully, reminding herself this was not a loving father. Robbie was lying in the arms of a man who must barely be aware of his presence and would care about it even less were he awake. Her son was too young and trusting to know the ills the world held. He had no understanding of the possible danger he was in, feeling only that he was warm and being held tight.

She knelt beside the bed and edged Sir Roger's hand down to his side until she was able to tug Robbie free. She eased him across her shoulder. The child wrapped his arms around her neck and did not stir. Sir Roger muttered and rolled his head from side to side, though his eyes remained closed. Now she had her son back, Lucy could breathe easily once more. She paused to look curiously at the man in her bed.

Sir Roger. But Sir Roger who? And of where? She had heard of no knight or lord of that name in Cheshire or Derbyshire. She had no idea where he had come from, or where he was hoping to go. He would not want to remain here long if he had slighted Lord Harpur, she knew that much. Instinctively she tightened her hold on Robbie.

'He'll never know he has you to thank for his life,' she whispered against the boy's ear.

Robbie needed his bed. Lucy, too, though where she would sleep was anyone's guess. Not in her bed, that was for certain. She felt the beginnings of a blush around the back of her neck as she remembered Sir Roger's hands on her body. The arm that had held her son was muscular and iron hard, the neck and chest well shaped. Robbie was not the only one whose bed was a solitary place of rest.

She eased herself to her feet and stepped away. As she did, Sir Roger gave a great gasp. His eyes snapped open and he jerked upright, clutching hold of Lucy's skirts. He bared his teeth and snarled.

'Run, wench, lest they take you, too!'

Biting down a scream, Lucy pulled away, but his grip was strong and he held her fast. Still holding Robbie in one arm, she could not tug her skirts free. In panic, she brought down the poker she held in her other hand, flailing at his chest to push him away. The tip was hotter than she had expected it to be and as it touched the bare skin above his heart there was a hissing, accompanied by the sickening smell of singeing hair and flesh.

Sir Roger cried out, loosening his grip on Lucy's skirts and falling back on to the mattress. The back of the arrow landed on the bed, driving the tip forward through his body, but not fully out. Sir Roger screamed at the pain—the angry, agonised roar of a felled boar. His head lolled back as he slipped into a deep faint.

Lucy dropped the poker in horror at what she had done and backed away. In her arms, Robbie began to whimper. She kissed his damp forehead, trying to quiet her own sobs, and backed against the wall by his cot. When Robbie had settled, she eased him into his bed. She slid to the floor and hugged her knees until she stopped trembling.

Sir Roger did not move. Lucy's assault had drained him of any remaining strength.

For now.

The room still smelled of charred flesh and Lucy's stomach heaved. She needed to see what damage she had inflicted and tend to the wounds, but she could not trust that Sir Roger would not awaken before she had finished. Her skin crawled at the idea of him seizing her once again and she thought furiously what she should do. She clambered to her feet and ran back down the stairs, returning with a length of thin rope and a knife.

Biting her lip to stop her heart leaping from her throat, Lucy tiptoed close to the bed and knelt on shaking legs. She worked quickly, passing one end of the rope under the bedframe and wrapping it once round the leg of the bed closest to her. She securely tied the ends round each of the unconscious man's wrists. To her relief he remained insensible throughout.

Lucy sat back on her heels and examined her handiwork. Sir Roger's hands lay at his sides on the mattress. His bonds would cause no discomfort, but the rope was short enough that he would not be able to bring his hands together to undo the knots. If he attempted to grab her with one hand, the other would be pulled beneath the frame of the bed by the motion.

Now she finally felt safe enough to examine him, she brought the lamp close and settled by his side. Asleep he looked less fearsome, the lines on his forehead smoothed. She wondered what he would look like without the thatch of beard. She pulled the sheet down to his waist and peered at him, her fingers hovering over his body. His chest was broad and the muscles that Lucy had felt as she had undressed him were well defined beneath the soft dark hairs that covered his torso. Lucy drew her hand back, examining the wound she had inflicted. The poker's tip had left a livid red mark on the skin above his heart. It had already begun to blister and she winced with guilt.

Lucy fetched a pitcher of water and pressed a damp strip of his torn-up tunic over the wound. Sir Roger's eyelids flickered, but he did not wake. The arrow wound had begun to bleed, but slowly. It oozed out around the wooden shaft that now stuck further out. She wetted more strips of cloth and contrived padding around the wound. Perhaps she should remove the arrow while he was unconscious and less likely to feel pain, but the lamp was beginning to sputter, almost empty. She would have to wait until morning and Thomas's arrival. She did not want to think what would happen if her brother was caught and never returned.

She watched until the blood stopped. There was nothing more she could do tonight, but if he died it would be from infection, not from his lifeblood ebbing away. Lucy shivered with cold, wishing she had been in bed long before now. She could not deprive her patient of the blankets in the state he was in so she leaned over and retrieved his cloak from down the side of the bed. Even cut and bloodstained it was of better quality than anything she owned herself. Wearily she dropped to the floor beside Robbie's cot and slept on the bare boards, wrapped in the knight's ruined cloak with the unfamiliar musky scent of man enveloping her.

* * *

Lucy woke early. Her body ached and she felt nauseous, her stomach churning after the night's happenings. She crept to Sir Roger's side, hoping not to awaken him, but he was still deeply asleep. So deep, in fact, that Lucy believed it must be the combination of alcohol and whatever Thomas had given him that accounted for his slumber. He could barely have shifted in the night as the blankets were precisely where she had placed them, halfway between his waist and shoulders.

Daylight edged through the gaps in the wooden shutters and in the light she could see his skin was ashen beneath the dark hair, except for the area around his bandaged wound. The flesh there was red and angry, with blood crusted around the arrow. Cautiously Lucy placed her fingers on the wound and found the flesh as hot as it was scarlet. She lifted the cloth from the burn above his heart and placed her fingers there, spreading her hand wide over the taut muscle. At her touch Sir Roger drew a rasping breath, his chest rising beneath Lucy's hand. Her skin fluttered as his firm muscles tensed. She drew back hastily.

No man had shared her bed here and she had no expectation, nor wish, for any to do so in the future, but the unanticipated longing for this man was confusing and his kiss had been intoxicating.

He was by far the finest-looking man she had encountered, but those muscles had been hardened in battle and the deep brown eyes had seen danger and death she could barely contemplate. Even half out of his mind with pain he exuded an air of danger. To imagine repeating such a thing would be akin to throwing herself into the middle of a dogfight.

Sir Roger murmured, his head tipping to one side. He half-opened his eyes and looked at Lucy, though she doubted he really saw her. His forehead creased and he gave a slight moan. Lucy reached a trembling hand and stroked her thumb tenderly across his brow. The creases vanished under her touch and he closed his eyes once more.

The cockerel crowed, his raucous interruption reminding Lucy she had other matters to attend to. Unexpected resentment rose in her—a much safer emotion than the ones imagining Sir Roger's touch had provoked. She was too tired for the start of the day and had enough tasks to keep her busy until nightfall without having to think of Sir Roger. This was a burden she did not need. One child was enough to manage, let alone a fully-grown man.

'You'll have to wait, my fine lord,' she told the sleeping man. 'I have ale to brew and a house to keep.'

She brushed her hands down her dress, which was creased and felt grimy from being slept in. She only had two and the other was lighter cloth better suited for warmer days. It would have to do as she could not bear to remain in this one any longer. She pulled the dress from the chest at the end of the bed and quickly changed with her back to Sir Roger in case he should awake and catch her in her linen shift.

Her eye fell on the small glass vial that he had drunk from the night before and she held it to the light. A few drops remained. She inspected the ropes on Sir Roger's wrists. He would be going nowhere when he awoke, but just to be certain…

She narrowed her eyes and looked down at Sir Roger.

'You'd rather sleep and be free of pain, wouldn't you,' she said. 'We don't want you waking before I'm ready to deal with you.'

She knelt by the bed and held the rim to Sir Roger's lips, parting them with her fingers to allow the liquid to slip into his mouth. His throat moved as he swallowed and his tongue darted out to lap up the droplets that remained on his lips, reminding Lucy of Robbie suckling in the night when asleep and unaware of what he was doing. Her breasts gave a sudden throb and she wrapped her arms tightly around her chest. Robbie had only recently given up nursing and she put her body's reaction down to the memory of that. It was most definitely not because of the idea of Sir Roger's lips on her breasts.

The thought of Robbie raised another issue that she had not previously considered. If Sir Roger was sleeping and drinking like a babe, there would be other needs that would arise. If it came to it, she would deal with those in the same manner she dealt with Robbie, but as she picked up her son and left the room she fervently hoped Thomas would return long before she had to assist with anything that involved more of Sir Roger's body than she had already encountered.

Lucy went about her daily tasks. She fed the pig and the chickens and put Robbie out to play in the yard behind the house, a long rope around his waist so he did not stray to the stream. Once or twice someone passed by heading to or from Mattonfield. She greeted them with a wave, calling brightly that there would be new ale within the week. Noon passed and still Thomas did not return, but neither was there a sound from the bedroom. Robbie began to wail and she spooned boiled apple into his mouth, sitting him on her lap.

'Mama will crush the malt next,' she told him with a smile, 'and you can go see if Gyb has caught anything.'

He burbled excitedly, pleased to be given permission to torment the burly orange tomcat that sometimes graced them with his presence. That would keep him busy while Lucy ran upstairs to check Sir Roger had not lapsed into a fever. His wound would need bathing and she should try him on some of her father's draught. Perhaps he, too, would take some of the mashed apples that her son was busily smearing in his hair.

She frowned. Where was Thomas? She had hoped him to be back by now so she could be rid of her burden as soon as possible.

She went to the shed and began crushing the malt and tipping it into the bowl to soak. When she heard a familiar whistling coming down the road she forced herself to finish the task, covering the vat with a damp cloth before wiping her hands down her apron and emerging.

The visitor was Widow Barton, an old friend of Lucy's father. She leaned on the stout stick she used for walking and tugged her cap into place, tucking wiry grey strands beneath it.

'Good day, Lucy.'

She was one of the few inhabitants of the nearby town who had remained on good terms with Lucy after she returned home with a swelling belly and no husband to save her honour—and the only one who knew the identity of the man who had caused her shame. The old woman took the leftover ale mash to feed her pigs, in return for an occasional flitch of bacon, without which Lucy's diet would have been scant indeed.

'Did you hear about the commotion in Mattonfield last night?'

Lucy shook her head truthfully. The news had not reached her, but her nerves jangled as she imagined who might have been the cause.

'Two men searching for two more. They tried to raise the hue and cry, but Lord de Legh refused as they would not account for why they were searching. He told them if they could not name the crime he would have no part in it.'

'Did they catch the man?' Lucy asked.

Mary gave her an odd look.

'The men,' Lucy amended. She averted her gaze, annoyed at her slip.

'No one was found,' Mary answered after a pause. 'They must have come past your way before they arrived in town.'

'I suppose they might,' Lucy agreed, 'though there are many ways to travel.' More on her guard now, she stopped herself from finishing the sentence '...from Lord Harpur's estates.'

Mary gave her a shrewd look. 'You'll meet a bad end living out here alone. Your father should have sold up when he knew his time was at hand.'

'Should he have left my brother nothing to inherit when he returns?' Lucy asked.

It was remarkably easy to speak of Thomas as if he was still in France. For years she had believed he would never come home and that most likely he was dead somewhere across the water. A guilty thought crossed Lucy's mind that if Thomas did not return to claim his friend, he would not claim the inn, either.

Mary glanced towards the inn, which was showing more signs of disrepair as each month passed. 'There's not much to inherit,' she said kindly.

Lucy's lips twitched. 'I keep it going as best I can.'

'I don't blame you. Your father should have found you a husband to help run it.'

'He tried. I refused,' Lucy reminded her. 'Besides, no man of any regard wants a wife with a bastard brat hanging off her.'

Any husband, whether of good standing or not, would have been suitable in her father's eyes to rid him of the shame of an unwed daughter with a child. Mary knew this already. Lucy suspected the widow even approved. She had five grown children and no husband for the past decade.

Mary sniffed, her beak of a nose flaring.

'Are you brewing again?'

Lucy held an arm out, glad of an excuse to

draw the older woman away from the house and off the subject of husbands.

'Come see.'

She led Mary into the shed, talking all the while of the new mix of yarrow and elderflower she was planning to use as gruit to flavour the brew, of Robbie's final emerging tooth—the goodwife had helped birth the boy and still took a keen interest—and of the fair to be held in Mattonfield at the end of the month.

Anything to keep the old woman from suspecting that upstairs she had a drugged nobleman tied to her bed who would very soon require her attendance.

Chapter Five

❦

Through the haze of pain, Roger became aware he was not alone in the room. He groaned weakly, trying to speak, but his throat was too dry. His arms were leaden and would not rise. He fought down panic.

Cool fingers stroked his forehead, brushing the hair from his brow and easing away his anxiety. A woman's voice, soft and high, murmured soothing words that jumbled in his mind. He felt something cool and damp pressed to his brow, stroking gently and he sighed.

'Joanna?'

The stroking stopped. 'No.'

An unfamiliar voice.

The hands moved down to his jaw, firm strokes cleaning away the grime from his cheeks. Despite the coldness of the cloth, Roger's skin began to burn hotter from within. He couldn't remember the last time a woman had touched him unbidden with such gentleness and desire began to awaken, tickling with devilish fingers at his groin.

Good. If he could still contemplate a spot of swiving between the sheets he was not yet dead. He opened his eyes to see who was caring for him, but his lids felt unaccountably heavy. He forced them wide anyway, but the brightness hurt and the woman was silhouetted against the window so he could see nothing of her features. He screwed his eyes tight, wincing.

A pale face framed with fine, light-coloured hair and the impression of a grey dress filled his mind: the girl from the inn who had been half-terrified to death by their appearance.

Lucy Carew. He hoped it was she who was nursing him. He remembered her mouth, hot against his, resisting at first in alarm, but quickly giving in to his kiss and meeting him with as much fire as he was exuding. It would be pleasant indeed if it were she.

Lucy—Roger would assume it was until evidence proved otherwise—removed the cloth from his forehead and put it to his cheeks, freshly damp. She began to bathe his neck and chest, lifting each arm to wipe it before moving down towards his waist, which sent shivers of bliss cascading over him. The sensation was so unbear-

ably erotic Roger felt he would be consumed by
the sheer pleasure of it. However, when he gave
himself up to the indulgence, he realised the reaction was in his mind alone. His body was refusing
to acknowledge anything was happening to rouse
him. Perhaps he was closer to death than he had
realised after all. He lapsed into sleep with this
troubling thought.

He woke again to find himself being bathed
still. Or perhaps a second time because now the
room was darker. The hands moved over his body
as before, but shifted now to his right shoulder. As
they probed the wound searing pain shot through
him, obliterating any thoughts beyond making the
torment end. He cried out, but his voice rasped
painfully.

'Thirsty…' he managed to croak.

Those bewitching fingers stroked his brow
once more. He felt the back of his head cradled
and lifted, firm fingers burrowing deep into his
thick hair. A cup was put to his lips.

'Not too fast,' a soft voice instructed.

It was ale. Cool and thirst-quenching. Roger
could not remember the arrow being removed,
or Thomas returning, but the pain in his shoulder was so intense it must be from the brand that
sealed the wound. Panic filled him once again

and he twisted his head from the cup. Lucy's firm hands guided it back and the cup was put to his lips once more.

'Drink this,' she commanded, her voice allowing no possibility of disobedience. 'It will ease the pain.'

Her voice brooked no argument. If it meant those delicate fingers exploring his body once more he would do anything she asked.

It was not the same cup. This brew was sickly and bitter at the same time. He was being drugged.

He groaned with relief. Wonderful woman, to ease his pain in such a way.

His head began to swim once more. Oh, he'd thank her indeed when he was back to strength with everything working as it should. He could think of so many ways to show his gratitude that did not even involve leaving this bed.

'The arrow?' he mumbled. His mouth now felt too small to hold his tongue.

She drew a sharp breath and the hand at the back of his skull tightened briefly. She muttered something to herself and Roger caught Thomas's name.

'I'm sorry. I didn't know what to do. It's still in your shoulder.'

He felt her move away and shortly the door closed, leaving him alone.

The news was bad, but the matter was out of

Roger's hands for now. However hard he tried, he could do nothing to fight the sleep that was claiming him.

He fell into a deep slumber and dreamed of Lucy.

When Roger next achieved full awareness, it was night once more and opening his eyes did not require the effort it had earlier in the day. The air that kissed his skin was cold, deliciously so, for his flesh felt hotter than he would expect, especially one spot just above his heart. His vision began to clear. He craned his head to search for Lucy, but he was alone. He shivered and pain surged through him, radiating from the wound outwards. The God-rotted arrow was still there, wasn't it? He bit down on his lip to stop the sudden trembling that began as he thought of what removing it would entail.

His stomach growled and he became aware of another discomfort; a clenching ache in his belly that demanded to be filled. He had barely eaten yesterday and by all accounts had slept the whole day away. No wonder his limbs felt leaden and his body weak.

'Hello! Is anyone there?' he called. His throat rasped painfully. He coughed and tried once more. 'Woman? Dove? Where are you? I'm hungry.'

Roger waited for her to arrive with increasing irritation. Possibly the wench would be serving in the room downstairs and could not spare the time immediately. The inn was unusually silent compared to those Roger had been in before. Perhaps that wasn't the reason. He would have to go in search.

He tried to move his arms, but they would not lift from beside his body. The right arm he expected to be weaker, but the left had nothing to hinder it. With mounting anxiety he tried again. Something was preventing him. He took a deep breath and tried to fight down his fear, but visions filled him of a life of paralysis, his body useless and relying on the goodwill of others to survive. A puppet being fed and wiped like a babe.

His father's form swam before Roger, his puckered eyes gazing sightlessly on Roger's face and his twisted arm hanging limply by his side.

'At least you have your sight. Be thankful for that.'

Roger moaned, remembering his father bellowing a warning, the lance splintering. Was a similar incapacity to be Roger's penance? He clutched at the rough blankets covering him. The relief that flooded him as he felt his hands curl about the homespun cloth was incomparable. He tried once more to bring his hands together and this time he succeeded in lifting them both, but bringing them together was impossible. A tugging at his wrists was confusing, but the last dregs of the painkilling draught Lucy had given him were wearing off and as a result his head felt less clouded.

Concentrating on what he felt, he came to the conclusion that he had not lost the use of his limbs. He was being restrained by something tied around his wrists holding him to the bed. He tilted his head to look at his arms. Cold sweat broke out across his body as he confirmed it.

The bitch had tied him down!

He jerked his left arm up and his right was wrenched from the bed, hitting the floor with a loud thump and bashing his knuckles. The movement caused further pain in his shoulder and he gritted his teeth to stop from crying out. He eased his hand upward to the sore spot above his heart that had mystified him earlier and his fingers touched blistered flesh. Someone had burned him.

Had he been subject to torture and blocked out the memory? He cast his mind back to Lucy's pale, frightened face that had filled his vision the previous night as she cut his clothes from him. In his earlier befuddled state he knew Lucy had bathed him, given him water, and soothed his pain away with her gentle hands and soft words. She had done all that knowing he was bound. Would the next thing she did be to slip a dagger between his ribs or slit his throat? It seemed unlikely. He could not imagine the quivering girl would have dared do something so rash as take him captive alone, so she must have been instructed to do it by someone else. If she was not responsible for his situation, who was, and was Lucy being mistreated also?

Roger's fists clenched. The worry for Lucy's wellbeing was so unexpected it brought him up sharp. He gave a wry smile. He had often been accused of dishonour. What a pity those who had laid the charge at his feet would never know how he had spared a thought for the girl before they both died. Memories of battles in France threw themselves about his brain, captured soldiers herded like cattle, roped together awaiting death. Innocent townspeople slaughtered, women and children among them.

Where once he had dreamed of glory in the lists, of prizes and cheers, the sights of carnage now featured regularly in his nightmares. Was that to be his fate? Panic flooded his limbs and he began to pant like a tethered dog. He twisted, rocking from side to side to try pulling free, but he was securely bound.

'Wait,' he commanded himself aloud. There

was no need to speak but it served to drown the silence and reassure him. 'Think, don't panic. It's rope, not irons. And it's a narrow bed.'

He dropped both arms to the floor and twisted them to reach beneath, trying to undo the knots, but the effort of contorting his right shoulder was excruciating. Cold sweat once again broke out across his body. He would not gain his freedom that way so his only option was to wait. And plan.

When he heard a footstep on the stair he dropped his head to one side so that his hair covered his face and eased his left hand close to him to give himself as much slack on the rope as he could. Lucy entered and he watched through half-closed lids as she placed a lamp and cup on the chest at the foot of the bed. She came to his side and knelt, placing a bowl beside her. If she was being instructed, someone would be waiting for her to return downstairs.

Roger closed his eyes, though the urge to watch what she did was tempting. She brushed his hair back from his face, slipping the jaw-length tangles behind his ear. He let her begin to bathe him as she had done before, first his brow and face, fingers tickling where they brushed against the growth of beard that felt too unkempt for his liking. Her hands travelled to his neck, her fingers tracing the cloth along a route from the sensitive flesh behind his ear to the hollow at his throat. The cloth was rewetted and wiped across his chest.

Roger clenched his fingers, readying himself to move as soon as the opportunity presented itself, but when Lucy removed the cloth and placed her bare fingers above Roger's heart he almost decided to abandon his plan, giving himself up to the sensations of pleasure at her touch.

Almost, but not quite. Lucy made a small circle with her thumb around the burn mark and gave a sigh of worry. Goosebumps rose on Roger's flesh. If he was about to die, no condemned man could ask for a better prelude to passing, however Roger did not intend to die. Carefully, so as not to be noticed, he eased his hand off the bed. He risked opening his right eye ever so slightly and saw Lucy's face was creased with anxiety.

As Lucy reached down for the cloth she leaned forward. Roger whipped his left hand up around her, ignoring the pain this caused his right shoulder as the rope pulled taut, and seized her around the back of the neck. She cried out, a mixture of surprise and pain. Ignoring the sound, Roger tightened his fingers and pulled her head towards him until her eyes were level with his and their faces almost touching.

'You have a lot of explaining to do!' he snarled.

He moved his thumb around until it pressed against the side of her windpipe. He could feel the blood pounding through her veins beneath his touch. Tears sprang to Lucy's eyes. Guilt writhed within Roger at the discomfort he must be causing her, but he bit it down. He had been forced into this violence by her actions.

'Set me free or I'll choke the life from you,' he growled.

Her hands came around Roger's, clawing at his skin as she attempted to prise his hand free. He held tight and she scraped the nails of both hands against his wrist. Ten sharp daggers. Time ceased to move as they glared at each other, her eyes fearful beneath the defiance that simmered in them.

Lucy's neck was slender, the skin smooth. If Roger squeezed the creamy flesh a little more she would lose consciousness before she drew his blood. He found as he looked at her reddening cheeks he did not wish that. He slackened his grip the slightest degree. She could not break free, but he would not cause her lasting ill if she did not struggle. He held her rigid with the same ease with which he steadied his gelding in the midst of battle, or set his destrier at the tilt, until Lucy knelt motionless, as obedient as the animal itself.

'We can stay like this as long as you like, or

you can save yourself time and pain and release me from my bonds. Do you have a knife? Any weapon?'

She could not move her head to shake it, but her lips formed the word 'no.'

Nothing she could use against him, but nothing Roger could seize to free himself. He held her, wondering what to do.

Lucy's eyes darted around the room before settling back on Roger. Instead of beginning to pull against him once more as he half expected, she lowered her hands to her sides. Lucy dropped her gaze and her shoulders slumped in defeat. Roger gave a tight smile. The last time they had been in such close proximity was when he had kissed her. Despite his anger at her betrayal he considered pulling her closer and doing it again.

He was not expecting her to bring the water bowl around and dash the hard pot against the side of his head.

Roger let loose a string of obscenities. Lights flashed behind his eyes and his grip loosened enough for Lucy to be able to twist free. She fell backwards, crashing to the floor in a tangle of skirts as her legs slid out from under her, giving Roger a glimpse of shapely calves encased in thick woollen stockings. He craned his neck to glare at her. She looked back from her position on the floor, her body spreading before him as if in offering, the contours of her full breasts and rounded hips contrasting with her slender waist. He'd wanted to take her in his arms, bury himself between her breasts and sate himself between those soft thighs, but even the loveliest woman lost her shine when she cracked him over the head.

'Who are you working for?' Roger snarled.

'I work for myself,' Lucy replied. 'This is my inn.'

Roger raised his left hand, pulling the rope taut. 'I mean who told you to tether me here?'

Lucy tossed her hair from her brow and her eyes narrowed. 'That was my idea also.'

'You must set me free. I'm working in the service of the King!'

'Don't lie!' Lucy spat. 'Thomas said you were mercenaries.'

Her voice dripped with scorn and suspicion. Why would she believe he had a respectable purpose, too, if she knew that.

'I'm both. Undo the ropes and let me free!' Roger cried in exasperation. A thought struck him. He pointed to his chest. 'Did you burn me, too? Was this your doing?'

Lucy paled. Wordlessly she twisted on to her front with a grace that reminded Roger of a cat and scrambled to her feet. She was through the door and gone before he could call her back.

That was all the confirmation Roger needed. He lay back on the mattress, furious at Lucy's betrayal and his own foolishness. He had conjured assailants who had forced her to act as they demanded only to discover she had taken it upon herself to imprison him and hurt him further. He had believed her to be a gentle, compassionate woman, not a calculating madwoman. Now he wished he had wrung her neck like a chicken while he had the opportunity.

Roger swallowed and licked dry lips. His throat ached with thirst and his belly constricted with emptiness. He should at least have waited until she had brought the cup to him. Now he would have to wait for who knew how long for the hellcat to come back before he could slake his thirst. Assuming she did return.

'You never did know how to charm a woman,' his brother remarked. 'Always pushing. Always demanding. Always forceful.'

'Go away, Hal!' Roger muttered. 'You aren't here.'

In which case the thought was his own, not his brother's judgement. Hal had once accused Roger of rape. He'd been innocent, but that Hal had considered him capable of such violation was something Roger still resented years after the event. Now his roughness had succeeded in terrifying Lucy. It was doubtful she would come back into his presence before Thomas returned. Assuming Thomas did return. Surely he would come back as soon as possible, knowing his sister was alone with Roger.

Roger clenched his fist and pounded the mattress in frustration. Too many possibilities, and all the while the arrow was still in him and the wound would begin to fester unless it was removed and cleaned.

And now he realised he needed a piss.

Like it or not, Lucy was his only company and the only means of getting what he needed. He had to entice her back and convince her to free him. Anger had not worked. That had been badly done. Roaring at the girl and threatening murder had achieved nothing. He had been too long in wars and not enough time in the company of respectable women. Orders and shouting might work on the men he had commanded, but he had lost sight of what women desired.

Roger gave his first genuine smile for days. If there was one thing Roger was skilled at, it was convincing a woman to do his bidding. It would take honey cake, not threats, to entice this little dove to his side. If he put his mind to it, he was certain he could make Lucy fall in love with him for as long as it took to gain his freedom, recover and leave.

She came back after a shorter time than Roger anticipated. Without a candle to mark the passing of time he had kept his mind busy by singing songs in Italian and French that he had picked up around various campfires, and cataloguing the location and number of men he had recruited to join the Company. If every man showed up to be recruited, and if Sir Hugh Calveley went to France as the King requested, Roger would be a richer man than when he left. Rich enough to afford a horse decent enough to win in the tournaments. Rich enough to overcome any nobleman's objections to him as a son-in-law.

So many 'ifs.' He sighed.

Movement in the corner of the room caught his eye and he stiffened. A shadow formed on the wall.

'I know you're there.' Roger kept his voice level and as free of any threat as he could manage. 'Come in. I won't harm you.'

Lucy's face appeared round the door frame, but she did not come any closer.

'I'm very thirsty.' Roger added a touch of self-pity to his voice. 'And hungry.'

She gave one nod and vanished. Roger waited patiently. He heard her voice and the sound of a child's cry rising in a wail. He gritted his teeth. He'd forgotten the brat. That had been the reason for the delay in removing the arrow.

After far too long, Lucy returned, looking weary. This time she entered the room carrying a bowl. In the other hand she held the poker at arm's length in the manner that people who had never held a sword thought they should be brandished. She took three steps, stopped and placed the bowl on the floor. She used the poker to push it towards Roger. It contained watery broth and wasn't meaty enough for Roger's liking, but he drank it eagerly. Remembering his intention to woo Lucy into freeing him he thanked her politely. She received the compliment stony-faced.

'Is there more?'

'Put the bowl on the floor and push it towards me,' Lucy instructed. 'I'm not stupid enough to come closer.'

Roger's cheeks flushed with annoyance. She spoke to him as if he were her equal. His stomach growled as the broth made its way down, waking the appetite that had been dormant. He pushed the bowl out. She hooked the handle of the poker round the brim and pulled it closer. A thought struck him as he watched.

'Is that what you burned me with?'

She folded her arms across her chest, hunching her shoulders defensively.

Roger shifted until he was sitting more upright. 'You tied me to your bed and branded me!'

'No,' she blurted out. 'I burned you, then tied you to the bed.'

Roger barked a laugh. 'I'm not sure the order makes much difference to me now. And you did this without instruction? Why?'

'Because you attacked me,' she answered. She raised her head, revealing troubled eyes that bored into him. 'You were crying out that I should run, but holding on to me. You wouldn't let go when I tried to pull free and I panicked. I didn't mean to hurt you.'

Roger sucked his teeth, a knot hardening in his guts. His memories of his arrival at the inn and what took place afterwards were confused, but to be presented with this scenario was disconcerting.

'I have no memory of that,' he said quietly. 'I was drugged and drunk. You cannot hold me responsible for what I did under those circumstances.'

Lucy's expression hardened. 'Perhaps not, but I wasn't going to take the chance.'

Roger raised his hands, wrists upturned and

palms flat in supplication to show the ropes. 'I swear you are at no risk of harm. Take these off.'

'I think not. I prefer you as you are for now.'

She raised her head haughtily as if she were a noblewoman and he the serf. He remembered he was supposed to be seducing her into freeing him.

'You prefer me this way, do you?' Roger asked. He twisted his wrist around to display his bonds, giving Lucy a flirtatious look. 'I've heard of men who find it stimulating to be pleasured under such circumstances and of women willing to oblige them so. I've never had the inclination myself, but perhaps we could discover the thrill together?'

Lucy's cheeks flamed scarlet. The blush came on instantly and crept down her throat, carrying on, no doubt, below the bodice of her dress. Roger could not take his eyes off the slender throat that he had held so recently. Oh, to replace his cruel fingers with his lips, tongue, teeth… To tease moans of excitement from her would be wonderful. The urge to bed her grew strong and he felt himself begin to grow hard.

'I prefer you that way because it keeps me and my son safe,' Lucy snapped. 'Making such unfitting and revolting suggestions only serves to prove I'm right. You kissed me against my will. You'll not touch me again in any manner.'

She hadn't been shocked at his words though, Roger mused. If anything, he'd seen a flash of something bordering on interest in her eyes. The kiss might have started unwillingly, however she had joined in enthusiastically until he had chanced his luck too far. He would let that lie for now. No sense in provoking the annoyance that seemed to consume at least two-thirds of her when he needed her to think fondly on him.

'I swear on my honour as a knight you are in no danger from me.'

'You are truly a knight like Thomas said?' Lucy sounded doubtful.

'I am.'

'Will I have heard of you?' Her eyes showed interest rather than suspicion for a moment and the familiar feeling of vanity awoke in Roger's breast. He'd swapped middling success at the tourney for the chance to grow rich abroad, but he'd switch in an instant to have Lucy look on him with admiration.

'Do you follow the tournaments? The joust?'

She shook her head. 'I don't have time for that sort of amusement.'

Roger's vanity deflated like a pig's-bladder target pierced with an arrow. 'Then you won't have.'

Even if she did, his name would mean little to her unless she looked at the bottom of the lists.

Still, she needn't know that. All women were the same when it came to knights and it would do no harm to bolster his name.

'My name is better known in Yorkshire. In fact, my skill on horseback was the talk of the shire before I retired from the contests. Perhaps one day you'll be able to boast you had Roger Danby sleeping in your bed.'

Lucy snorted. 'I'll be sure to mention he slept there alone.'

She stared at him suspiciously. 'The men who came said you were a killer, not a gallant knight.'

'A man can be both,' Roger answered. 'In battle he has to be.'

She sniffed contemptuously. 'Oh, in battle, of course! They said you had killed three nights ago.'

'They lied!' Roger jerked forward at the blatant falsehood. An accusation of adultery he could live with, but if John Harpur sought to blacken his name in such a way there would be consequences.

'Three nights ago I was a guest in a noble household not far from here. I did not break the laws of hospitality in so odious a manner.'

Lucy's mouth fell open and her eyebrows shot up. She edged closer to the bed, still not within Roger's reach, but she had lost the air of anxiety.

'Either you're lying or you're still confused. I don't know which, but three nights ago you arrived here with my brother. You've been here ever since.'

Chapter Six

Her words had the same effect on Roger that the arrow had when it pierced him. He froze, ice chilling his limbs and weakening them before fire rushed through, sickening him.

'You must be mistaken,' he gasped. All the time he had spoken, in whatever state of consciousness or pain he had been, he believed his voice had been steady. Now it shook for the first time. He clamped his jaw shut tightly, shocked at the outward sign of weakness.

'Of course I'm not!' Lucy exclaimed. She came closer to the bed, hands on her hips and face thunderous. Her voice dripped with resentment.

'Believe me, I have counted every hour! I've spent three days not knowing if you would be dead the next time I came up here. Trying to keep your presence—which I could well have done without—hidden from anyone who might be searching. Tending to your needs…'

'My needs?' Roger interrupted, furrowing his brow. His bladder, which had begun increasingly to trouble him, should have been fit to bursting after three days. A horrifying thought crossed his mind and his hand moved downward.

'*All* your needs,' Lucy confirmed, following the movement with a smirk. 'Don't worry, I have a young child so I've done such things before. It was no great matter.'

'I hope it was a matter a little greater than your son's!' Roger exclaimed. He caught a flash of a smile before Lucy stalked to the door.

'Where are you going?'

She whirled around in a swirl of skirts, no trace of amusement on her face now.

'I told you. I don't need that sort of talk.'

Roger sucked his teeth. All the barmaids he had known had been coarse drabs or merry harlots who needed little persuading to slip between the sheets. Could Lucy Carew be that rare thing: a virtuous woman? As she held herself haughtily, her breasts jutting forward and her hands resting on her slender waist in a manner that invited him to slip his hands over hers, Roger fervently hoped not.

'Come back. I was teasing,' Roger called. The idea of being handled in such a way made him feel oddly vulnerable. The thought she might have been assessing him and found him wanting was insufferable.

'No man likes to be referred to as a small matter.'

'It was the act I meant,' Lucy retorted. She stopped and clamped her mouth closed. Her cheeks reddened as she realised what she had inadvertently admitted. Roger hid his smile, though inwardly he crowed as exultantly as the morning cock. She might deny it, but he had seen the flash of interest in her eyes more than once.

'I'm grateful for all your ministrations, but why didn't you wake me sooner?' Roger asked.

'You needed to sleep,' Lucy said, as if she were talking to a child. 'Though sleeping is too light a word to describe what you've been doing. You were so hot to touch I feared you had started a fever or the poison had got into your blood. I thought it safer to let it burn off.'

'Or let it claim me,' Roger muttered. He had been hot in his dreams. Her fingers had been barbs of ice across his flesh. He felt again the odd curling of desire that rippled in his guts at the thought of Lucy's hands on him.

'Not that! I kept the wound as clean as I could and hoped Thomas would return before you woke.' She raised her eyes to meet his demandingly. 'Were those men lying? Did you kill someone?'

Roger delved into his memories of the chase

through the forest, remembering the crunch of steel against bone as he lashed out blindly with his sword.

'If it was the night I came here, I bloody well hope so. I slashed the throat of the man he meant.'

She paled visibly. 'Why?' she asked, eyes wide.

'Because the whoreson had just shot me though with an arrow!' Roger thundered. 'I wasn't going to let that go unanswered or give him the chance to strike with more accuracy.'

He jerked his head towards his shoulder, greater concerns than his loss of days now consuming him.

'Why didn't you remove the arrow while I slept?'

'Me!' Lucy's eyes grew wide. 'I didn't dare. I don't know how.'

Roger bit his lip. 'That's probably as well. Leaving it there stopped the blood flowing. It probably kept me alive, but I cannot leave it indefinitely—I have to get this arrow out. I will not be able to do it alone. Lucy, you have to help me now. You will have to be the one to pull it free.'

She paled, edging away from the bed. A moment more and she would be out of the door.

'I can't do that. I don't know how.'

'It's not hard. I've done it in the midst of a battle,' Roger said soothingly. 'You will do well out of it.'

She looked suspicious, but stood still.

'I'm a rich man, or will be one day. I can reward you.'

Lucy came a little closer.

'With money?'

'Of course. Unless you'd prefer me to show my gratitude in a different form...'

Roger left the suggestion hanging. Lucy wrinkled her nose, but did not retreat any further.

'The reward I suspect you mean would most likely leave me with a fuller belly than a purse,' she remarked drily. 'Can you think of nothing else but that?'

His eyes flicked to her face. 'Lying here like this, I can hardly contemplate making my fortune or planning my future. There is little else to think of.'

She rubbed her hands across her eyes with an air of weariness. Roger resisted the urge to prompt her. She seemed to take against that. When she looked up her expression was icy.

'Tell me what I need to do. I don't want your money. The greatest reward will be seeing you gone and leaving me and my son in peace.'

Sir Roger blinked. He looked as though Lucy had slapped him. What sort of response did he expect from her?

'We'll need more light. Refill the lamp,' Sir Roger ordered abruptly, gesturing to the wooden chest at the foot of the bed. 'Bring a knife, fresh water, cloths, something to serve as bandages and that hot poker you so like to wield.'

Lucy edged closer to the bed. Sir Roger's eyes followed her with a look that reminded her of Gyb planning to raid a nest of fledglings. At the foot of the bed she stopped and snatched up the lamp, half-expecting him to pounce in the manner the cat did.

'Still wary of me, dove?' Sir Roger laughed. He lifted his chin and smiled, revealing his teeth. Three days with little food had left his face leaner, his cheekbones sharp beneath watchful, intelligent eyes.

'You've given me no cause to be otherwise,' she answered. 'Don't call me that. I'm Mistress Carew.'

'Can't I call you Lucy?' He gazed at her through half-lowered lids, rolling her name around his mouth, the tip of his tongue lingering on his bottom lip a touch longer than necessary, elongating the word. She didn't really care what he called her, but the sight made her shiver deep inside as she remembered the sensation of his tongue on hers.

'If you must,' she replied. 'Do you want me to

bring you more of the sleeping draught? I have some left.'

He shook his head, scowling. 'No. You've taken three days from me. I'm not losing any more.'

The accusation was barbed and Lucy was about to object until she saw the fairness in it. The use of her father's concoction had been as much for her peace of mind as the comfort of her patient.

'But won't it hurt when I take the arrow out?' The hairs on the back of her neck stood on end at the idea.

'I imagine so,' he grunted. He swallowed and his expression darkened just a touch before a ghost of his cocksure smile flitted across his lips once more. 'Don't fear though, dove. I've been bruised and beaten at the tilt until my entire body was as purple and tender as autumn plums. Men are able to withstand what would make a woman faint to contemplate. I will be able to endure it.'

Lucy eyed him with interest, letting the familiarity slide for once. She tried to imagine the unkempt, bearded, dishevelled figure, more akin to a vagabond, as a knight in his glory. She failed, but could not help wondering if he had been any good. His condescending manner set her teeth on edge.

'I know all about pain,' she retorted. 'I've birthed a child and unless it will take from now until daybreak to remove your arrow I wouldn't be making any wagers about who could endure the most discomfort! We'll do it without any help if you wish.'

'Very well, woman,' he said grudgingly, as if he was doing her a favour. 'Bring wine, or anything stronger if you think it will help, but I'm done with potions.'

He still spoke with bravado, but Lucy saw a flash of real anxiety cross his face. She felt a burst of sympathy. So much of his posturing was just that.

'I'll be as quick as I can,' she promised. She left, feeling his eyes on her until she was through the door.

She gathered what he had listed, her hand pausing as she added her short kitchen knife to the pile, glad that Thomas had not stolen that, too. She tucked it inside the pouch at her girdle, determined to keep it from Sir Roger's reach. She still didn't trust him. If anyone had asked, she was uncertain what she thought he would do, but knowing he was tethered securely gave her peace of mind. She would have to free him at some point, but not today.

At the top of the stairs she paused and rested her head on the door to the second room where she and Robbie had slept since their own cham-

ber had been invaded. He had been restless for
nights and she whispered a quick entreaty that
he would stay asleep and safe while she did what
needed to be done.

Sir Roger had manoeuvred himself upright
and was leaning back against the headboard.
The blanket had fallen to his waist, revealing the
firm, defined muscles of his chest and belly. His
eyes were closed and his head lolled to one side,
pulling the tendons in his throat tight where they
appeared from beneath the shaggy beard. The
blackened scab of blood around the sharp tip of
the arrow made Lucy feel sick to see.

'I've got everything you asked for,' she whispered. Perhaps he was unconscious again and she
should let him sleep until morning. 'Your shirt
was beyond saving so I think it will serve to bandage the wound.'

When she began to lay things on the chest he
opened his eyes and gave her a smile of such unexpected sweetness that she hesitated, suspecting trickery.

'It's a pity. It was a good shirt.' He stretched his
hands out towards her. 'Will you free me now? It
will be much easier if I'm able to use my hands.'

Lucy looked at the ropes, and the wrists they
bound. The muscles in his arms were as well defined as the rest of his body. On the wrists she

could see red welts where he had strained to free himself.

'I still don't know if I can trust you.' She frowned. 'I don't even know your real name.'

He raised his eyebrows and his mouth twisted into a crooked grin. 'You know my name is Roger.'

'When the men came up here I had to explain you. I masked their view and said you were my husband and they asked what you were called. You shouted a different name.'

'Whatever did you tell them that for?' He gazed at her in astonishment. Lucy squirmed.

'You were in my bed. I had to think of something.' She bit her lip. 'I said you were my husband and a drunkard and wastrel at that.'

She stopped short of explaining the part Robbie had played in making the fiction believable. Sir Roger looked thoughtful.

'Blackening my character to save my skin. I should wonder if that tells me more about your experience of husbands than anything else. Where is yours, by the way? You're the only person I've seen here.'

If he was hoping to glean information he was going to fail. Lucy narrowed her eyes.

'That's my business. I pleaded with them not to reveal my shame at having such a man and that if they disturbed you I would feel the brunt of it.

They never came close enough to recognise you, but when you cried out they believed I was speaking the truth. They asked what you were called and you shouted the name Henry.'

He sucked his breath and glanced away, the skin at the side of his eyes tightening. The information seemed to be a surprise to him and an unwelcome one at that.

'I said that? I don't remember. My memories of that time are fogged.' He grimaced. 'In truth, I don't trust you either, but I have little choice except to put myself in your hands.'

'You don't trust me?' Lucy exclaimed. 'Why not?'

He spread his hands before him. 'What reason have you given me? I woke to find myself your captive with days stolen from me and I only have your word that what you said has happened is the truth.'

He made a good point. His loss of days clearly bothered him and the situation he had awoken in would have alarmed anyone.

'You were drugged. That's why you won't remember.' She edged round the bed and offered him the cup of wine with an outstretched arm, snatching her hand away once he took it.

'I swear what I have told you is the truth and I acted for the best to help your pain. If I invented the incident and the name, how could I choose one that hit you in such a way? Are you Roger or Henry?'

'I'm Roger. Roger Danby. Henry is…' He tilted the cup back, draining it with an aggression that was startling. 'He's someone else. Do you have more?'

'Do you have the means to pay for it?' Lucy asked, indicating the cup he held out. He pouted and Lucy folded her arms in annoyance. It was the best wine and did not come cheap.

'I'll pay, though you're a hard woman to ask a man in such a condition.'

Lucy thought of the sack of flour growing emptier in the pantry, the holes in her thrice-mended undershift and the leak in the roof of the brewing shed. A knot of anxiety clutched at her belly at the thought of how she would pay for replacements or repairs with so few customers to bring in money. If Sir Roger had accepted another bowl of stew, she would have gone hungry herself.

She wondered whether to tell him that, but decided against it. Her affairs were none of his business, but if Sir Roger was as rich as he claimed to be, he could well afford to buy his wine, whatever his condition.

'I can't give my wares away. I need to live,' she said. 'I won't charge you for what you've had so far, but from now on you pay for what you drink and eat.'

'That seems fair,' Sir Roger said agreeably. He shifted uncomfortably, wriggling a little higher on the bed. 'Speaking of such matters, I have that need we alluded to before coming on me again. I would rather attend to it myself, however if you don't want to let me loose I'm more than happy for you to assist.'

Lucy felt the heat spread across her cheeks as understanding dawned. She had only been able to do what had been necessary while Sir Roger was drugged and unaware she was touching him. The thought of handling him while he was conscious was excruciating, especially after his earlier indignation at her insult to his manhood. A slur she had neither meant nor which, in truth, had been warranted. Far from it. She kept her eyes fixed on his face, in case they began to stray to the area under discussion.

'You only need one hand for that,' she snapped. 'The pot's under the bed. Call me when you're done.' She dragged the pot out and edged it within reach of his hand with her foot, then left the room.

At the top of the stairs Lucy leaned against the wall and ran her hands across her hair, smoothing it back from her forehead. She had been more at ease with his presence while he had been under the control of the sleeping draught and she had forgotten how relentless his ribald comments had been when he arrived. Even lying down and weakened, he was the most masculine man she had ever encountered and his vitality was disturbing. His words had the ability to set her heart beating with the pace of the drummer playing on market day. Despite her best intentions to ignore his words, a flash of his roguish grin or glint in those deep brown eyes caused her body to respond of its own accord. The battle was increasingly harder won.

Sir Roger called her name and she took a couple of deep breaths before going back in.

'Let's get this over and done with while we still have light,' she said briskly. 'Tell me what to do.'

Sir Roger looked taken aback by her change in demeanour.

'First I'll have another drink of wine. Don't worry, I'll add it to my account,' he smirked.

Lucy poured one and handed it over.

'Now you have one as well,' Sir Roger instructed. 'You're as pale as the moon and your hand was trembling. I don't want you passing out before we're done.'

'I don't need wine to settle my nerves,' Lucy admonished.

He laughed. 'Really? In that case you're a rare

woman as well as a modest one. It works for me every time. Drink!'

Lucy perched on the end of the bed, knees pressed together, and sipped from the cup. Despite her protestations to the contrary, the taste was welcome.

'You'll have to come closer,' Sir Roger instructed. 'Bring everything to this end, including the wine.'

Lucy shuffled down towards Sir Roger, unwilling to put herself within his reach, but knowing she had no other option. She laid the equipment out beside her, save for the knife, which she kept in the pouch at her waist.

They sat face to face, Lucy twisting round on the bed to sit beside the reclining man. They were as close as lovers exploring each other as the prelude to lovemaking. The dark curls that framed Sir Roger's face lifted as she exhaled and his wine-scented breath was soft on her cheeks. It would take only the slightest motion forward and their lips would be close enough to touch.

They both raised their eyes at the same time and when they met a jolt passed through Lucy as violent as the lightning bolt that had split the old hawthorn tree the winter previously. It reached down inside her, tugging at her stomach and more intimate parts, stirring feelings she had long forgotten existed.

She lifted a shaking hand to his shoulder and brushed a finger alongside the crust of blood, taking care not to touch it. The skin was cooler than when she had feared he had a fever and no longer slick with perspiration. He inclined his head to follow the gesture and his breathing sped up. Lucy held the lamp close so she could see the arrow and peered at it, her fingers probing with more firmness as she examined the area.

'I think it missed the bone completely.' She raised her eyes to his. 'Someone must be looking out for you.'

'I seriously doubt I warrant that privilege,' Sir Roger said with a curt laugh.

He blinked rapidly and his gaze dropped to his right arm, which hung motionless down the side of the bed, the hand curled into a loose fist. He covered Lucy's hand with his left one. The gesture was gentle and there appeared to be no flirtation in what he did. He had made no further request to be freed.

'Why did you kiss me the other night?' Lucy asked.

'I thought I might be about to die. It seemed a better way to leave this world than expiring on the floor in my own blood, don't you agree?' Sir

Roger replied after a pause. 'Any man would have done the same.'

And any woman's lips would have sufficed, Lucy thought, with an instant clarity that caused her stomach to writhe with self-contempt. She was simply a convenience.

'You said you didn't want to die unmourned. Don't you have family?'

'Family doesn't equate to grievers,' Sir Roger said tersely. He lowered his head, but when he raised it he gave her a crooked smile that was more like the man she had become familiar with.

'You could kiss me again now. For luck.'

He eyed her intently. Once again Lucy felt the intense drive to do as he asked but it was tempered now with the knowledge that it was not she herself that he had wanted. She shook her head.

'You're not going to die today so there's no need.' She hoped it was true.

'Check the back of the arrow,' Sir Roger said, lowering his hand. 'If it isn't completely smooth use the knife to cut away the splinters. I can't risk infection. When that's done you twist and pull from the front, gently and slowly, and get ready to staunch the bleeding.'

'Should I get the poker?' Lucy asked.

He grunted a laugh.

'You're fixated on the thing, aren't you? It will

be too cold by now. You wouldn't even manage to burn me like you did before.' He stroked his finger across the mark she had left in illustration. 'No, I'd prefer to save that for a last resort. Dress it with honey if you have any, pad the wound and bind it as tight as you can. Will you remember all that?'

'I think so.' She tried to make her voice brave and to exude a confidence she was far from feeling.

Sir Roger sat forward. He leaned his head against Lucy's shoulder, his chest pressing against hers. His beard was scratchy against the side of her neck when he turned his head. It tickled the soft flesh below her ear, causing her heart to race with the sensation. Gingerly she reached her hands around Sir Roger and ran her hand along the protruding length of wood. Thomas had almost completed the task and it took only a few strokes to ensure the wood was smooth. Sir Roger grunted once or twice and gave a sharp hiss, but urged her to continue each time she paused. When she was satisfied, Lucy slipped the knife back in her pouch and helped Sir Roger lean back once more.

'It's done.'

He nodded. His lips were white from where he had pressed them together. It must have been more uncomfortable than he had revealed.

'Do you want more wine?' she asked, reaching for the flask and pouring it before he had a chance to answer. This time, when he passed her the half-empty cup she did not hesitate, but drained it in one.

Sir Roger felt for her hand resting in her lap. 'Lucy, when the arrow comes free it is going to be painful. I might behave as an animal would and lash out.'

He looked deep into her eyes. She studied the brown depths ringed with thick dark lashes. They radiated honesty that she was not sure she could trust.

'If I do anything that hurts or scares you, it is not intentional. I mean you no harm, Lucy. Will you trust me in this, if nothing else?'

Lucy bit her lip and nodded. A ragged whimper escaped her and to her horror her eyes blurred.

'What's wrong?' Sir Roger asked with gentleness in his voice that surprised her.

'I don't know what to do. I've never had to do anything like this before,' she admitted, her voice beginning to quiver. 'I'm afraid I'll do something wrong and hurt you.'

'You won't.' He smiled and his hand tightened momentarily on hers, his thumb coming to rest against the hollow of her wrist where the pulse galloped.

'I trust you.'

Lucy grabbed a handful of cloth, ready to stem the flow of blood, and folded it into a thick pad. Sir Roger guided the hand he was holding to the arrow, easing her hand around the wooden shaft between the iron tip and his flesh and enclosing it in his. He raised an eyebrow questioningly. She nodded. He drew his knees up behind her to brace himself for what was to come.

Impulsively Lucy dipped her head forward and brushed her lips against his. The hairs of his beard were soft against her cheek and she tasted the trace of wine as she enclosed his lower lip between hers.

'For luck,' she whispered. She pulled back before he could draw her into a deeper kiss. Enjoying the astonishment that suffused his eyes, she smoothed her hair back.

'I'm ready.'

Chapter Seven

It was not easy and it was not quick. The arrow had gone clean through the flesh as Lucy had suspected, but because it had remained for so long it took a lot of twisting and pulling before it was free of the crust of blood. At the first twist, Sir Roger bit down on his lip, drawing blood. He jerked his head to the bundle of cloths and demanded Lucy give him one. She wiped the trickle of blood away, hushing him as she might comfort Robbie when he fell in the yard. Whenever she had attempted similar with her father he had brushed her away angrily, but Sir Roger's eyes filled with pained amusement.

'I'm not your babe in arms. Just give me the damned cloth to bite on.'

There was blood, but less than Lucy had feared. It oozed rather than spurted, welling up between her fingers as she pressed the cloth to his back against the hole. Sir Roger did none of the things he had warned Lucy he might do. He swore loudly and repeatedly, using expressions Lucy had never heard, not all of them in English, but he directed none of his ire at Lucy.

When her fingers became slippery with gore, Sir Roger pushed Lucy's hand out of the way and pulled the arrow the rest of the way by himself, leaving her to reach around behind to staunch the bleeding. When the shaft came loose with a stomach-churning, sucking pop, Sir Roger gave one final resounding roar. The arrow dropped from his hand, the iron tip clattering on the floorboard. He wiped his arm across his now-pale brow where sweat had slicked his hair down and lay back, eyes closed.

'Now do what you need to,' he said brusquely.

Lucy realised her own body was clammy, whether through effort or tension. She shivered, but had no time to dwell on it as the blood was welling and trickling down Sir Roger's chest. She pressed the remaining cloth bundle against it with her free hand and found that she had somehow ended up half-lying across Sir Roger's lap. If she moved she would lessen the pressure on the wounds. She wrapped the strips of cloth beneath his armpit and around his shoulder.

'Keep pressing on the pads,' Sir Roger wheezed.

'How long do I need to do this?' she asked.

Sir Roger half-opened one dark-ringed eye. His complexion was ashen and he looked weary. 'Until the bleeding has lessened and the bandages are sufficient to keep the pressure. Or longer, if you like.'

His voice sounded thick with exhaustion. 'You can stay there all night if it pleases you. I make a point in never passing up the chance for a companion.'

He closed his eye again. Lucy pulled back the cloth covering the front of the wound to see if the bleeding had stopped, but the rapid welling confirmed she would have to stay where she was for the time being. Her shoulders were aching from the uncomfortable position she had been holding them in. She switched arms, so that her right passed behind Sir Roger's back, and let the heel of her left hand push against the wound on his front. It was easier to apply the pressure this way, even if it did mean she was now almost lying chest to chest with him as if they were embracing.

Beneath the blanket that covered him, Lucy was becoming intensely aware of the shape of his legs and his hips pushing against her. She wriggled to get more stable and felt him move in response, hips tilting. An increase in firmness beneath the blanket made her remember the other things she had done for him. An aching throb of desire caught her by surprise.

She shifted her gaze to Sir Roger's face. He was lying motionless. He appeared unaware of her presence and had given no indication he was aware of what his body was doing. As long as that state remained she could ignore it herself and the improper ideas that it gave her. She yawned and let her eyes close as tiredness whispered that she should rest. The events of the evening had left her drained and this was now beginning to make itself known. She would not allow herself to sleep, or to stay longer than necessary, but it would do no harm to rest for a short while. She was still telling herself this as her eyes closed and she drifted into sleep.

Roger woke to find the top of Lucy's head pressing against his cheek. His first, confused urge on finding a woman lying face down in his arms was to decide which part of her body to caress first in order to wake her up to continue whatever pleasures they had enjoyed before sleeping.

His brain caught up with his instinct, overtook it and pulled sharply on the reins before he slid his hand down her slender waist to begin fondling her rounded thighs. He recalled who she was and why she was there. Lucy would not welcome his

attentions, at least not at this moment in time—
though, remembering the flashes of interest she
had failed to hide, he did not give up all hope.
More than this, the fact he was contemplating
morning adventures was a good sign that he was
alive and recovering.

It was starting to grow light and Roger let his
eyes drift in and out of focus staring at the strands
of brown, gold and tawny of Lucy's hair that had
come loose from her braid. It was better than concentrating on the sensation in his shoulder, which
had changed from the dull throbbing ache to a
sharper, more insistent pain. He flexed the fingers
on his right hand, then tried to lift his arm. The
resulting pain drew a shameful gasp from him and
he dropped his hand again. It would take a day or
two before he was able to use it at all.

The tugging at his wrist reminded him he was
still tethered. For all her softening towards him,
Lucy had not been persuaded to release him. He
doubted that she would and resentment swelled
in him. He was not prepared to remain her captive until she decided to free him. He could not
imagine a more alluring jailer, but she was a jailer
nonetheless.

He shifted and Lucy slid downward a little.
Her hand, still pressing against his shoulder, was
limp. She showed no sign of waking, but fortu-

nately the pressure she had applied before she slept must have been sufficient to stem the flow of blood. Roger grinned, remembering he had seen Lucy stow her knife back in the pouch at her waist after using it. The pouch was now within reach of his hand.

With exaggerated care, he crept his fingers along her girdle until he came to the leather bag. Slipping three fingers inside, he eased it open until his hand closed about the short, thick handle of the knife. Suppressing his elation, he drew it out. Still Lucy did not stir. She must be exhausted to sleep so deeply, but soon the cock would crow or her child would cry and she would wake. He would need to be quick.

It took a lot of effort and muffled muttering, and caused waves of sickness to flood over him as he braced his useless right arm, but Roger succeeded in pulling the rope beneath the bed taut and sawing at it until the threads split and gave. The relief that soared in his heart eclipsed any of the pain that coursed through him as a result of his endeavours. He stretched his left arm wide, feeling the muscles begin to spasm, then sing with the satisfaction of free movement. Roger was unused to inactivity and he needed to exercise, to ride, to swing a sword and wake the blood in his veins.

He pictured the look on Lucy's face when she woke face to face with the tip of her own knife and realised what he had done. The woman was obstinate and rude, showing none of the deference he would expect from one of her rank to one of his. If she wasn't so endearingly pretty he'd…

He'd what? Threaten her again? Beat her until she begged for mercy for her insolence? What would that achieve, other than to prove him to be the sort of man she had disparagingly described him as to the men hunting him? The sort of man his brother thought him to be. He could never harm the woman who slept so peacefully against his breast.

Besides, Roger knew he needed to rest, at least for the morning, and while Lucy believed she was at no risk she would feed and care for him. He returned the knife to the pouch and pushed the end of the rope out of view beneath the bed. When Lucy rose she would see everything as she expected to. When the time was right, he would reveal he had been free all along.

He closed his eyes, drifting back into sleep and enjoying the sensation of a soft, warm body nestling close to his.

When the sun warmed his face, he awoke for a second time, feeling better than he could remember, even before Thomas's rude interruption in Lord Harpur's house. Lucy was still asleep against him.

'Lucy...' he breathed, dipping his lips close to her ear. 'Lucy, it's morning.'

She sighed, her shoulders rising and her breasts swelling against Roger's naked chest with a maddening sensuousness. Her head burrowed against the hollow beneath his jaw. He'd had a woman beside him at John Harpur's house, he recalled, though with Lucy so close he could not bring her to mind. Perhaps before long he would convince Lucy of the benefits of sharing his bed for purposes beyond nursing him. It gave him something to hope for at least.

'Is it morning?' Lucy mumbled. She rolled her head sideways and opened her eyes. As they focused, Roger stared down into them, examining the fine, pale lashes surrounding eyes that fought a constant battle to be either blue or grey. They widened further as Lucy became aware of how intimately she was lying with Roger. She sprang back, moving away from Roger to get to her feet, but inadvertently brushing against his lap and causing all manner of sensations to awake within him. He almost gave up his intention of hiding his freedom as the urge to bed her came upon him.

Lucy wiped her hands over her brow, smoothing tendrils of hair that had stuck to her forehead. She dipped her head modestly, but not enough to disguise the roses that blossomed in her cheeks.

'I apologise! I didn't intend to fall asleep here.'

'Ordinarily I would take it as a personal affront if any woman fell asleep in my arms before I'd finished with her,' Roger said. 'However, under the circumstances...'

He grinned at her, not caring if she noticed his arousal. Lucy looked Roger up and down and an expression of worry crossed her face, as if unsure what had passed between them.

'You remain unsullied, don't fear,' Roger said.

Her lips pursed slightly. Her eyes slid to his shoulder.

'Does it hurt?' Her voice was terse.

'A little.'

He lied. It hurt more than he intended to share with her. 'The bleeding has all but stopped, I think. You managed well last night, Lucy. I won't forget what you did.'

She gave a faint smile, but her eyes became hard. 'Good. You can rest for the day. I'll bring you food when I have time.'

She walked towards the door, pausing by the end of the bed to gather the empty wine jug.

'You're leaving me?' Roger asked.

Lucy looked back over her shoulder with disdain in her eyes. She had changed from a sleepy kitten to a haughty cat in the space it had taken to cross the room.

'Yes. I have a child to tend to and ale to brew. My last batch was tainted somehow. Filled with dust.' She frowned, a small crease bisecting her brow. 'I have an inn to clean and run. I don't have time to stay talking to you.'

'It wasn't talking I had in mind,' Roger muttered beneath his breath as she went out.

He lay back and closed his eyes. He slept again, on and off, fitfully, as sounds from outside reached his ears and wound into his dreams. The wails of Lucy's son from outside, a clattering noise from the room below, the sound of conversation and laughter that took him by surprise. Lucy had been either serious or angry when he had been in her presence and he had not imagined her being merry. He wondered who had provoked it and was taken aback to realise that he was jealous.

Lucy returned at midday, bringing bread and cheese that she placed on the floor within his reach. He feigned sleep, though watched through slitted eyes as she moved around the room, her hips swaying sinuously and her step light. She tensed as she came closer to the bed even though she must have believed him asleep. He felt her hands on his bandage, fingers probing his flesh with a light touch that was unbearably teasing. That she was capable of such gentleness yet could transform into a fury at the slightest provocation fascinated him. Which side would come to the fore when she was making love? He was desperate to find out.

He should have got her into bed by now. Why was she so determined to resist what she so clearly wanted? Perhaps the voice that caused her laughter was the reason. The boy must have a father somewhere after all.

Later on, he felt a pressure on his shoulder that alarmed him until he opened his eyes to see a burly cat coiling in a circle on his chest to settle for a sleep. He hissed and it glared back at him with malevolent orange eyes. He shooed the animal off and it slunk to the floor grudgingly, but the activity served to make Roger feel restless. If he had ever spent this long in bed it was because he had a woman to occupy his time and, if the woman who currently absorbed his thoughts was not willing to join him, he needed to get his sluggish blood moving once again.

He swung his feet to the ground quietly so as not to make any sound that might alert Lucy. His head spun as he stood and he almost returned to the bed, but he set his jaw and succeeded in keeping his balance. He rolled his head around, feeling the muscles protest at the unaccustomed exertion. He walked across the floor, barefoot. His boots had been placed side by side in the corner of the room. A cold draught blew across him and he shivered. His cloak and jerkin were folded alongside his boots and the scrip with its pitiful contents was on top. He remembered his shirt had been cut to shreds. He wrapped the blanket around himself, wishing there was a fire to heat the room.

Once again Lucy's voice floated up the stairs, but this time the tone was different to her earlier laughter. Roger edged closer to the door, recognising the wariness and anger that he had been on the receiving end of more than once. The sound of a man's voice reached him, the words muffled but the tone irate, followed by Lucy's answering voice, higher and more urgent now.

He'd heard no voices besides those of Lucy or her child and Roger's senses became alert in a way they had not been for days. He had assumed any threat was done with. Was the danger not past after all? He attempted to pull his boots on, but gave up, discovering he had little strength in his right arm. He pushed the worrying thought to the back of his mind.

The voices increased in volume, Lucy's becoming more indignant and urgent. Roger looked around the room for his sword, but could not find it. The only thing that might serve as a weapon was the poker that Lucy had forgotten and which had rolled under the bed. His fingers closed around it and a glint of metal caught his eye. He pulled out the arrow, shaft streaked with his blood. He tucked it inside the waistband of his breeches and pulled the blanket snugly to mask his semi-nakedness. He paused at the doorway to reflect on his state of undress. He'd bargain a year of his life for a simple mail coat. The polished armour he had worn when tilting in the lists seemed a dream. He was glad there was no one from his past to see the level to which he had sunk.

He crept down the stairs, clutching the poker in his right hand. The stairs were dark and the door was half-shut. Roger stood in the shadows, waiting to see what was occurring. Lucy was standing with her back to the stairs. Her spine was straight and her head erect. Her long braid was twisted into a roll and peeked out beneath the linen cap she wore. It gave Roger an unspoiled view of the elegant curve of a neck that he'd enjoy kissing. Her arms were folded across her chest and she stood with her feet planted apart. Roger did not need to see her face to picture the expression of cold fury it would bear. He enjoyed the prospect of witnessing her directing her ferocity at someone else besides him for a change. Ready to move if he needed to, he paused and watched to see how the situation would play out.

'You drank it, you pay for it,' Lucy said firmly.

'It tastes like dog's piss. Why should I pay for that?' sneered one man. The other gave a croaky laugh.

Roger craned his neck to look at who had spoken. The two male voices belonged to a couple of bedraggled-looking men, rangy and lean. Their clothing was poor quality—Roger would not have looked twice at it in the marketplace—and looked well worn. Across their bodies both wore belts and criss-crossed straps of leather and rope hung with trinkets. They had the red-eyed look of day-long drunkards. The bench in front of the counter lay on its side where they had seemingly tipped it.

'You drank three mugs before you passed judgement!' Lucy snapped, moving her hands to her hips. Her sleeves were pushed to above her elbows, giving Roger a glimpse of her bare forearms. 'If you didn't like it, you should have stopped at one.'

The argument was only a couple of pedlars arguing over their bill, nothing more sinister. Roger relaxed, his shoulders releasing the tension he felt he had been carrying for days. This was nothing to do with him and Thomas, but an affair of Lucy's own. Whoever had been chasing them would be long gone. He hoped Thomas was dining in luxury at Calveley's house. As soon as he felt able to ride, Roger would leave Lucy's inn far behind and make his own way there. He'd wasted too much time lying around already and surely he would be feeling well enough after one more night of rest under Lucy's care.

Roger turned to go, but two steps back up the staircase he stopped. His mind flashed back to the night he had arrived and Lucy barring his way upstairs with a ferocity that had surprised and impressed him. Later that night she must have assumed a similar position when she protected him and allowed Thomas to escape.

'D'yer want us to spread the word yer serve bad drink?' he heard one man sneer. 'We're heading into Mattonfield from here.'

This matter was nothing to do with him, but he had not liked the look of the two men, and Lucy was alone. He crept back down the stairs in time to see Lucy make a move past the men towards the doorway.

'There's nothing wrong with my ale,' Lucy insisted.

Her eyes blazed, her pale skin making them

seem all the brighter. The foolish girl looked like she intended to bar their exit. Roger whistled, low and quiet, between his teeth, torn between a sense of admiration for her doggedness and exasperation that she would put herself at risk for the sake of a penny's worth of ale.

'Going to stop us, are yer?' scoffed one.

The two pedlars exchanged a glance. They laughed in unison in a way that made Roger's hackles rise. Before Lucy found herself in a darker situation Roger pushed the door open and stepped into the room.

'Gentlemen, good day,' he said pleasantly. 'Is anything the matter?'

A gasp of alarm burst from Lucy. Roger slid his gaze to her. She was standing rigid as a statue, her face paling further than he would have thought possible. Only her expression showed signs that she was a living, breathing woman. It changed from the indignation she had been showing to horror as she looked at him. Roger was used to reading the eyes of men as he faced them in the tiltyard or on the battlefield and in Lucy's he saw a flash of genuine terror. And why wouldn't she, when she believed him still captive upstairs?

He flashed her a brief smile designed to comfort her, but which caused her to look more terrified. The two pedlars stood uncertainly, their previous mirth turning to confusion. Calculating that the men were strangers to Lucy, Roger stomped into the centre of the room. Time to play the layabout husband she'd portrayed him as.

'What's going on, woman?' he asked angrily. 'Can't I sleep without being dragged down here to deal with matters on your behalf?'

'Her 'usband, are yer?' asked the shorter pedlar. He scratched his crotch and grinned.

'Yes, and if there's trouble I want to know. No man drinks here for free,' Roger growled. 'Give the lady her payment and be off before I boot you out the door.'

The man looked down and, seeing Roger's bare feet, gave a mirthless grin.

'Like that, will yer?'

'If it comes to it.' Roger relaxed his glare, his voice laden with fake camaraderie. 'I've talked my way out of a bill enough times so let me tell you, that isn't the way to do it. You have to coax the lady into wanting to let you have her wares for nothing.'

He flashed a lustful grin at Lucy, who closed her eyes and looked away in distaste. He'd done it often enough in his time and a ripple of disgust shot through him at the idea of these two trying it with Lucy. Roger brandished the poker, ignoring the fire that streaked from his shoulder to wrist as he held it aloft.

'Out! You're not welcome here, and tell anyone that Mistress Carew doesn't suffer attempts to cheat or blackmail her. The drink here is as good as anywhere.'

His head was beginning to feel light and the pain in his arm was increasing. This worried him more than he liked to consider now. He was used to lifting a sword four or five times heavier, to say nothing of the lances he had once wielded. If it came to it the men could probably beat him in a fight—then beat him senseless. He lifted his jaw, baring his teeth and jerked his head towards the door. He thrust the poker towards them, motioning to leave.

To his relief the men nodded at each other and sauntered to the door. Lucy stood her ground, unfolding her arms and holding one hand out. The thin pedlar dipped a hand inside his shirt and flourished a farthing. He flipped it into the air with a sniff. Lucy snapped a hand out, plucking it mid-fall with a practised air.

Until they had vanished from sight, she stood as gracefully as a queen dismissing her courtiers to let the men pass. When they had gone, her whole body wilted. She looked smaller, more vulnerable, and Roger's muscles sagged in sympathy. Or maybe it was the effort of standing upright after so long lying down and on an empty stomach. Nausea washed over him. He'd seen men taken like this after battles. Fine during the skirmish when their minds were occupied, but losing their breakfast or keeling over into a faint once the fighting was done. He was determined not to be one of them.

He looked at the woman standing rigid by the doorway and realised with a sinking heart that she looked more terrified of him than she had of any difficult customer. He cursed his stupidity at charging downstairs and revealing his freedom so soon. There was nothing to be done now but get Lucy to help him once again. Though it pained him to be so reliant on her, he jerked his head towards her.

'Come over here, Lucy Carew,' he growled. 'I'm not going to hurt you but if you don't help me sit, I'm going to fall down where I'm standing.'

Chapter Eight

Lucy's stomach lurched at Sir Roger's words, the deep growl reaching inside her with the ferocity of a fist embedding itself into her guts.

'How…?' She swallowed, her words sticking in a throat that grated like a well-used grindstone. 'How did you…?'

Sir Roger held up his arm holding the poker. The length of rope dangled from his wrist.

'How did I free myself?' His voice was cold. 'I borrowed your knife while you slept and cut the rope. It was not an easy feat one-handed, but I was careful and you noticed nothing.'

She'd returned the knife to its home earlier today, but instinctively her hand moved to the pouch. His eyes followed the movement.

'I put it back straight away, naturally,' Sir Roger said, smirking. 'I don't like to show my hand unless I have to. Quite literally in this case.'

He raised an eyebrow and looked at her as if he expected her to laugh at his feeble jest. Lucy had never felt less like laughing. Her skin crawled at the thought of his hands having such freedom while she slept. She told herself that taking the knife was the only liberty he had claimed and hoped it was the case. She wrapped her arms around herself. Shaking already from her dispute with the two pedlars, she backed against the wall beside the open door, unsure if her legs would bear her weight much longer. Her sole comfort was that the man standing before her looked equally frail. He still held the poker out, but the tip was beginning to waver and he looked like he was having to concentrate on keeping it still.

As she remembered the way he had raged at her, demanding to be freed and his powerful hands tightening around her throat, bile curdled her stomach. Now he was free without her leave and his wound was dealt with. He had no reason to treat her kindly. She had faced down the vagrants alone and plenty more before them without being reduced to a quaking mess, but she'd seen the muscles that were now concealed so oddly beneath Sir Roger's blanket and had felt the strength in them to her cost already.

'Please don't hurt me,' she whispered.

An expression flashed across his face, but she read it as irritation rather than anger. He lowered the arm holding the poker, which was now visibly shaking, and leant on the end, supporting his weight as an old man might use a cane.

'If I wanted to hurt you I could have strangled you as you slept,' he said with exaggerated patience. 'Or used the end of this rope on your backside and thrashed you until you cried for having the impudence to tether me like a dog. It's what you deserved and the fact I didn't should prove you're safe in my company.'

Lucy met his eyes. His face was changing from ruddy to ashen and his forehead shone with sweat. Swathed in the heavy blanket he cut a strange figure, but not a threatening one. He brought to mind one of the monks who sometimes passed through the town, though the expression in his eyes was anything but holy. She noticed his feet were bare and somehow it was this that comforted her more than anything.

'If you're trying to reassure me, you've got a strange way of going about it,' she remarked. 'How long were you planning to keep up with your deception?'

He shrugged, winced and blinked as the gesture obviously caused him discomfort. Lucy scrutinised him. He must still be weak and the longer he stood there, the less able he would be to attack her at full strength.

'Until I was stronger and didn't need to rely on you. Until Thomas returned and we could leave. Honestly, I'm not sure.'

'So you were happy to lie there idle while I waited on you. Very gallant of you, my lord!'

He gazed at her through glazed eyes. She pictured him how he must be in his everyday life. The young nobleman with his fine clothes and haughty attitude. Of course he would behave in no other way towards someone like her.

'I wanted to prove to you I wasn't a threat,' Sir Roger explained. 'That I could have done anything but chose not to would have signified that.'

'You were going to prove to me that you could be trusted by deceiving me,' Lucy said tartly. 'How cunning! What made you change your mind?'

He pursed his lips, glancing at the doorway. 'I heard voices. I thought it might be the men who came the other night, or others like them. I decided it best to be ready to deal with them if necessary.'

'But you must have realised they weren't?'

'I was going to go back up, but I didn't like the way they spoke to you.'

He looked almost embarrassed as he admitted it. How curious that a knight who must have sworn vows to honour and protect would seem ashamed to be caught in an act of gallantry. For a moment they faced each other uncertainly. He leaned against the poker, seemingly content to wait for as long as she liked. His knuckles were white though, and he swayed ever so slightly back and forth. His appearance now couldn't be taken as guarantee, however.

'Before I come closer I want you to swear I'm safe from harm for as long as you remain under my roof. I'll only help you after that.'

'I won't let anyone harm you,' he said.

'I meant harm from you.'

He blinked in surprise. A line of sweat began to trickle from his temple. 'I've already said I don't intend to hurt you, but I see that isn't going to be enough. I have many faults, but I don't break my word.' He placed his left hand over his heart and looked deep into Lucy's eyes. 'I swear on my house, on my name and in the name of King Edward you are at no risk of harm from me. Will that suffice?'

'It will.'

Sir Roger flashed her a grin, but his eyes tightened with pain. 'Good. Now get over here quickly, dove, because I'm about ready to drop.'

He looked as if he was speaking the truth because by now he was swaying more obviously. Lucy crossed the room and righted the bench beside the counter. She held an arm to Sir Roger. His hand gripped before he pulled her close and threw his arm around her shoulder, his hand holding— no, *caressing* her upper arm. His sudden weight took Lucy by surprise and she slipped her arm around his waist to prevent them both falling to the floor. His skin was warm and where her fingers touched the smooth, bare flesh of his waist they began to tingle, the heat spreading along her hand and through her arm. Sir Roger's stomach muscles tightened in response to her touch and a quiver passed through her at the transformation from relaxed to firmness. He bowed his head and the long exhalation of breath he gave was cool upon her lips. They were as close as they had been when he had forced his first kiss on her and Lucy realised she was parting her lips in readiness, but he made no move.

Feeling foolish, she cocked her head to the bench. 'Sit down there.'

He did not move, but slid his eyes to hers. 'You're stronger than you appear for someone so slight.'

'I spend half my day lifting barrels and sacks of grain. I have to be. Come on, I can't hold you forever.'

She helped him to the bench and he sank on to it, stretching out and spreading his legs wide before him. He leaned his back against the counter and let his head loll back, closing his eyes. He really was very handsome, even beneath the greyish pallor that his loss of blood had given him. Lucy perched on the bench as far away from him as possible. She tucked her skirts beneath her so that not even the slightest part touched him.

'Still wary, dove?' he muttered. 'Don't you trust me?'

'Is it any wonder? I thought you were asleep upstairs and you appear at the doorway, brandishing a weapon?' She shifted a little further away until her buttocks were almost hanging off the end of the bench. 'And knowing what you did while I was asleep, how your hands could have been anywhere and I'd never know…'

She drew her arms tight across her breasts. Sir Roger rolled his head so he was facing her.

'You'd have known.' He smiled and raised an eyebrow, his face lighting with amusement. 'If I'd had that in mind, I'd have made sure you were awake to appreciate it. I don't waste my efforts on a partner who can't thank me afterwards. And you would thank me.'

Lucy watched his full lips curl into a smile and recalled his kiss that had been delivered with an intensity that had left her breathless. Her throat tightened at the memory. She snorted, determined not to let him see the effect his words were having on her.

'You seem very confident in yourself. After what you've been through you can barely stand without assistance and your arm was trembling. How do you know I'd want to thank you?' she scoffed.

'I don't need to stand to do what I'm talking about and I have more than one arm. And other parts, too. And let me assure you, if you take me into your bed you'll be begging me not to leave it! Every woman I've bedded has enjoyed herself.'

'Every woman! You talk as if the number is a recommendation!'

'Isn't it?' He looked confused. 'Don't women want a lover who has taken the time to perfect his skills?'

His words wound themselves around Lucy's mind like the rope around his wrist, beguiling her and reminding her of pleasures she had not experienced for so long, tempting her to play the wanton. It had been a long time since anyone had watched her with such open interest, but the result of accepting the attentions of the last man of any standing who had done so was now playing outside with the chickens. That was not a mistake she intended to make again. Lucy pushed herself from the bench and spun to face him.

'Women don't want a man who will bed them, then leave, or deny the association afterwards. Skill is no substitute for constancy.'

He opened his mouth, then closed it abruptly. When he looked at her again, the desire in his eyes had all but vanished, but she had no doubt it was not quenched, merely simmering beneath the surface ready to boil again if the opportunity presented itself.

'I'll add to my earlier vow, if it pleases you. I swear I will respect your virtue as long as you demand it.' He licked his lips and grinned. 'But if you change your mind, I'll be more than ready to answer your call.'

Fingers of flame began creeping around the back of Lucy's neck, daring her to test him at his word. She remembered the sight of parts of his anatomy she found difficult to forget. Knights were supposed to be honest and keep the vows they made. She fervently hoped he would keep this one.

'Thank you. Now I have work to do.'

He dipped his head in acknowledgement.

'Of course, but since I dragged myself from my sickbed to save you from assault, I think I deserve a reward. Can I have a drink?'

Lucy filled Sir Roger a cup from the flagon the two pedlars had left. He took it left-handed and sniffed it.

'Smells fine to me.'

'Of course it does,' Lucy snapped. 'There's nothing wrong with it. Those two cheats were just trying to get out of paying.'

She watched him drink it, knocking the brew back in one swig, seemingly revitalised after his brief show of weakness. He wiped the back of his hand across his lips, gazing at her over the top of his hand.

'It isn't the best I've brewed,' she added. 'I'm trying a new balance of gruit—that's the flavourings— but I've been too busy this week and didn't have the time to tend it.'

She watched the realisation dawn on his face that he was the cause of her extra work. Some men might have apologised, or at least offered thanks, but Sir Roger said nothing. He leaned forward and the blanket slipped from his shoulder, revealing the bandages and padding she had applied. It must have taken effort to drag himself from his bed so soon after his ordeal.

He did not look like a knight. She could not picture him in armour, urging a charger into battle— though admittedly she had never seen anyone do that in reality—but when he had stood brandishing her poker, his blanket thrown over him like a cloak, she had glimpsed the fierceness in him. She gave him a slight smile.

'Thank you for your defence. It wasn't necessary, but I appreciate it all the same.' She refilled his cup. 'This one won't go on your account.'

Instead of thanking her, he adjusted his blanket and gave her a stern look, his dark eyes boring into her.

'If I hadn't intervened when I did, what were you intending to do?'

Lucy sat back on the bench, still taking care there was a gap between them. 'I'd have insisted as long as I dared, or perhaps accepted payment of another sort.'

He raised an eyebrow questioningly.

'A new length of rope or a knife sharpened,' she clarified, sensing the inevitable innuendo he was no doubt forming in his mind. 'Round here people trade what they have when they haven't the coins.'

She turned away, not wanting him to see the thoughts that churned through her mind. There had been times she had resorted to methods of an unsavoury nature to clear her own debts. She bit down on her lip, reminding herself she had sworn to feel no shame over what she had done. She sighed, dropping her shoulders, and faced him once more.

'Most likely they'd have refused, laughed and left no matter what I said. It wouldn't have been the first time. My father kept a stave beneath the counter in case he ever faced that problem.'

'You'd have had it taken and used on you!' Sir Roger's voice took on an edge she was not expecting. A warning and a prediction but also, surprisingly, a touch of concern. 'Better to lose your profits than an eye or your teeth.'

'That's why I don't use it,' she said, chilled at the idea of what he described and the memory of a hand across her cheek or backside on more than one occasion. He stared at her gravely. She stood and paced around. Agitation flowed through her limbs, tightening them and making them feel too short. Resisting Sir Roger's advances had left her feeling like a flagon corked too tightly, threatening to explode.

'Now you're up, at least I can sweep the room,' she said. Without a further word to him she picked up the besom that stood in the corner and stalked upstairs. She began to sweep the dust, determined to work off the energy that had built inside her.

Roger waited until the thudding of Lucy's feet from above stopped before following. She had her back to him, her broom attacking the wooden floor with violence. She jumped when she heard him, spinning around with her hand rushing to her breast.

'What do you want?'

'I need a bath and fresh clothes,' Roger began, indicating the blanket he wore.

Lucy's expression eased. 'I can find you some clothes,' she said. Before he could explain he had his own wherever his saddlebags had been stowed, she had opened the lid of the chest and was on her knees delving inside. She produced a tunic and held it out to him.

'Here. It was my father's. He was a shade taller than you, but it should do for the time being.'

Roger ran the cloth between his fingers. The linen was thin and a rougher weave than Roger would have liked. Ordinarily he would have scorned something so threadbare, but he bit back his objections. He began to shrug off his blanket, but stopped when it became clear Lucy was not about to grant him privacy. He tilted his head to one side and met her eyes, expecting her to look away in embarrassment.

'Is there something *you* want?'

'I thought I should examine your dressing. On your shoulder.'

'Or just watch me dressing?' Roger asked suggestively.

'That's a good shirt. I don't want you to bleed on to it.'

She reached out and unfolded the edge of the blanket with the same determined care Roger would take over undressing a lover. He stood naked to the waist, feeling disconcertingly exposed. That Lucy had no interest in what should follow only added to his sense of vulnerability.

His thoughts of lovemaking were replaced with anxiety as Lucy's forehead wrinkled.

'How does it look?'

'I'll give you fresh bandages. Sit down, you're too tall for me to do it standing.'

Too tall without coming closer than she was now, Roger thought. Nevertheless, he obeyed and sat as she unwound the old dressings and replaced them.

'There's no infection that I can see.' She wound the long strip of bandage across his shoulder and beneath his arms. 'How does it feel?'

Roger raised his arm and felt the same pulling ache in his shoulder that he had when holding the poker aloft.

'I have no strength in my arm.'

He looked at Lucy and the unexpected pity on her face curdled his stomach. He sighed and began to pull the tunic over his head. His arm spasmed and he gave an involuntary gasp. His head was inside the tunic so when he felt Lucy's hands close over the hem and skim his upper arms he almost moaned aloud in astonishment as her fingers on his bare skin awoke his desire. She helped him lower the tunic, pulling it down to his waist. She smoothed the tunic. Completely unnecessary, but Roger did not protest.

'The strength will return in time.' Her voice was too comforting for Roger to bear, not when pity rather than desire was governing her actions.

'Not soon enough,' he snapped. She jerked her hands away as if he had struck her. It was too much to stand. He began pacing around. Six paces covered the room. 'In the meantime I'm stuck in the middle of nowhere in ill-fitting clothes with a woman determined to rebuff my advances.'

Lucy's lips twisted. She crossed her arms tightly.

'There's nothing keeping you here. Leave when you like.'

'I will as soon as I am fit,' Roger retorted. 'In the meantime I'll wear my own clothes. Lucy, where are you keeping my horse?'

She stared at him in confusion. 'What do you mean?'

'Horse,' Roger repeated. 'The large, brown animal I arrived here on. Four legs. About as tall as you, but less contrary. Carrying my saddlebag. Where is it?'

'I know what a horse is.' Lucy huffed indignantly. 'It isn't here.'

'I can see that he isn't in the bedroom,' Sir Roger growled. A sense of unease was beginning to grow. He walked to the window, but the oiled linen frame was nailed to the ledge and he couldn't see anything. His throat constricted.

'What have you done with him?'

'I've done nothing!' Lucy exclaimed. She twisted her hands and took a step away as if fearing his reaction. 'I told you before. Thomas left, causing a commotion. He took both horses with him.'

Roger felt the blood drain from his face. He shook his head in disbelief as the implications of Lucy's words sunk in. Beneath the tunic his skin was clammy and hot. He felt a hand on his arm and raised his head to find Lucy gazing up at him, her large grey eyes filled with unhappiness.

'I should have explained better.' Her voice was gentle, comforting, as if she was speaking to her child. Keeping control of his temper took more effort than Roger felt capable of after everything else he had endured.

'I don't remember you telling me at all,' he said, struggling to master his unease. 'Was this when I was half-insensible?'

She nodded slowly, biting her lip and the expression in her eyes changing to anxiety. Roger put his hands on her shoulders and attempted to pull her towards him. She resisted. Raising his right arm high sent waves of nausea cascading over him. He ground his teeth to dismiss the discomfort. He loosened his grip and it was only then that she faced him of her own volition.

'Tell me everything I don't know,' Roger urged. 'You've teased me with revelations, but I'm tired of learning little by little. I want no more gradual surprises.'

Beneath his palms, the muscles in Lucy's arms tensed. 'I don't know what that is until you discover it yourself. I thought you would have realised. Thomas had left the horses outside as you know. He went to see to them while you made me—'

She broke off. A hint of rose began to bloom on her cheekbones. 'When I helped you to remove your clothing. You do remember that, don't you?'

Roger nodded. He remembered that well enough, but savouring the memory was not uppermost in his mind. He gestured for her to continue.

'I know you say your memories are uncertain, but I told you he had gone when you woke at one point the next day. Thomas took both horses and tried to make it look as though you were both riding away.'

'How did he manage that?' Roger asked, curiosity getting the better of his dismay at being stranded.

'He had followed me downstairs when the men knocked at the door. While I was trying to prevent them seeing your face close, he was busy outside. He tangled the reins of their horses and contrived to make it look like there was another rider on the horse beside him.' Lucy's eyes lit with a teasing glint. 'He tied an old sack to it. From a distance and in the dark it looked near enough like you were slumped over the saddle.'

Roger ran his hands through his hair, gripping his fingers at the roots. Thomas had shown more initiative than he had expected, but perhaps not enough sense. 'Tell me one final thing. Did he leave the saddlebags?'

'No. He left nothing.'

'Bull's pizzle! Are you telling the truth?'

'Of course I am,' Lucy shouted, her voice rising and her cheeks colouring. 'I'm no liar. Or perhaps you think I've hidden them to spite you?'

Roger swore. Lucy paled, but he ignored it, giving full vent to the frustrations he felt as he let out a stream of obscenity aimed at Thomas and the world in general. He looked around him at the low-roofed room that was shabbier than he had realised at first. Beyond it was the wood and beyond that nothing worth regarding. Even his father's home on the barren moors of Yorkshire was not this isolated. Being stranded in a town, or even a village, would have been a trial when he had so many tasks to accomplish, but here it was intolerable.

He swung round and thumped his fist on the door, relishing the rattling sound it made. The impact made his fist smart, but he ignored it, the pain at least being some sort of sensation. His muscles, long unused by his enforced bed rest, began to sing beneath his skin as blood flowed through his veins. This was not the exercise he wanted, but to be moving freely felt wonderful. He ignored the light-headedness that lingered and flung his arms out.

'Stop that now!' Lucy's command cut through his rage.

'Don't order me around, woman,' Roger growled.

'In my house I'll order you as I please!' she yelled back. 'And if you don't like it you can leave.'

Her retort brought him up short. No woman had ever spoken to him in such a way. Few men, either, of rank so far beneath his own. Roger faced her. Her hands were now on her hips, her sharp face as thunderous as the rage that churned inside Roger. There were not more than two paces between them and Lucy was shorter by a head.

To look up at him caused her head to tilt back, displaying her slender throat and delicate jaw that practically begged to be kissed. Her eyes glinted with unspoken warning. Beneath his temper Roger felt a flicker of excitement. He narrowed his eyes, but instead of looking away as he would expect a modest woman to do, Lucy narrowed her own.

'What do you think you're doing behaving in such a way?' Lucy asked.

Roger drew a deep breath through his teeth. He forced calmness into his voice that he did not feel. His outburst had been satisfying in the same way a bout of swordplay—or lovemaking—was, in that it had relieved some of the agitation he felt, but ultimately solved nothing.

'I'm expressing the frustration I feel at finding myself abandoned in the middle of nowhere with little more than the breeches I'm standing in. Does it surprise you that I'm less than delighted at the discovery? I have nothing! I have no means of knowing how long I am trapped here. I have places I need to be and errands I must complete. What am I supposed to do?'

'You aren't trapped here. Not since you freed yourself,' Lucy growled. 'You can leave any time you like. Thunder all you want, but do it somewhere else. Mattonfield is four miles away. Go throw yourself on the hospitality of Lord de Legh. He'll doubtless take in a man of your standing.'

'Then that's what I'll do!'

Roger grabbed his boots from where they lay. He fished inside and found his remaining money.

'I apologise I can't pay you everything I owe, but you see I am left with nothing.' He held his farthing up and flicked it towards Lucy in the same manner the pedlar had. She made no attempt to catch it, but watched it fall to the floor, her face thunderous. The sight was the final indignity Roger was prepared to suffer. He stormed down the stairs, out of the inn and out of Lucy Carew's life for good.

Chapter Nine

❦

Blasted woman!

Roger stalked towards Mattonfield, somehow finding the energy to seethe at Lucy's unjust behaviour despite the challenge of the steep incline ahead of him. He was halfway up the hill before he realised he still had the ropes dangling from each wrist. He worked at the knots as he walked, discovering them hard to unpick. Lucy had definitely intended him to remain bound! If he hadn't freed himself, he wondered just how long she would have kept him tethered to the bed. His confidence that he would have talked her into freeing him with honeyed words diminished the more he remembered her scathing responses.

When he reached the top of the hill he stopped, doubling over to rest his hands on his knees and drawing a deep breath into his aching lungs. His head swam and as he stood upright his shoulder throbbed and he was assailed by nausea. Every twinge served to mock his failure and emphasise his impotence.

He glared backwards to where the inn nestled in the valley. As he watched, Lucy's slight figure appeared and vanished around the back of the building, returning a while afterwards bowed down with a large bucket. She did not even glance towards the hill to see if Roger had managed to find his way or was still within sight. He should have been lying in bed being cosseted, not forced out on foot. He caught his petulant thought and checked himself with a growl. A hard march wasn't unusual to a man who had travelled to France and he'd recovered from plenty of injuries in less luxurious places than Lucy's bed. He knew it wasn't the lack of comfort that rankled, but the lack of tenderness on the part of his hostess.

While she had believed him unconscious or incapable Lucy had displayed the most caring heart and the change once he awoke still unsettled him. How dare Lucy speak to him in such a manner! The insolent woman had treated him as a child— or worse, an equal rather than a man far superior in rank. No deferential *milord* from her! Come to think of it, she had never called him anything. She had somehow avoided using his name or title, or referring directly to him in any way. If that was how she treated her guests it was small wonder her inn had so few visitors. And to throw him out when her brother had offered him refuge there was scarcely believable.

Roger had reached the hilltop where the ground had levelled. The forest he had ridden through to evade his pursuers was to his left. He shuddered at the memory of how close to death he had come that night. He'd suffered falls at the tilt and survived many battles, but he sensed the sheer terror of that night would remain with him long after the scars had healed. He hoped Thomas was safe. The youth was far too green to be carrying out the task they had been assigned alone.

'Where are you, lad?' he asked aloud. 'Hurry yourself back here so I can stop fretting.'

To his right a river wound through low ground around the bottom of a hill where sheep grazed. It must be the same one that passed by Lucy's inn. Beyond him he could see a cluster of rooftops and the spire of a church nestling into the side of the hill. A handful of homes were spread further out between the inn and the main group of buildings, though none was as remote as Lucy's inn. Mattonfield was a town barely worth the description.

Roger found a convenient clump of bushes and rested back against it, burying himself in the undergrowth away from the rough stone path. His shoulder was protesting and his belly was empty. He should at least have demanded something to eat before leaving. A short sleep would see him right.

He closed his eyes and planned what he would say to Lord de Legh when he arrived at his door. The man was not one the King had instructed him to visit and the name was unfamiliar to Roger. He hoped his own connections would be sufficient to gain admittance to the household. His name had made scarce difference to Robin de Monsort when he had changed his mind about granting permission for Roger to marry his daughter five years ago.

His hand felt for the folded letter in his scrip, though he knew the humiliating words off by heart. He noticed absentmindedly that dwelling on that particular cut felt less raw now. Jane de Monsort's plump, soft face was becoming indistinct in his memory. He closed his eyes, trying to bring her to mind, but the only woman who filled his vision had angular cheekbones beneath angry grey eyes that were filled with contempt for him.

'Begone, you bad-tempered dove. I'm done with you,' he muttered.

Lucy Carew was doubtless as glad to be rid of Roger as he was of her. At least, he thought he was glad to be out of her company, but the further from the inn he walked, the less sure he was that leaving had been the right decision. Even as they had argued he had felt a thrill whisper through his veins as his blood speeded up. The sure hands that had ministered to him would have been enough of a draw by themselves to convince him she was worth bedding, but usually he would have scorned a woman who behaved in such an immodest manner.

With Lucy he found himself increasingly drawn towards her. His instinct recognised a kindred spirit, a temper as quick as his own. He found himself wondering how alike they were in other passions and felt a strong urge to discover the answer. What a pity he never would. He envied whichever mysterious man had had the pleasure of fathering her child on her.

The sound of hooves galloping closer roused him from what had been a deeper doze than he had realised. The creak of a cartwheel and off-tune whistling disturbed him further. Because he was lying off the path he was unnoticed when the two travellers met almost directly in front of him and began to speak.

'Good day, master. Have you travelled far today?'

Roger opened one eye out of curiosity. The accent was northern. The voice might have been familiar and Roger dug into his memory to locate the owner, but found no one. He craned his head, but from his position could see only the legs of the horse. There was a pause before the driver of the cart answered suspiciously.

'Mebbe. Not so far as you, I'll warr'nt.'

'No, for certain. I am seeking my companions who I became separated from a few days past.' The voice was charming and exuded innocence. The soldier in Roger warned him to remain silent. He burrowed a little further into his nest.

'Is that the only town nearby?' the first voice asked. 'My friends—one or both—may have gone there. I am concerned that one might be injured. Have you seen such a man? Who is the lord of this manor?'

Roger shuddered. It sounded like the man was looking for Roger or perhaps the assailant who he had slashed at in the forest.

'That's a lot of questions,' the driver answered, more guarded now. 'Some might pay well for answers.'

Roger grinned at the man's boldness. He, too, was keen to find the answers and if someone else would pay that was even better. The horse was motioned closer to the cart and money presumably changed hands because the cart driver coughed and directed the rider to Mattonfield, adding further directions to the home of Lord de Legh.

'I've seen no injured stranger,' the cart driver added.

'I may return, so please keep in mind what I have asked,' the rider said. 'If there is talk of strangers in these parts, I want to hear of it.'

Roger let go his breath, though his heart was racing. If he had a sword he might have jumped from his hiding place and demanded answers of his own from the questioner, though remembering the way his arm had shaken holding the poker, he feared he would not be able to wield it effectively enough. In any case the rider dug his boots into the horse's flanks and galloped towards the town.

'You'll have to pay more than that,' the cart driver laughed to himself once the man was out of earshot. 'Now, sweetness, let's find out if you've got what I want.'

With that strange endearment to his ox, the cart moved away, too, heading down the road towards the inn. Roger waited until both men were safely away before sitting up. He scratched his beard thoughtfully, feeling both heartened and disturbed by what he had overheard. The rider might have been entirely unconnected to Roger's business, but deep in his bones Roger felt sure he was involved and this told him a number of things.

He knew Thomas had not yet been apprehended.

The seeker had not known the area so their pursuers likely had not been sent by Lord Harpur.

Which meant they had another purpose in hunting Roger. He could think of several men who would be glad to be rid of him, but no one who would go to so much trouble. The stranger could be intent on preventing Roger delivering his message from the King, but the accent was English so it seemed unlikely. The Northern Company, then?

Perhaps, though Roger wasn't aware he had earned anyone's ire.

Whatever the case, he was still in danger and seeking hospitality with Lord de Legh might prove difficult or unwise. Getting there would be at the limit of his endurance, too. He sat motionless, knees drawn up to his chest as he ran down all the possible paths he could take. Each time he arrived at the same location. The only place he was sure to be safe was at Lucy's inn.

He groaned. After the way he had departed, Lucy would doubtless be unhappy to see him return. Other than the possibility of getting her to agree to a quick tumble with him, he did not relish the idea of spending more time in her company, bad-tempered as she was. Nevertheless, that was what he intended to do. The sleep had done him good and he felt much better than he'd expected for it, not that he needed to reveal that to Lucy. He pulled himself to his feet and brushed himself down before beginning the walk back the way he had come on lighter feet.

Halfway back he encountered the cart returning. The burly driver was whistling the same approximation of a tune as when he had stopped the first time. Roger eyed him with interest as he approached. The man wore a wine-coloured tunic to his knees. It bore streaks of white dust that could be flour. The miller or baker, perhaps. He stared back at Roger, whose scalp prickled as he remembered the stranger's promise to return for further information. If a stranger was being hunted, Roger's best chance of self-preservation was to be anything but that.

'Good afternoon.' He beamed at the driver. 'A fine afternoon for a walk, though I'd rather be on your cart than on foot.'

Both men looked at the sky where dark clouds were gathering and heading towards them.

'Still,' Roger continued, as if he had been asked, 'I'll be glad of a drink when I get to the inn down the road. Best in Cheshire.'

'Old Carew's place?' the driver grunted. 'His daughter runs it now.'

'When a man has been abroad for a while, any

English beer is welcome and Mistress Carew brews fine ale.'

The driver looked interested in Roger for the first time. He pulled a hand through straggly, greasy hair. 'Know her, do you? You'll find her at home if you make haste.'

If the man had completed his errand and was returning home it was likely he had been visiting Lucy. A miller would deliver grain to the brewer, naturally. Roger hoped the subject of her recent guest had not come up. 'Oh, yes. We're fine friends, Mistress Carew and I. There's no hurry to get there.'

The driver cackled. 'Friends, are you? Well, I'll agree she's a friendly hostess indeed.'

He picked up his reins, making it obvious the conversation was at an end. Roger wished he had a hat to tip, but settled for a nod and carried on. He would hardly have described Lucy as friendly, but perhaps when her customers did not arrive in the middle of the night bloodstained and demanding she undress them, she was more welcoming. Remembering the way she had cared for him, he could not help believe there was the capacity for kindness within her. He would have to play a careful game, but if luck was on his side Lucy might greet Roger with more warmth than when they had parted.

* * *

Lucy hummed as she scrubbed the table on the ground floor, lighter-hearted than she had been for days. Sir Roger's departure had felt like a stone lifting from her chest. There would be no more fears of strangers arriving to question her with threats of violence, no more need to wait hand and foot on an irritable patient, and no more beckoning glints in the knight's eyes that threatened to awaken emotions she had long since buried.

Robbie laughed and sang along to her tune, making up nonsense words to accompany her. Lucy dropped her brush into the bucket and picked him up to swirl around in a wide circle. He squealed with delight, but squirmed in her arms when she tried to clutch him in a tight embrace. Already he was independent enough not to tolerate being treated like a baby. She held him a moment longer, needing to treasure him as he was now, before letting him down. He gathered his wooden animals and ran outside without a backward glance.

Seeing her son content was worth the whispers and sneers she had endured when she had returned in shame, refusing to name the father. She congratulated herself for not succumbing to seduction by another nobleman who would undoubtedly treat her in the manner John Harpur had.

When someone hammered on her door, her first thought was that Sir Roger had returned. Annoyed at the direction in which her mind had leapt and set her heart racing, she threw the brush back into the pail. He would be miles away by now. She opened the door and found Samuel Risby, the miller.

'Good tidings, Mistress Carew.' His eyes openly fixed on her breasts in a manner that made Lucy's toes curl in repulsion. He always managed to make her name sound squalid.

'I've brought your malt. Pour me a mug of ale and I'll unload it.'

He swaggered to his cart and heaved a sack over his shoulder. 'Into the brewing shed?'

'Yes, please,' Lucy answered. She speeded inside and filled a mug, intending to take it to the cart, but Risby met her on the doorstep. He eased his hefty frame on to the bench, spreading his legs wide, and accepted the mug.

'It looks like you're about ready for this sack judging from the other,' he said. 'Have you been brewing double?'

'I've had to,' Lucy replied, thinking of the cobweb-strewn brew. 'I lost a batch.'

'So you'll be able to pay me for this sack as well as the last? And the one before that?'

Risby named a price that made Lucy draw an angry breath.

'That's more than before.'

'Prices have risen. If you don't like it, find someone else to supply you, or malt your own barley. Either way you still owe me for three sacks.'

Her debt to Risby had grown without her realising. Lucy thought of the farthing Sir Roger had given her. That had not covered the ale he had drunk or the food he had eaten by a long way. Even considering the pedlars, she had barely earned anything.

'I can give you half for this sack now. When I've brewed it, I'll be able to give you what I owe.'

'Confident you'll get customers, are you?' He smirked. 'You aren't scurrying around a full house now.'

Lucy forced a smile although anxiety filled her voice. 'I'll find the money.'

'I feel sorry for you, living out here alone. No husband or father to help you. I know you struggle for money.' Samuel rested his hand on her knee, fingers flexing and unflexing. 'I've heard talk that you don't mind paying in other ways when you haven't coins. I'll take payment any way you wish if you'd rather. I'll even give you the next sack on account if you do everything I ask.'

Lucy's stomach threatened to empty. She stiffened, hoping Samuel would feel her disgust and remove his hand, but he didn't. She knew which man in Mattonfield had been at the root of such rumours. Desperation caused by the need to put food on the table and buy medicine to ease her father's pain had forced her to perform acts for the physician that had made her throat fill with bile and her cheeks burn with shame when she thought of them in the dead of night. She had hoped he would have kept her degradation a secret, but clearly she had been wrong.

'I'll do no such thing!' she exclaimed.

'Don't play the virtuous maid with me,' Samuel sneered. 'That brat of yours didn't appear from nowhere. Everyone in town knows you're not the innocent you once were. Assuming you ever were…'

Lucy's cheeks flamed. She had been innocent once, had planned to remain so before events took over and she had fallen for a winning smile and coaxing words.

'You'll get your payment in coins,' she snarled. She bit down on her lip and shrugged Risby's hand off her knee. She stood and gestured to his hand. 'Count the mug you're drinking now as part of it and get out.'

Samuel pushed himself off the bench. 'I'll be at St Barnabas Fair. I'm sure you'll be there. You can pay me then, one way or another.'

He bunched his tunic over his copious belly

and sauntered out as if he owned the building. Lucy sagged back down on to the bench and put her head in her hands, no longer strong. Her hands trembled and it took all her strength to stop tears from spilling out. She imagined leaving the inn behind, running far from Mattonfield and the reputation she had made—a reputation of her own doing—but there was nowhere she could go and no one to turn to.

Robbie toddled into the room and pulled on her skirts. She looked into his solemn brown eyes, glad he had not witnessed the exchange that had taken place.

'Robbie's hungry.'

Lucy smiled bleakly at her son.

'I'll bring you some bread if you go play outside with the chicks, my pet.'

He waddled out. Now the tears Lucy had been holding back fell freely. Robbie's tunic was growing too short and she had no means to buy or sew another one. She could have cut down her father's old shirt except she had given it to Sir Roger. She heaved a sigh, annoyance momentarily causing her tears to cease. A throb of desire pulsed within her at the memory of the knight standing before her, bared to the waist. The bandages had not diminished his attractiveness in any way but accentuated the shape of his muscles half-hidden beneath.

She broke a morsel of bread from the small loaf and chewed it. It was a day stale and too hard for Robbie's few teeth. She crumbled some into a bowl and added a splash of milk and water to soften it. That, too, tasted on the cusp of souring. She wrapped her hands tightly across her breasts, still high and full even though her milk had ended. They were useless now for anything other than enduring the fondling of men such as Samuel Risby and the physician as the price to pay for not starving.

Stinging tears streamed down her cheeks, but pitying herself would do no good, nor brew any ale. She had four days until Samuel would demand his payment and anything could happen in that time. Thomas might return. He would not let his sister starve or be forced into degradation, surely? Sir Roger had mentioned becoming rich if their mysterious task was completed, though explaining how she had thrown the nobleman out would surely put Thomas into a bad mood. Perhaps she had been too hasty in acting.

Lucy straightened her skirts, wiped her eyes and walked to the yard behind the inn, blinking in the afternoon sunlight. Robbie was in the chicken run arranging and rearranging pebbles in rows. He babbled a greeting as Lucy handed him the bowl. She blew him a kiss and went into the brewing shed.

Dust hung in the light. Even without looking she knew the thick wooden rafters overhead were heavy with filth. Cleaning those would be a tiring job, but one that could wait until another day. Brewing was the most important task now.

She inhaled the heady aroma of fermenting barley. Samuel had put the sack inside and she dragged it alongside the almost empty one. Her mood lifted slightly. The batch she had in the vat would be ready in a day or two. That would give her time to make another for the St Barnabas Fair in Mattonfield. She gave her attention to the ale, picking up the wooden paddle to skim the surface.

'That smells wonderful. Perhaps I'll get to try it when it's ready.'

Lucy stiffened, hoping her mind was playing a trick on her. The voice had become ever so familiar to her over the past few days, but she had thought never to hear it again. Now the deep tones reached inside her and stoked fires in her belly that heated her breasts and sent her innards hot and cold at the same time.

Sir Roger had returned.

Chapter Ten

Lucy waited until her heart found its way back to her chest after trying to leap out through her throat. She wiped her arm across her eyes, roughly brushing away the evidence of her tears before she faced him. He stood in the doorway, leaning against one doorpost for support, his broad frame blocking the light. If she had not known his strength was lacking, she would have thought he was paying a casual visit. His eyes raked over her, taking in the swollen eyes and red cheeks.

'Is it me you've been weeping over, dove?' He grinned.

'Of course it isn't,' she said, loading her voice with scorn. 'Why would I ever cry over you?'

'Something else then?' His smile vanished, his brow furrowed and he gestured towards her with his good arm before withdrawing it hastily. 'Tell me, if you like.'

His voice was gentle, as if he actually meant his concern. Lucy's eyes pricked. This unexpected show of feeling was more unnerving than any innuendo or threat. The promise of pity or comfort from such an unusual source threatened to tip Lucy back into misery and she spoke more curtly than she intended.

'It's nothing that need concern you.' She wiped her face again and straightened her cap. She gripped the paddle firmly with both hands like it was the stave she kept beneath the counter.

'What are you doing back here? I thought I told you to leave.'

Sir Roger didn't answer immediately, but studied her for a moment longer, eyes still full of concern. She looked away first and he made a curious sound that she couldn't interpret.

He looked around the shed curiously. Lucy let him stare, glad of the chance to master the confusing mix of emotions that seeing him had prompted. She moved to the other side of the large vat so it acted as a barrier between them.

Sir Roger sniffed deeply and gave a sigh of appreciation. 'It really does smell tempting, doubly so after a long walk.'

'I asked why you're here,' Lucy muttered through gritted teeth.

'I fear I am still being hunted.' Sir Roger clenched

his jaw. Lucy could see the muscles in his neck tensing. 'I dislike this as much as you will, but I must throw myself on your mercy and ask you to take me in once more.'

'No! I told you before I don't want you under my roof. I have troubles of my own without you adding to my lot.'

She bit off her words in case Sir Roger asked her once more to share her troubles, but his own needs were preoccupying him. He slumped wearily against the door, looking so weak that Lucy almost rushed to his side.

'I thought we were rid of each other and I was as glad of it as you were. It pains me more than you will understand to discover I cannot make it as far as Mattonfield on foot, much less to Lord de Legh's house,' he said. He truly sounded as though the words were excruciating to say. 'Believe me, I would not be here if there was any other choice.'

'What if I refuse?' Lucy asked.

He closed his eyes and rested his head against the door frame, looking as though he might fall to the ground. Now she looked closer, Lucy saw his face was pale and sweat glistened on his brow.

'Then, Mistress Carew, I believe you will be condemning me to death.'

Lucy gasped aloud. Sir Roger slowly raised

his head, baring his teeth in a grimace of despair. He fixed Lucy with dark eyes that bored into her with an intensity that made her shiver. Something pulled inside her, tugging her towards him, again wanting to take him in her arms, soothe his pain away against her breast. She reminded herself why she had made him leave in the first place and forced her heart to harden.

'If you're hoping to make me feel guilt over your situation, it won't work. You brought it on yourself.'

'How did I do that?' He sounded genuinely puzzled.

'You seduced Lord Harpur's daughter and caused him to send men chasing after you.'

Sir Roger swore; a single, curt explosion of anger that made Lucy jump.

'Who told you I did that?'

'Thomas.'

Sir Roger looked furious.

'And you believed him without question?'

'The first time we met, you pushed me against the wall and kissed me,' she pointed out. 'It seemed the sort of thing you would do.'

Sir Roger appeared to be wrestling with some dilemma, then smiled coldly. 'The charge of depravity has been levelled often enough. Best you know what you're dealing with, dove. Roger

Danby is the sort of man who would bed a maiden in the house of her father, the rogue who would attempt to grope the woman who stands between him and death, a seducer of any woman who takes his fancy. I'm a man not to be trusted.'

His honesty was unnerving. No man could accuse himself of so base actions without shame. He must be playing a trick to persuade her to let him stay, but if portraying himself as a scoundrel was his plan, it was absurd.

'Do you really mean that?'

Sir Roger pushed himself upright from his position against the frame. He was in silhouette against the doorway. A fine figure, broad and straight backed, despite the slight lift of his injured shoulder. Lucy was unable to see the expression on his face, but his tone was more embittered than she had heard since they first met.

'Have I given you cause to think anything to the contrary since meeting me?'

'Not at all!'

He looked taken aback by her outright agreement, but grinned down at her before the smile vanished to be replaced by his serious expression once again.

'Having said all that, I don't think it is the wronged father who is after my blood in this instance. I now think my pursuers are from a different source.'

Lucy wrinkled her nose in thought. Something that had nagged at her mind on the night he had arrived came back to her. 'The men who came here didn't look like men of Lord Harpur's,' she agreed.

Sir Roger gave her a thoughtful look. 'How do you know what Lord Harpur's men should look like? Do you know anything of him?'

Lucy's mouth twitched. There was plenty she could say, but saw no need to go into any details of how much she knew of John Harpur, even to this unwanted nobleman who felt less like a stranger every time they talked.

'Everyone knows of him.'

Sir Roger gave her another odd look. Lucy glanced away.

'I worked on one of the farms he owned, before I returned here.'

'Am I on his land? I thought it belonged to de Legh,' Sir Roger said.

'It is de Legh's. I wouldn't be living on Harpur's,' Lucy said. 'Pass me that ladle.'

He blinked and showed surprise at her change of subject, but passed her what she had requested. She took it at arm's length, not wanting to get too close to him. She returned her attention to the vat in front of her, skimming the froth off the top into the pot on the floor.

Head safely bent over the vat, she spoke. 'What you have to do with Lord Harpur is none of my business and if you now think your troubles are nothing to do with that matter I care even less. There is no reason for me to help you.'

Sir Roger had not stepped back and he put his hands on the rim of the vat, peering at her over the top.

'No reason apart from kindness and compassion. I know you have that.'

'What makes you think that?' Lucy laughed bitterly.

He tilted his head to one side. 'I remember the care you gave me when you thought I was unconscious. Your touch was so gentle and you treated me kindly then. However furious you have been with me—not without reason, I might add—I don't believe you would cast out a helpless man.'

Her stomach shuddered at the thought that he had been aware of her hands on his body. The memory of those firm muscles made the tips of her fingers tingle and her heart beat faster. She could not meet his eyes and bowed her head.

'I don't want to put my son in danger.'

Unexpectedly Sir Roger placed a hand on her shoulder.

'I swear I won't let any danger befall you.'

'I can't risk that.'

His fingers tightened the slightest amount. Lucy glanced up. Sir Roger was looking at her intently.

'Like it or not, dove, I'm afraid you're already involved in this matter.' His eyes hardened, banishing the weariness from his face. 'You lied for me. Today while I rested I overheard an exchange between someone from the town—the miller, I am guessing from his clothes—and a man asking after strangers. Money exchanged hands. I met the same miller as I returned here and I told him I was coming here to see you. I also told him we were old friends.'

'Why did you do that?' Her hands tightened on the handle of the ladle as fury set her skin on fire. The notion of Sir Roger exchanging pleasantries with Samuel Risby was not something she wished to imagine. He could not imagine the effect his words had on her, far beyond seeking to tip the balance in his favour once and for all.

Sir Roger resumed his position leaning against the door frame. 'The rider was looking for a stranger. You had already passed me off as your husband. I thought it safer to continue to pretend familiarity.'

'You told Samuel Risby you were my husband?' she asked, appalled.

'Of course not! I'm not so loose lipped.' He gave her a stern look, giving Lucy a glimpse of the man he must be at full strength. 'I didn't want to be caught in an obvious lie by people who would know we were not husband and wife.'

She could guess what Risby would have supposed her relationship to be with a man as handsome as Sir Roger. Her throat flamed with shame. Sir Roger could not have known that, however, and his attempt at caution was oddly endearing, if unnecessary.

'The whole town is aware I never had a husband. It took me months and months to even become tolerable to them.'

He looked confused. She jerked a hand to the yard outside the shed, hating to have to make it so clear what she meant.

'No one here knows who fathered Robbie. I refused to name him when I returned home.' She squared up to him and smirked as she spoke, preempting his disapproval.

'I suppose that shocks you. Perhaps you believed me a respectable widow? Perhaps you don't want to live under the roof of a woman with such low morals after all?'

She heard the note of hope in her voice, that

perhaps the knowledge of what she was would persuade him to leave. He shrugged, then winced as the gesture caused him pain.

'It doesn't shock me. Besides, at the moment I'm not in a position to demand better. I'll live anywhere that will house me. Your brother and I aren't the only men returning from the wars. What better story than that your son's father is one of them. A husband would be an ideal disguise.'

'I'm not pretending you're my husband!' she exclaimed. 'That was the only reason I could think of for you to be in my bed, but no one will be searching there for you again.'

Sir Roger smiled, lighting his whole face. He ran his hand through his hair, brushing it back from his face. He looked momentarily less care-worn and ill.

'Again? So you're considering letting me stay?'

'I didn't say that,' Lucy said cautiously.

'Lucy, will you give me sanctuary in your home once more?'

He lapsed into silence, waiting and watching. Lucy glared at him, hating him for putting her in the position, yet unaccountably drawn to him. This nobleman with his smile that made her shiver inwardly and the dark penetrating eyes that turned her legs to water. A man who would use her while she was necessary, just as all men did, then discard her. The same sort of man who had put her in the position she was in and from which she could see no escape.

As she was thinking how to respond, Sir Roger said a single word she had not heard him utter before.

'Please.'

She jerked her head up in surprise. He reached across the vat for her hand. Lucy felt the flutter that raced up her arm as she resisted slightly, but did not pull away. 'I have no one else to turn to but you.'

He had demanded before; when her brother first brought him into her life, he had ordered her around as he would any servant and been ungrateful and rude. Now he spoke simply, without cajoling, with no attempt to seduce, and with none of the bravado she had come to expect. Lucy shifted uncertainly.

'I don't know, let me think.'

She let go of his hand and picked up the bucket of slops.

'Wait here,' she instructed. He drew back courteously as she passed by him, but she was acutely aware of how close she came to him. At the stream, she swilled out the bucket and refilled it, but waited longer than necessary before returning, sitting back on her heels to decide what to do. Sense told her to refuse. To allow Sir Roger in would inevitably be to invite danger, to say nothing of temptation that she might not be strong enough to resist.

Emotions would do her no good, not when every touch sent her mind spiralling down paths best avoided and her body seemed to burst into life of its own accord. She turned her mind to practical matters. He had been useful that morning when he intervened with the pedlars.

A helper might be useful to have around in the busy period before St Barnabas Fair. Even if the townspeople ignored her wares, now the weather was warmer, more travellers would be passing: people who were less particular about drinking the ale of a disgraced woman with a bastard. Even taking his injury into account, a one-armed man would be able to fetch and carry and ease her work.

There would have to be conditions of course. She listed them to herself as she walked back to the brewing shed. If he did not agree, she would have no obligation to allow him to stay and he could take his chances with whoever he thought was chasing him.

She was weakening. Roger knew enough about women to recognise the moment when downright refusal turned to hesitation and would soon become acquiescence. He would have her agreement before long. He had expected the fight to be harder, but perhaps he had caught her at a moment of weakness brought on by whatever had upset her. He wondered briefly what were the troubles she had referred to and what had caused her tears. Then his mind drifted to the thought of her long-lashed eyes made all the more piercing and attractive by the redness surrounding them and pushed his concerns to the back of his mind.

Roger took a final look around the brewing shed, tilting his neck back to try to ease his sore shoulder. Dust floated down and filled his nose and eyes. Lucy seemed to have begun cleaning the central beam and given up halfway through because one end was free of cobwebs while the other was thick with them. He went outside and took a deep breath to fill his lungs and rid himself of the pungent, mealy smell of ale and dust.

Lucy's small son was peering over the top of the wicker fence of the chicken run. Roger leaned his arms on it and stared down at the boy. His curls, much darker than his mother's hair, tumbled across a grubby forehead and his brown eyes were wide. He reminded Roger of someone, but he could not think who it was.

He wondered if he should say something, but

children were an unfamiliar experience to him. He knew from the last letter from Yorkshire that his half-brother had fathered two by now. Meeting them would be another trial to endure when he finally arrived in York. If he ever managed to get there.

He heard Lucy's footsteps and smiled at her. Lucy stopped as if instead he had slapped her. Her body tensed, reminding Roger of a cat ready to pounce. He had no doubt that her claws would come out if she thought her child was at risk.

'I'm not going to hurt your boy,' Roger muttered, stung by the unspoken accusation.

'Robbie doesn't know many people.' She tore her eyes from his and glanced towards the child. 'I don't... We don't have many friends here.'

Loneliness oozed from her words, causing Roger some puzzlement and opening a pit in his belly. This was her home and where she had grown up. She should have companions.

The boy didn't look particularly scared. As Roger looked at him he blew a spit bubble and held up a wooden figure.

'Hoss!' He grinned.

The anger in Lucy's eyes melted and her face took on an expression of such affection it made Roger's heart twist to see it. Robbie looked at Roger, sticking his bottom lip out. Roger felt his lips curl into an unexpected smile. Robbie blew another bubble and sniffed. Roger wrinkled his nose in mild disgust at the stickiness on display.

'Hoss!'

The boy was becoming agitated, his voice on the cusp of becoming a wail as he held the toy out. His face was reddening. Roger gingerly took the toy between his fingertips. It was a roughly carved horse, slightly damp from some source Roger preferred not to consider. He jiggled the toy and made a clopping noise with his tongue. To his surprise and pleasure, Robbie's face split into a wide beam and he cackled.

'Thank you,' Roger said in a serious voice. 'If only your horse was my size I could ride away and leave your mother in peace. That would satisfy us both.'

Behind him Roger heard Lucy snort, whether in amusement or annoyance he could not tell. Roger trotted the horse back to Robbie. He turned to discover Lucy had moved closer to him than he had realised. She had one hand across her mouth. Her eyes were unreadable. Roger held his breath. Lucy lifted a hand and for one moment Roger thought she was going to touch him. His stomach tensed with excitement, anticipating the softness of her fingers against his flesh, but she reached past him to stroke her son's cheek.

She looked at Roger and her eyes briefly crinkled at the corners.

'You can stay here. But there are conditions.'

Roger mastered his impulse to cheer aloud.

'Name them.'

She held a hand up and raised each finger to list the conditions.

'I'll expect you to pay for what you eat and drink. I know you have no money at the moment, but when you do you can settle your account.' Her angular, serious face was tilted back to look into his eyes. She licked her lips nervously, the tip of her tongue skimming around them in a manner that sent Roger's heart thudding.

'You sleep in the other room. I want mine back. No one goes up there so you can hide well enough if I have customers.'

Roger held a hand up to stop her mid-flow, raising his eyebrows. 'I'll gladly sleep in there, *if* that's where you want me to sleep, but I don't intend to hide. I've been caged long enough.'

Lucy lowered her fingers, clenching her fist into a ball. She pursed her lips, forming them into a perfect bud, which only increased Roger's desire to kiss them.

'Then how shall I explain your presence?'

Roger's lips curved into a smile. 'I've already

told you. We have a story that has worked before. It will work again. I'll play your husband.'

She did not answer, but skirted around him and bent over the fence to lift her son into her arms, nuzzling the top of the child's head.

'The lie worked when I saw off your unwanted customers,' Roger said. 'It could benefit you, too, for me to be here.'

The ginger cat slunk from the direction of the stream, something between its jaws. Robbie twisted to break free, waving his arms at the animal. Roger winked and the boy gave a toothy grin that pleased Roger more than he was expecting. Lucy put Robbie down and he lurched off in pursuit of the cat.

'Very well.' Her cheeks grew a shade pinker, reminding Roger of early roses. 'If it becomes necessary you can act as my husband. But in name only.'

'Of course,' Roger said. 'If that is what you demand. I am here on your goodwill. I'll do whatever you ask of me to keep it.'

He hoped his tone would make it clear that if she demanded anything else he would gladly provide it. 'Are there any more conditions?'

'One. If you live in my house you help with the running of it.'

'I've already agreed I'll pay you,' Roger exclaimed. 'Why should I work?'

He'd envisaged time to rest and regain his strength, the freedom to think and plan what to do when Thomas returned, and where his life would take him next. Stirring and serving ale was not part of his plan.

'Because it needs doing. I'm not sure I trust you not to leave when it suits you and never return,' Lucy said.

'Why would I leave?' he asked.

Lucy crossed her arms and gave him a sceptical look that reached inside him as though his deepest thoughts were laid bare on the ground between them.

'You seem the sort who would. A man who will brag about his seductions and conquests hardly presents himself as reliable, wouldn't you agree? I might wake one morning to find you gone and me out of pocket.'

Roger opened his mouth to protest and closed it again. It was a fair charge, but it stung nevertheless.

'We parted badly. It was a quarrel that shouldn't have happened. If I'm staying here I'd like to be friends. I won't leave without telling you, but if it makes you happy I will help as you ask. Do you want me to brew the ale?'

She gave him a stern look but had a hint of mischief in her eyes. 'Oh, no. I wouldn't trust you with something that important. I do the brewing.' She indicated the bucket. 'Fill the water trough and bring me another bucketful inside.'

She slipped past him, skirts and hips swaying, and walked around the front of the inn without bothering to see if he followed. Roger watched her go, suppressing the words that sprang to his lips. He took a deep breath. He braced himself, bent and picked up the bucket in his good arm, then obediently made his way to the stream.

Chapter Eleven

'I want to bathe.'

'Now?'

'Why not? It was the second thing I requested besides clothes, if you remember. It's almost dusk—are you likely to get more customers at this time of day?'

Lucy gritted her teeth. He could not mean to rub her nose in how empty the inn was, but it rankled all the same.

Sir Roger lowered the bucket to his side and scratched at the thick thatch that covered his face. 'I stink.'

He cocked his head towards his armpit and sniffed, wrinkling his nose.

'No, you don't,' Lucy said indignantly. 'I kept you perfectly clean.'

Sir Roger's mouth twitched at one corner and he flashed her a wolfish grin, perhaps remembering how Lucy had ministered to him. A shiver raced down Lucy's back as she remembered it, too.

'Well, perhaps I overstate it,' he said grudgingly.

'You know where the stream is now,' Lucy said. 'You needn't ask my permission.'

Sir Roger raked his hands through his tangled curls and rubbed his cheeks. 'I want to remove this beard. For that I'll need hot water.'

Still annoyed from his mention of the empty inn, Lucy folded her arms, disinclined to help. 'In that case you'll need wood to heat it.' She gestured to the door again. 'The axe is inside the shed. I'd thank you not to take all my supply. I don't have a large tub, but it should serve your needs. You can use it by the fire.'

She watched him carefully as he digested her words. Someone with his rank and privileges likely never drew his own bath. Servants would wait on him, carrying out his wishes. She counted a dozen heartbeats before he nodded curtly and spun on his heel. He had forgotten the bucket. Lucy emptied it into the iron pot that stood over the hearth, then waited a dozen more heartbeats before taking it outside.

What she saw outside made her belly curl in shame. Sir Roger had his back to the building,

looming over the small stack of logs, and had
begun to chop. Lucy watched as he grasped the
axe in his right arm and raised it level with his
shoulder. He grunted and swung. The axe stuck
in the log, barely making a mark. After a few
attempts the grunts became louder, but the axe
swings no more effective. Lucy expected him to
cease trying, but Sir Roger proved to have more
stamina than she gave him credit for and continued to make his attempts. After a half-dozen
more blows he muttered beneath his breath and
dropped the axe to the ground. He arched his
back, resting his hands on his hips, and stretched.
As he did, Lucy saw a small red stain on his
shoulder.

'You're bleeding!'

Sir Roger gave a start at her voice. He looked at
Lucy over his shoulder before craning his head to
inspect the tunic. He spread his hand wide, covering the area at the front, which was mercifully
free of a similar marking.

'At the back,' Lucy said. She stepped closer to
stand behind him and reached a hand out to indi-
cate the spot. Sir Roger's eyes followed her hand.
When she touched his shoulder, spreading her fingers wide around the stain, the corner of his lip
twitched. She found herself curious to discover
what he looked like without the beard.

Sir Roger reached over his shoulder to touch the wound, then inspected his fingers.

'It's only a little. I count myself fortunate there was not more at the time. You never needed your poker after all.'

His eyes grew weary, serving to remind Lucy that it was only the day before that they had removed the arrow and not long before that when he had been insensible. Sir Roger picked up the axe and raised it once more, but before he could take a swing he paused and lowered it. He shook his head.

'I fear it will be a cold bath for me after all as I have no strength in my arm to continue.'

'Why didn't you use your left hand?' Lucy asked.

Sir Roger looked down at the axe. 'Why? It won't make my right arm any stronger. I'll try again shortly.'

'And how will making yourself bleed help you to heal? Unless you're well you won't get your strength back.' Lucy covered his hand with hers and tugged the axe free.

Sir Roger's shoulders dropped and he looked defeated. Lucy felt the unexpected urge to take him in her arms and comfort him.

'It isn't the wood that matters.' Sir Roger sighed. 'I am not used to being inactive, or failing in what I want to accomplish. I dislike it.'

He gave Lucy a wry smile. 'I was a soldier. I've bathed in cold water before. I used to do it all the time in the beck as a child in Yorkshire. I'll take your earlier suggestion and make use of the stream.'

He spoke without any self-pity or complaint, but began walking towards the bank. If he had shown any resentment she would have left him to make do with that, but understanding what had compelled him to push himself, Lucy ran after him.

'Wait. You don't have to do that. I was unfair to make you chop the wood. I'll do it for you.'

'I told you, the wood doesn't matter.' He looked her up and down. 'I don't need you to exert yourself out of pity.'

'It isn't out of pity!' Lucy soothed. She winced inwardly, hearing the lie. 'You're my guest and I've treated you poorly as such. If you collect the water, I'll bring the logs.'

He wrinkled his brow. 'You don't have to do that.'

'I know,' Lucy answered. 'But I will.'

She had split the largest log when an unfamiliar voice cried out, summoning the innkeeper. A lone traveller was standing by the door. He settled himself on to the bench in front of the house while Lucy brought him ale, her spirits rising at the thought of a customer. She handed the guest his drink with a smile and dip of her skirts, old habits of enticing customers springing easily to her. She was sitting close beside the man, listening attentively to his description of what he would be selling at the St Barnabas Fair, when Sir Roger appeared round the corner, carrying his bucket. He stopped on seeing the man and glared at him suspiciously.

'Who is this?' he asked.

'A customer,' Lucy answered. She gave the man a warm smile. 'One dearly needed, too, *husband*, so don't drive him away with your surliness.'

Sir Roger glowered. The man on the bench paid them no mind. Lucy could not imagine why Sir Roger was so hostile when he knew guests were the purpose of the inn.

'Take the water inside, then go fetch Robbie,' she instructed Sir Roger. 'Our son will be hungry.'

The look of astonishment on Sir Roger's face was extraordinary to behold, but he did as she asked, leading Robbie by the hand into the inn.

'Pay no mind to my husband, sir,' Lucy simpered to the traveller. 'He's been in a tiresome mood ever since the water scalded him last week when he was brewing.'

'Perhaps he had better stick to men's work and let you get on with yours,' the man answered.

Lucy feigned a merry laugh, drawing closer and tilting her head flirtatiously.

'That he should. Now, why don't you try another cup and see how well I make it?'

'Not tonight. I have to be on my way,' the man answered. He paid and left.

As Lucy tidied his cup away Sir Roger emerged from inside.

'Who was that?'

'A customer. Why did you behave in such a way?'

Sir Roger looked after the departing man. 'You don't know who he is and you sat so intimately with him.'

'And why should that concern you?' Lucy asked in surprise.

'It could have been the man who was asking after me.'

Lucy straightened her neckline.

'It wasn't. I saw them, remember. But you didn't know that when you saw him, so if you don't want to invite suspicion don't make such a show of yourself.'

Sir Roger frowned mutinously then gave a gesture of resignation. He sat where the man had been.

'That's a fair point, I suppose,' he admitted grudgingly. 'But all the same, you were very sharp to me. If I'm acting as your husband we should appear loving. A kiss or cuddle to keep the fiction.'

A tremor ran through Lucy, tipping her stomach upside down and causing her to shiver at the thought of Sir Roger's hands slipping to her waist, pulling her close into his arms. The idea appealed more than it should. 'You clearly don't know many husbands and wives!'

'I know some wives,' Sir Roger retorted. 'It can't be that hard to feign affection for me, can it?' He pushed his hair back and gave her a serious look. 'If you even have to pretend, that is.'

Lucy rounded on him. 'What are you implying?'

'I know you find me attractive,' Sir Roger said, his voice low and husky. 'It shows plainly on your face when you look at me. Your cheeks colour and your eyes grow wide.'

Lucy drew a sharp breath. She had not been aware her feelings were so easily observed. The treacherous heat that he spoke of was already rising to her breast.

She gazed at him openly. As he had almost invited her attentions she would not deny herself that pleasure, but if he thought she was about to swoon into his arms he was mistaken.

'You're a good-looking man, but don't fool yourself. Anything that my body might reveal is instinctive and nothing to do with my mind,' she said. 'If I got a nose full of pepper I'd sneeze. That doesn't mean I'd welcome the sensation or choose to dip my nose in the pot again.'

Sir Roger burst out laughing, his eyes sparkling.

'I'm pepper, am I? You have a lot of experience of rich spices?'

'Enough to know that they seem tempting, but should be used sparingly.'

'And is that the only reason?' He caught hold of her sleeve as she moved to go past, his expression now intent. 'The night I arrived, even through the pain I felt, I could sense the desire growing inside you like a flame lapping at kindling. Or are you scared you won't be able to stop if you kiss me again?'

The breath caught in Lucy's throat and a sharp throb of longing caught her by surprise.

'I could stop,' she said, uncertain if she spoke the truth.

Lucy had time to feed Robbie on pottage and egg and ready him for bed before the tub was a quarter full of warm water. Sir Roger sat on the bench by the fire, chewing on the hard heel of the loaf and the remains of a cheese. Gyb sidled into the room and jumped on to the table. He dropped a dead rat in front of Roger. Lucy swiped him away with an angry snarl.

'Your cat is far too forward,' Roger remarked.

'He isn't mine.' Lucy watched the cat saunter off, rat in mouth. 'He showed up one day unasked and unwanted and decided to stay. I might as well make use of him. If he doesn't like it, I'm sure he'll leave.'

'So I'm not the first stray you've taken pity on,' Roger observed in mock seriousness.

'Not the first battered tom who would have his end away with any female that takes his fancy?' Lucy asked scathingly.

'Is that what you think of me?' Roger asked, grinning, his eyes bright.

'Aren't you?' Lucy held his gaze with a challenge.

Roger laughed and carried on eating.

When Lucy picked Robbie up and bade Sir Roger goodnight he looked at her in surprise.

'You haven't eaten.'

'I ate before you arrived.' Her stomach threatened to loudly proclaim her lie. She scraped her finger round the bowl, scooping up the remains of Robbie's egg and licked it, then gathered the crumbs of cheese. 'Your bath is prepared. I should give you some privacy.'

'You can't go. I'll need help redressing my wound.'

Sir Roger began tugging at the hem of the tunic to pull it over his head. Lucy caught a glimpse of the dark hair fanning from the waist of his trousers to his chest before she dragged her eyes away. Desire fluttered through her. She had seen him half-naked, and more besides that, but the notion of being present while he bathed made her cheeks flame.

'You can call me when you're done,' she muttered. She fled with Robbie in her arms before he could object. She waited in the bedroom until she heard her name called, trying not to picture Sir Roger's hands moving across his broad frame as he bathed.

She settled Robbie in his bed and rushed to the door. She flung it open and stopped short, colliding with Sir Roger who was standing outside the room. He was facing away, but turned at her footstep so they were face to face, bodies close.

He was naked from the waist up and his tunic hung loosely around his neck, soaking up the drops of water that clung to him. As Lucy watched, a droplet fell from his hair and landed in the hollow of his collarbone. She bunched her fist to stop herself reaching out to wipe it away. He had not removed his whole beard, but had shaped it neatly and had cut away the length of his hair to leave it curling around his jaw as it began to dry. The effect was to make him look younger and more innocent. And twice as attractive as usual.

'I didn't hear you come up.'

Sir Roger was holding the wad of dressing to his wound. Fixing her eyes on the area in question, Lucy peeled it back. It looked better than expected. The hole was deep and the area red, but with none of the inflammation that had been present as he lay unconscious. Lucy ran her fingertips across his shoulder and chest, gently examining the area, causing Sir Roger to give a soft sigh. Could he be as aware of Lucy, of the way the sensation of his still-damp muscles made her skin awaken?

She folded the pad so the clean side was against his skin and, as she had done before, rewrapped the bandages around it to hold it in place. This was easier now Sir Roger was upright rather than lying in bed. He followed her every instruction, lifting his arm, tilting his head, silently obeying her and never taking his eyes from her. Lucy was glad of the near darkness to mask the flames that ignited in her cheeks. She tied the end of the binding and stood unmoving, hands still on Sir

Roger's chest until a soft cough brought her to her senses. Sir Roger craned his head to look down at her work. He brushed his hand over the dressing, fingertips briefly touching hers. Lucy lowered her hand rapidly.

'It's clean now. Keep it dry,' she murmured.

'That should be easy enough to manage.' His lips slid into a suggestive smile. 'I'm clean also.'

He was, as he had pointed out, clean and fresh, damp and enticing. Without answering, Lucy dipped her head and plunged back into her room. She pressed her head against the cold wall, feeling feverish with desire that threatened to spill over.

When Robbie woke in the night as he always did, he found his mother already awake and pacing the room, unable to sleep because of the tug of her senses towards the room beyond and the man inside.

Lucy proved to be a tiring mistress. She was already awake and moving around downstairs by the time the daylight woke Roger and he dragged himself from his mattress. Robbie had been wailing again in the night, his cries disturbing Roger's rest and awakening him while Lucy's soft singing to comfort her child served to lull Roger back to sleep. In the morning light her eyes bore dark circles that told of her sleepless night. She nodded to Roger silently as she passed him a cup of ale, seemingly too tired to make conversation.

'He was noisy last night. Does he ever sleep peacefully?' Roger grumbled, indicating Robbie who was drawing with his fingers in the fire ashes. Spit mingled with the ash, creating a paste that he swirled into patterns.

'When his tooth comes he'll be happier. I kept him as quiet as I could, but it's hard.' Lucy answered. She narrowed her weary-looking eyes. 'Of course, usually it doesn't matter as there is only me to hear it.'

She stifled a yawn and Roger bit back his next grumble. Her night had been more disrupted than his and he sensed any further comment would earn him a less than friendly retort. They drank quickly, chewing on hard bread, the silence only punctuated by Robbie's demands and Lucy's attempts to occupy him with small tasks.

Women's work was both harder and more tedious than Roger had expected. He was set first to raking out the hearth, despite Robbie's protests at the disruption of his game.

'Be patient,' Roger instructed. He carried the ash bucket outside, returned and picked the child up under his good arm, carrying him like a barrel to where he had made a small pile of ash beside the front step. 'Play here and tire yourself out so that tonight you might let your mother and me rest!'

Robbie giggled and set about covering himself in the mess. Roger set about lighting the fire. He bent over the pile of wood and kindling as he arranged it, conscious of Lucy's eyes on him. Fortunately for his pride the kindling caught quickly. He sat back on his heels and smiled triumphantly.

Lucy's response was a nod of the head. 'Smartly done, my lord. I wasn't sure if a nobleman would know how to do a servant's job.'

'I was a soldier,' he pointed out. 'I know how to take care of myself when there is no other option.'

'That's good as there's more to be done,' Lucy answered. 'You can start on the rushes.'

Roger bit back his disappointment that his work had barely raised a smile or word of praise from Lucy, puzzled why he should feel it so keenly. Lucy scrubbed the table and every surface with vigour, though her sleepless night must have affected her. Determined not to prove himself lacking, Roger began to lay fresh rushes on the floor, stamping them down until a sweat broke out. He paused, resting against the wall as a wave of light-headedness overtook him.

Lucy came over to peer at him.

'I'm not as fit as I hoped,' he admitted grudgingly.

Lucy's forehead wrinkled and Roger wondered if he looked as weak as he felt. She raised a hand to his brow with a feather-light touch. Her eyelids fluttered rapidly.

'I'll do this.'

She set him instead to chopping vegetables in preparation for their meal. He recognised the knife as being the one he had taken from her and used to free himself.

'You trust me with a weapon now?'

She lifted her long-lashed, grey eyes to him. 'You have no reason to harm me so I have no reason not to. Besides, you're already in a borrowed shirt. I don't think there's anything else you'd want to cut off.'

Her voice lacked humour, but her eyes were dancing with some private amusement. As soon as Roger smiled, the humour vanished and a hint of rose touched her cheek. She fumbled the knife out blade first towards him.

'You can't cut cabbage by hand. I'm sure you'll be capable of the task.'

'Don't hold a knife like that, unless you're planning to stab someone,' Roger chided, reaching around to take the knife by the handle.

His hand closed over hers as he waited for

her to loosen her grip. They were standing close enough that he noticed when her eyelashes flickered as he touched her skin. Roger would have felt triumphant at the proof that she was not insusceptible to his presence except for the way his stomach answered with a flutter of its own. Lucy slid her hand free, leaving a trace of heat on Roger's palm. He investigated the meagre bag of vegetables, wondering how exactly onions were to be dealt with. After Lucy's scathing reference to his capabilities and his dismissal from rush-laying he was determined not to ask for help.

He managed the task, to his relief. Holding a sword might be beyond him, but he was able to grip the short-bladed knife firmly enough and slice the cabbage and onions. It felt a dreadful deterioration for a man who had once entertained dreams of glory in the lists. He pictured the neck of the man who had shot him lying on the table instead of the vegetables, slicing with vigour.

Roger carried the pot to the hearth and set it on the stand over the fire, adding ale, a handful of barley and the sparse ham bone that Lucy indicated. His stomach tightened as he gave the iron pot a stir, but from the amount of food going in he did not hold out hope for a full belly that night.

Bending over the table had given him a crick

in his neck and a dull throbbing in his shoulder. He leaned back against the wall by the hearth and dug his fingertips deep into the muscles to loosen them. He took a brief moment of respite, enjoying the view of Lucy's legs as she twisted her feet to grind the rushes firmly into place. In the time it had taken him to finish his task she had completed half of hers. She looked as though she was working her way through the measure of a dance.

Roger began to whistle the tune to a French jig that sprung to his mind. Lucy stopped midstep, one leg bent with heel raised in a pose that twisted her hip to the side and caused the curves of her waist and breasts to command Roger's attention. The effect was only spoiled by the manner in which she glared at him suspiciously. He explained what he was doing and she rolled her eyes as if it confirmed her opinion of him as a wastrel, lowering her leg and smoothing her dress down.

'We could dance together and finish in half the time,' Roger suggested with a bold grin. Despite the soreness of his wound he suddenly found himself yearning for further movement. The idea of taking Lucy in his arms and pulling her close as they worked through the steps made his spirits lift. Some dances involved more than handholding and polite bowing. She did not refuse immediately and looked almost as if she was considering his suggestion seriously, but then shook her head.

'It's been too long since I danced. I fear I'd make a poor partner for a man used to fine company.'

He'd expected refusal, but not this excuse. Denial that she had time to spare for such diversions, possibly. Suspicion that it was a ploy of some sort, almost certainly. A criticism of her own abilities, not at all.

'I don't think you would,' Roger said.

He walked to stand opposite her, adding a slight swagger to his walk. He took his time as if he was taking his place in the middle of a dance floor in front of assembled nobles, enjoying Lucy's eyes on him. Lucy shifted her stance, straightening her back and letting her hands drop to rest at her sides, watching as he crossed to her. As much as she might deny it, Roger recognised she was readying herself to dance. His pulse began a low drumbeat in his ears.

The skin at the creamy hollow of Lucy's throat flickered as she lifted her head to meet his eyes, gazing intently at him through pale lashes, before glancing away in a show of modesty that made his blood begin to race all the more for doubting it was real. The room grew hotter, smaller, enfolding them both in a moment that had sprung from nowhere. Roger swallowed, acutely aware of how much he wanted the woman standing before him.

'Some things you never forget how to do, no matter how long it's been since you tried.' He held a hand out, cocking his head to one side. 'I was always reckoned to be a partner worth having. If it pleases my lady, I could instruct you.'

Lucy folded her arms across her body. Her lips were set into a line. Roger ground his teeth in frustration. He had said the wrong thing and once again she had raised the drawbridge around herself.

'I'm no lady, Sir Roger, as well you are aware!'

Roger had meant nothing by the term beyond play-acting, but she was right. Lucy might hold herself like any of the noblewomen he had flirted with, but she wasn't one of them. She was better. She had more fire in her than any of the simpering, mild-eyed women he had encountered. How he would love to see the expression on his brother's face if he walked into their father's house with Lucy on his arm. Dressed in fine silks or cloth of gold, Lucy would capture the attention of every man. The challenge in her voice ignited the furnace in his belly. He withdrew his hand, but his heart skipped a beat.

'That's the first time you've addressed me directly since we met.'

She wrinkled her brow at his words. 'Is it really? I hadn't noticed.'

He nodded and stepped closer. 'It is, but it won't suit. If I'm to play your husband I cannot be a sir. Call me by my name alone.'

She stepped back from him into the shadows of the corner, eyes growing wide. 'But you have a title.'

Irritation consumed Roger at this unexpected consideration for etiquette. She'd ordered him about, scolded him and done him all manner of injuries with no concern for the distinction he was owed by his station. Now was not the time to develop a sense of what was appropriate, not when his hand almost trembled visibly at the idea of taking hers. He licked his lips thoughtfully. His title had always mattered to him. Knowing he would one day become Lord Danby, he'd scorned women of a rank lower than him before. The distinction had always been important to him, but hearing his name on Lucy's lips was a greater need than he had realised.

'*Fitting* be blowed! Three generations ago my ancestors were little better than yours. My great-grandfather raised sheep. My grandfather left home and earned his knighthood by fighting and my father…' A lump filled his throat as he thought of the man he had not seen in so many years. What would the current Lord Danby think to hear Roger dismiss the name they bore so easily? 'My father now keeps sheep and no longer chooses to leave the village he grew up in.'

He eyed Lucy sternly. 'If I want you to call me Roger, that's what you'll call me!'

She looked wary. Roger held his breath, sensing that to push her now would drive her away for good. After what felt like hours she licked her lips then formed the word silently, testing it out, tasting it.

'What's my name, dove?' Roger asked, dropping his voice to a whisper and making his tone as gentle and seductive as possible. Lucy's lip twitched, the slight curve at the corner that appeared every so often made him shudder with longing. The cream of her throat grew pinker, her skin transforming from pale to alluringly rose-tinted where it vanished below the bodice of her dress, crying out to be stroked or kissed.

'Roger.'

There was uncertainty in her voice. No warmth—certainly none of the love that a wife should show, much less the breathless, unrestrained, exclamation caused by a moment of passion that Roger yearned to hear, but it would suffice.

'Thank you,' he said.

Lucy raised her eyebrow. 'That's the first time you've said *that* to me,' she remarked. 'Roger.'

'It must be a good day for trying new things. So, shall we dance after all?' Roger asked boldly, holding his arm out.

Lucy's cheeks dimpled. Her hand twitched at her side, a small jerky movement that caught Roger's eye before she slipped both hands behind her back where they were safely away from being captured. Roger stepped closer and reached around behind her. He firmly drew her hands forward, lacing his fingers between hers, and raised their linked hands to chest height. Heart pounding at being so close, he began to whistle the tune again. He made the first advance, she stepped back, keeping the proper distance. They circled slowly, one way then the other, eyes locked. When it came to the measure where the man slipped his arm around his partner's waist to lift her high in a circle, Lucy twisted free.

'You're not strong enough, you'd hurt your shoulder again.'

'I'll risk it,' Roger said.

She shook her head, though Roger sensed there was a hint of regret in her gesture.

'Don't you know when you've pushed a situation as far as you can? Thank you, though; it's been a long time since I danced with anyone, let alone a nobleman. Finish this yourself, if you please. I'm going to search for eggs and see to the ale.'

She dipped a curtsy that seemed unaccountably meek, rushed past him with her head down and was out of the door calling for Robbie before Roger could stop her. Through the doorway he could hear her scolding the boy for the mess he had made before both voices moved away.

Was being in his arms so unsettling that it had caused Lucy to scuttle out with such urgency? He hoped so. It had unbalanced him for certain. There had been plenty of times he had beguiled women off the dance floor and into dark corners that he would gladly have owned to, but he had not intended to do such a thing with Lucy. Still whistling, Roger continued where Lucy had left off, grinding the stalks with his heels and trying not to imagine Lucy in his arms, dancing or otherwise.

Chapter Twelve

It was growing chilly when Lucy returned with three eggs. Roger was sitting on the bench resting his back against the wall beside the hearth. He began to form his excuse for sitting idle, but Lucy walked to the hearth and cracked the eggs into the pottage, careful to avoid catching Roger's eye. She stirred the pot over the fire, keeping her back to him.

'We should eat soon. I may get customers and I want to be ready.'

Roger heard the hope in her voice beneath the weariness. Privately he was doubtful. No one had called all day. Roger listed the ones he knew of: voices while he lay in bed, the unfriendly pedlars and the passer-by yesterday who had caused Roger a stab of jealousy on seeing Lucy sitting so close. He was not aware there had been any other customers since his arrival at the inn. This was not the prosperous place Thomas had made it out to be.

Roger was glad of it. No company meant no need to deceive anyone and perhaps reveal something that could lead his pursuers to him. He was content to hide for now, but when he had the strength in his arm he might consider letting it be known he was there and drawing the men to him. King Edward would doubtless give a reward to learn who was trying to prevent his messengers doing their duty, if that was the motive.

'No one has called all day. It's unlikely,' he said.

Lucy looked miserable. 'Do you think I don't know that?'

She began to light rush tapers, holding the spill with a hand that shook. Roger beckoned to her with a finger.

'Sit for a moment and rest. I'll do that.'

He plucked the spill from her fingers and finished the task while she took his place on the bench. Roger filled two cups with ale. He returned and sat alongside Lucy, leaning back beside her. They drank in silence, each lost deep in their own thoughts, but content to sit as companions. A rare feeling descended on Roger that it took him a moment to identify.

He was at peace.

He'd spent most nights during his time in France in camps and many others in the company of loud men and loose women. Even in his father's home in Yorkshire there had been the animosity between Roger's mother and his half-brother, and resentment between his parents for the existence of the bastard boy. To feel no anticipation of an argument was a new and welcome sensation.

Keeping his head still, he risked a sidelong glance at Lucy. She had her eyes closed and her face was serene. When she opened them and made to stand up Roger caught hold of her sleeve.

'There's no rush.'

'There is if you want to eat.' All the same she settled back on the bench and made no further attempt to leave Roger's side.

'Do you always work this hard or were you doing it to make a point?' he grumbled good-naturedly.

'I wasn't making a point!' Lucy exclaimed. Her eyes softened a little as she caught her tone. She rubbed her eyes and looked at him wearily.

'Perhaps I was. It's hard work managing everything myself.'

She dipped her head down before sliding a sideways look at him. 'While you're here I intend to make use of you.'

Roger bit back the response that sprang to his

lips about other uses she could make of him. They were sitting close and the atmosphere was intimate. He sensed that to throw out a careless innuendo would ruin that and for the time being he was happier to share Lucy's company without trying to entice her into the nearest bed. He took a swig of ale and looked round the room.

'Thomas described this as the finest inn in Cheshire.'

'Do you have to mock me?'

Lucy jutted her chin out. Her eyes brimmed with fury once more. Negotiating Lucy's temper felt like pushing blindfolded through a thorn bush, never knowing when the next barb would prick him. She was exasperating, but how, how enticing! Her anger brought a vivacity to her face that excited Roger and made him hunger for her more than for any woman in as long as he could remember. More essential to him at this moment was restoring himself to her good graces. The peace that Roger had been enjoying was in danger of being shattered and he was determined to broker a truce.

'Don't be so fierce. I meant no mockery.' Roger rested a hand on her wrist and looked at her questioningly. 'I'm surprised, that's all, after what your brother said.'

Her shoulders sagged as her rage subsided a little. She gave him a sad smile.

'I'm sure Thomas will be surprised, too, when he understands how things have changed.'

She glanced at Roger's hand. He removed it with regret.

'It was grand once.' Lucy bit her lip. 'Now I'm little more than an alewife in a house that is too big for me to keep.'

'You really run it alone. When you said that at first I didn't believe you.' Roger ran his hands through his hair, which felt better for the knife he had taken to the length.

'My father is dead. Thomas was abroad. No man takes charge of my affairs.'

She sounded proud. Roger bit back the retort that if one did the inn might be more prosperous.

'What happened to your father?'

'A canker in his belly took him last summer. Since then I've lived here alone with Robbie.' Lucy's voice was tight. 'Now Thomas has returned home, the inn belongs to him.'

Roger leaned back against the wall, crossing one leg over the other.

'Would you like me to take him back to France?' he offered. 'I could doubtless persuade him to come back to the Northern Company if it would please you.'

'Is that what you're planning to do?' Lucy twisted round to look at him.

Now it was Roger's turn to take a sudden interest in his hands. 'Sometimes I intend to, then I don't, then I change my mind again. I could return abroad to try to make my fortune or stay here and settle.' He snapped his mouth shut before he began telling Lucy about Robin de Monsort's daughter. 'It's only a handful of days since I believed I was dying. Too soon to plan a future.'

'Whatever Thomas decides, the inn will always be his when he returns,' Lucy muttered.

Roger nodded in understanding. Thomas was another younger son like himself whose rights exceeded his older sibling's, however morally lacking that claim was. Lucy had worked, but he would reap the benefit. No wonder she was angry.

'You resent your brother?'

'No!' She raised an eyebrow. 'Perhaps. I'm fond of him, but he's my father's son and he claims everything, despite the fact that it is only my work that has kept the inn standing. He never disappointed my father the way I did.'

'I know how you feel, dove.' Roger sighed.

'You have a brother, too?' Lucy stared back at him curiously.

'Hal.' Roger sat forward, examining his fingernails again and thinking of his half-brother who had no claim on his father's estate, but all of his love. He wondered, not for the first time, if he would swap places with Hal were he able. Be baseborn, but loved for himself rather than as the continuation of a line.

Lucy looked at him sharply. 'Is Hal short for Henry?'

Roger nodded.

'So that's why you called the name when you needed one. How nice to have a brother so readily in your thoughts.'

'I suppose so,' Roger agreed. Tension knotted his jaw. He doubted Hal would feel so happy to have been called to such use. Had Hal forgiven Roger for his attempted seduction of Hal's wife? Had the small part he had played in reconciling them been enough to earn that? Roger did not know and would not until he faced Hal on his inevitable return to Wharram. He wondered if Lucy detected any irony in his tone, but she seemingly took the words as an honest appraisal.

'Thomas and I are three years apart. We got on as well as most brothers and sisters, I expect,' Lucy said. She frowned. 'He used to steal my dolls for fun. He'd take anything he fancied from the larder and try to blame me. He never had much time for me growing up. He thought girls were a waste of time that could be spent gaming.'

Thomas had certainly developed time and taste

for girls after leaving the inn, but his sister did not need to know that.

'Plenty of men are returning to France as mercenaries in the Free Companies. Your brother might be one of them if all goes as we hope. You might yet get to keep your inn.'

Lucy clutched the cup tightly in her hands and stared beyond Roger at the shadows dancing across the rushes. She seemed melancholy now and dark circles were showing beneath her eyes, lending her a solemn air. If Roger was tired after the day, she must be more so for being up earlier than him and awake longer in the night. She must have spent every evening sitting here with no company since her father had died. Perhaps she enjoyed the solitude. Roger knew it would have consumed him.

'At least when Thomas returns you will have some company,' he ventured, attempting to console her. She did not receive this idea with the joy he would have expected.

'Is that likely? The matter is out of my hands and yours.'

She had been sitting still, but abruptly jerked her head upward and twisted further round on the bench until she was facing Roger in the position he had found her in with yesterday's guest.

'What have you got Thomas caught up in?'

Roger swallowed down the unfair accusation that it was he getting Thomas into trouble. The lad had been the cause of them leaving John Harpur's house so hastily after all. He remembered that he had foolishly taken the blame for what the boy had done rather than let Lucy know what a fool her brother was. Hearing her talk about him now made Roger wish he had saved himself the bother. Perhaps Thomas had left a similar trail of angry fathers or husbands across Italy and France that Roger didn't know about.

Most likely the men chasing them had nothing to do with that and Lucy was correct in her beliefs. He reminded himself to investigate when he was able. Lucy was watching him keenly and feeling her interested eyes on him relit some of the flame of pride that he had once felt at being admired in the tournaments.

'Thomas and I met when we were fighting as mercenaries in the Northern Company.'

'You told me you are working for the Crown,' Lucy interrupted.

'That's right. King Edward's most recent campaign in France was ending and we joined the Northern Company in the hope of becoming rich.' He examined his fingernails. 'My family would be appalled to hear I'd sunk so low. It is not a profession for a knight. Most are foot soldiers. Rough men who had little to call them home.' He had kept himself apart from some of the more common men, but grimaced remembering some of Thomas's drinking companions.

'The matter of the Breton Succession needs to be settled and Edward is keen to give his support to the Duke of Brittany. He gave me the chance to work for him again and instructed me to visit certain nobles in the north of England on his behalf. He is requesting them to join him in support for the Duke. Thomas wanted to return to England so came with me.'

'You're messenger boys.'

Roger's cheeks coloured at her dismissal of his task.

'I'm more than that.' He sat forward, resting his hands on his knees. The motion sent a twinge of discomfort through his shoulder and he sucked his breath in. Lucy's eyes flickered to his wound and her brow wrinkled. Roger hoped it was concern that prompted it. He fixed her with a serious look, determined to impress upon her the importance of his role.

'If the noblemen King Edward has asked me to visit answer his summons, I'll claim a payment from him. It won't be big, but it will be more than I've earned any other way. Even you must realise the importance of what I'm doing.'

'I don't care about politics or the wrangling of kings.' Lucy hugged her arms around her chest. 'What difference does it make to me who rules France or Brittany? Or England, for that matter?'

'How could it not matter?' Roger asked.

'To men of your rank it probably does, but to me it makes no difference,' Lucy said. The familiar light of annoyance was back in her eyes. 'I pay my taxes and try to earn enough to feed Robbie and myself. The affairs of men I'll never meet makes no difference to the way I live. Was that why you were visiting Lord Harpur?'

Roger confirmed it. Lucy gave a short laugh.

'He'll send men. You'll get your commission from his attendance, I'm sure, though the lord is unlikely to fight himself. He's well reputed round here for not venturing too far from his home for any kind of pursuit.'

Lucy gave a sudden shiver, though the room was not particularly cold. Roger reached out to touch her shoulder, spreading his fingers wide. What use were cold rooms if you couldn't take the opportunity of snuggling up to a woman? She did not shrug him off. Her frame was rigid, but when he spoke her name quietly, questioningly, her shoulders softened and she drooped against him. She gripped the edge of the bench with both hands and looked at the floor.

'Do you know when Thomas may be back?'

If Thomas had evaded their assailants he would have made his way to Calveley's home. That would take at least two days, another for the inevitable hospitality, then another two to return. All that assuming he was no longer being tracked or had been intercepted. If he decided to continue with their original plan to travel further north to recruit men for the Northern Company, the lad could be gone for weeks. Roger did not want to add to Lucy's unease by telling her this so simply shrugged.

'I should have insisted he found a way to send me a message, but I was not thinking straight. I was more intent on him leaving and reaching safety than what happened after.'

'Thomas should have taken you elsewhere. You brought danger to my home when you came. I should never have let you come inside in the first place.'

Her body was trembling beneath Roger's fingers. It confused him until he remembered the tales she had told of facing down the men who had come in pursuit of him. For all her ferocity, however much she met his arguments and challenges head on, she was frightened. What must the intrusion have been like for a woman living as she did? Roger wished Thomas had indeed taken him elsewhere so Lucy had not had to endure that.

Roger slipped his arm further around her shoulders, yearning to ease her anxiety.

'But you did let me in and for that I thank you.'

He attempted to draw her head on to his chest, but she resisted that intimacy, for which Roger could hardly blame her given the frequency with which he had tried to seduce her. No doubt she believed this was another such attempt. He wished he could make it clear it was not.

'I told you I won't let any harm come to you. I mean it,' Roger said earnestly. 'I'll protect you as long as I'm here.'

Her eyelids flickered. She did not ask how long he intended that to be. Roger knew it would be too long for his intended interrupted mission, but not adequate to satisfy his need to comfort the woman beside him. She tilted her face to stare at him. Shadows flickered across her face, brushing her sharp cheekbones, thick lashes elongated and accentuating the grey-blue eyes that regarded him solemnly. The soft lips were half-open in a trembling pout that awoke Roger's senses. He swallowed to moisten his unaccountably dry mouth and drew her closer.

'A woman should not live alone,' he whispered, lifting a hand to her jaw and running a thumb over the ridge of her cheekbone. 'You shouldn't be alone.'

Lucy tensed, eyes narrowing. She drew back. Roger cursed inwardly at the gulf that had arisen between them once more. He would not let her withdraw into anger, however. He held his hands up to protect his face in mock defence with a grin, determined to make light of his blunder.

'Before you get your claws out, I mean for protection, not companionship.'

'I have no need for either.' She sniffed and straightened up. 'I can take care of myself if need be.'

Roger's hand crept to the side of his temple where she had once struck him with the bowl. He flashed her a grin.

'With your bowl and stave and knee? I dare say you could.'

Lucy bit her lip once again. Roger longed to capture it and do the same.

'Those of us too poor to afford servants must make do.'

Lucy pushed herself from the bench and crossed to the fire, briskly stirring the pot as if to illustrate her point.

'Why don't you get a girl in to help?' Roger suggested. 'There must be plenty in the villages round here.'

'None who would be allowed to come here! What respectable mother would send her daughter to live and work with such as me? Before I disgraced myself and brought shame on my family we had more customers. While my father lived some still came, but since I took sole charge the people from Mattonfield will not drink here.' Her lip quivered. 'Thomas will not find a thriving business when he returns.'

Roger ground his teeth. He found himself caring nothing of Thomas. The lad would have to shift himself to get customers if he returned. That should not be Lucy's burden.

Lucy dropped the ladle into the pot and walked outside, returning with Robbie in her arms. The child's head lolled against his mother's shoulder. Lucy looked at Roger over the top of his curls, holding him tightly to her. Her face was bleak.

'I'm tainted forever because of what I did. Because of Robbie.'

'Where is his father?' Roger asked quietly.

She'd brushed off the question before and he expected to be rebuffed, but she simply sighed. In truth, he cared less about whom the child belonged to and more about the man who had possessed Lucy long enough to father him. He was curious to discover what kind of man she had invited into her bed to risk ruin in the process.

'He was…' An odd expression filled her eyes. She wrapped her arms tightly around herself, enclosing her child in an embrace that excluded the world. Such fierce love was moving to witness and it struck Roger that to be loved by Lucy would be a considerable prize.

She settled Robbie on the bench and moved to the fire where she began ladling the pottage into bowls. With her back to Roger she carried on speaking. 'I knew him when I worked in Lord Harpur's manor.' Her voice was hard. 'I meant nothing to him and I prefer it that way.'

She walked to the table and slammed the bowls on it. Her cheeks bore two bright spots of anger, a far cry from the delicate blush that he had seen on other occasions. Roger said nothing, taken aback that the love she bore for her son was so darkly reflected in the alarming animosity towards his father. She settled at the table on the other side of Robbie and began to coax the boy to eat, taking alternate mouthfuls herself.

Roger began eating. The food was warming and flavoursome, but like everything he had eaten since arriving did not go far to filling his belly or providing the pleasures he usually took from a good meal. He thought back to his father's table and his mouth watered.

'What I would give for some good Yorkshire

mutton,' he said with feeling. 'Boiled hogget...
roasted new lamb...forcemeat rissoles...'

He lost himself in a reverie, imagining such delights, and was brought up sharp by Lucy's angry interjection.

'Stop that!' She glared at him, spoon half-raised to Robbie's lips.

'I'm only daydreaming,' he said, affronted. 'I used to scorn my father's obsession with breeding his stock, but now I look back with more fondness than I expected.'

The moors of Yorkshire beckoned him as they so often did, purple edged and rugged, dotted with grazing sheep that made him long to be there.

Robbie pulled at Lucy's hand, making indignant demands to be fed. She spooned more pottage into his waiting mouth. 'You have no idea how tantalising all that sounds to an empty belly,' she muttered.

Roger had not seen her eat since the small morsel of cheese and egg Robbie had left the night before. It was small wonder Lucy looked so slender. The delicate cheekbones and waist that he could reach around one armed were the product of hunger. Even now she gave more to the child than she took herself. Roger's bowl was fuller, too.

'You think I'm spoilt, don't you?' Roger said ruefully, placing his spoon in the bowl.

Lucy paused before answering. 'I think you're used to being obeyed and getting what you want,' she said with a frankness that Roger found disarming.

He could have told tales of hardships he had faced in France with no idea where the next meal might come from, of hours spent as a young squire in Northumberland living at the beck and call of his lord, of the scorn he had faced for every failure in the tournaments.

'Perhaps I am,' he agreed. 'When your life involves courtesies and privileges simply because of who you are it's hard not to expect that as an entitlement.'

He indicated the bowl in Lucy's hand.

'You should eat more than you do. You finish what you have. The boy can share with me.'

'I don't…' she began, but Roger raised a finger and gave her a stern look. She stopped, her eyes wide in surprise. Roger took her free hand. Her palm was chilly, but heat danced through his fingertips. Lucy curled her fingers around his and Roger's chest tightened. He looked up and found her eyes watchful, but with a hint of the interest she seemed determined to hide.

'I'm used to getting what I want, as you say.'
He smiled.

He expected a caustic retort, but she lowered
her eyes, studying their linked hands. A smile
played about her lips. If he lifted her hand to his
lips would her eyes harden or grow soft with longing? He ran his thumb around the centre of her
palm, then with great self-possession guided her
hand to the bowl.

'I want you to eat.'

He enclosed his hand around hers a beat longer
before reluctantly withdrawing it.

Roger took hold of Robbie's knees and spun
the boy to face him. Lucy watched closely, eyes
flicking from boy to man and back. When it became clear Robbie did not care who fed him as
long as he could distribute the pottage between
his mouth and ears she began to devour her portion with enthusiasm that made Roger's heart
swell.

When she had finished she stood and held her
hand out for Roger's empty bowl. Her fingers lingered beside his on the rim as he passed it. She
smiled.

'You must think I have a bad opinion of your
sex and your rank in particular. Perhaps I do, but
my experience has not given me much opportunity to form a favourable one. A man can swive

who he likes and ruin any number of women and no one censures him, but *she* is ruined forever unless the father acknowledges his child,' she said. 'Robbie's didn't, so we are both shamed.'

That explained her hatred of the man.

'Perhaps he doubted the boy was his,' Roger suggested.

Lucy whipped her head up. 'Do you intend to insult me so blatantly? Robbie's father was my first, my only—'

'I mean no insult. Many women with the prospect of a fatherless child seize on one they hope will shoulder the burden.' He looked at Lucy, simmering with righteous indignation. She deserved the explanation for his unfair accusation, even though it would condemn him in her eyes. He braced himself and spoke.

'It happened to me.'

'You have a child?' Lucy sank to the bench beside him.

'I *may* have fathered a child. I wasn't going to acknowledge her without definite proof.'

'*Her?* A daughter? And you left her unclaimed?'

'A child who I was not sure was mine!' Roger protested. 'The woman was my brother's lover, though she came eagerly to my arms when he was absent.'

Hal's expression on discovering their betrayal

hung heavily in Roger's memory. At least he had never shared that truth with Hal. The one good thing he did in the whole shameful affair. He rubbed his hands over his eyes.

'I knew mine was not the only bed she had taken comfort in, but I did not care. I didn't expect faithfulness from a woman who was already cuckolding someone else, but when it became apparent the child could not be Hal's she attempted to name me as the only candidate for fatherhood. I told her I had no proof the responsibility was mine and…I sent her away.'

Roger frowned, recalling the cries and tears, the pleas and assertions he had hardened his heart to.

'So you let her and her child live in shame?' Lucy's voice was low with horror.

'Kitty did not survive the birth.'

Roger's first thought on hearing that news had been relief. He put his head in his hands, knocked sideways by the revulsion that flooded him now. It seemed unbelievable that he had been so callous.

'I never saw the child, but I hear she does resemble me, so perhaps Kitty spoke the truth. My brother believes she is mine.' He sighed.

'Do you regret how you behaved?' Lucy asked.

Roger folded his arms defensively and looked

away. Was this an accusation or was she offering him absolution? 'I can't change the mistakes I made.'

'You could see the girl, though. It might do her good to know her father,' Lucy said with more gentleness than Roger felt he deserved under the circumstances.

'A man like me? I doubt it!' Roger shifted uncomfortably in his seat, trying to imagine himself as any sort of father. 'The child is well cared for and if she never learns of me, her life will be better for it.'

'An easy thing to tell yourself to salve your conscience,' Lucy said. She stood abruptly and drew Robbie into her arms. She eyed him coldly. 'I'm going to bed.'

Roger followed, unwilling for this to be her final word to him, but she kept her back to him. As she reached for the door latch he called her name. She turned slowly.

'Would you have married Robbie's father if he had acknowledged the boy?'

She bit her lip and gazed at him with solemn eyes that made Roger want to draw her into his arms.

'He was already married.'

Roger waited until she had closed the door before going into his own room and collapsing on to the mattress. He imagined he would sleep instantly, but every time he felt the drag of slumber, his mind jolted him awake and dragged his thoughts to the woman sleeping so close. She had invaded Roger's brain like ivy round an oak and her scathing judgement echoed in his mind.

He flexed his arm, feeling the discomfort of stiffness and the throb that was ever-present, coupled with the desire building inside him that demanded to be sated but for which he could foresee no release.

He had succeeded in easing his mind and body into a state of drowsiness when a high-pitched wail pierced the silence, causing his body to be at once alert. He growled under his breath when he realised it was Robbie beginning his nightly assault. He rolled over, covering his ear with his arm in the hope of drowning out the sounds, but to no avail. Would the child never be quiet!

Pulling his shirt and braies back on, he stomped to Lucy's room and pushed open the door. Lucy was standing by the window, holding Robbie and rocking him gently. Her hair was loose and she was barefoot. Her linen shift stopped at mid-calf, giving Roger a good look at shapely ankles. Despite the cold night air Roger felt himself grow warm with desire. When she saw Roger Lucy's eyes widened. Her lips slid into a smile that vanished as she began to apologise for the disturbance.

Roger's irritation melted. He held his hands out and stepped towards her.

'Give him to me.'

Lucy clutched her son to her chest, looking fearful. 'Why?'

'Because you look exhausted and I am less so,' Roger said gently. He placed a hand on her shoulder, aware with every part of his body how smooth her skin felt beneath his fingertips. She gave a shiver, like a bird struggling to break free, though Roger had known enough women to recognise it was desire that caused the flutter.

'Go to sleep. I'll keep watch on him. He'll come to no harm with me.'

Lucy's hesitation lasted almost no time and before he could draw breath Roger found himself holding Robbie. Lucy flashed him a look of relief mingled with some other emotion Roger couldn't identify. She took a step towards him, one hand reaching out, then withdrew it hastily. With difficulty Roger tore his gaze from the beguiling curves he could make out beneath Lucy's shift and left the room. At the top of the stairs he gave Robbie a stern look.

'Now, child,' he said in a firm voice. 'I know you'd rather be in your mother's arms. If it comes to it, so would I, however neither of us are getting what we want tonight.'

Robbie stopped crying, curious at this man who seemed unperturbed by his tears and wails, confirming Roger's suspicion that at least half the fuss was for Lucy's benefit alone. The boy attempted to cram his entire fist into his mouth, studying Roger to see what reaction this would cause.

'Your teeth hurt. So does my shoulder,' Roger said agreeably. 'I suggest we go downstairs and find something to ease the ache.'

By the glow of the embers Roger located the almost empty bottle of liquor. He poured the remains into a cup and settled on the stool beside the fire. Roger dipped a knuckle into the cup, reasoning that what eased his own pain would surely work for the child. Cupping Robbie in the crook of his arm, he gave the boy his knuckle to chew on. The sharp stab of an emerging tooth explained Robbie's general displeasure at the world.

Robbie sat placidly on Roger's lap, head beginning to droop. Minding the boy was easier than Roger had anticipated. He closed his eyes, occasionally sipping his own cup and letting his mind drift to Lucy who he hoped was sleeping peacefully upstairs.

Despite all attempts he had not been able to rid himself of thoughts of her. Worse, every moment he did, Roger felt increasingly drawn to her. The realisation of the extent of his feelings chilled him, unwanted as they were. He was besotted with Lucy. Infatuated.

He would go further and venture to call it love, other than to declare such a thing even to himself was a danger far greater than any he had faced on the fields of battle.

Remembering Lucy's stark condemnation of men such as himself, he writhed with shame. When he had been accused of fatherhood he had been so intent on denying the claim that he had never stopped to consider the desperation Kitty must have felt. Kitty's daughter was cared for. Hal, with his conscience and determination to do good that made Roger grind his teeth with envy, had seen to that. There was no one to care for Robbie besides Lucy and no one at all to care for her. Little wonder she was constantly angry, eternally argumentative and simmered with rage like a pot with the lid on too tightly.

Lucy had no Hal. No good man to bear the responsibility. Not even a bad man who paid and left. Well, tonight Roger would bear her burden. The knowledge caused a feeling of warmth in his heart as much as the liquor warmed his belly.

* * *

Roger could not say whether he or Robbie fell asleep first, but he awoke to find the soft head nestled beneath his own, a warm heaviness on his chest and the light beginning to creep beneath the gaps in the door frame telling him they had slept through the entire night.

Chapter Thirteen

Robbie was rolling around on the floor by the hearth, still in his nightclothes, when Lucy came downstairs. She hesitated before entering, unsure of what she would see and with an unnerving squirming sensation in her belly at the thought of seeing Sir Roger after the previous night.

The evening had been like no other she could remember: a curious mix of heated accusations and intimate admissions. What Sir Roger had told her about his behaviour towards his former mistress was reprehensible, so why was she drawn to him despite that? Perhaps it had been the slight hesitation before he had admitted he could change nothing. Only a small sign that he perhaps regretted that, but a sign nevertheless. She took a deep breath to settle her nerves and entered the room.

Robbie had captured Gyb who had returned from his nightly explorations and involved the cat in his game. Roger sat on the stool beside the dead fire, watching him. He, too, was clad only in knee-length braies and the shirt Lucy had given him. His expression was thoughtful, sombre even as he stared at the boy. As Lucy drew close he smiled, holding her gaze with eyes that were a little shadowed.

Lucy had awoken for the first time since Robbie's latest bout of teething without having to drag her eyes open and a rush of fondness for the knight took her by surprise. When Roger had burst through the door her heart had stopped beating, then begun to hammer twice as hard as he drew closer to her. She had not known what to expect, but to have Robbie taken with such assured hands was not one of the scenarios that she had ever considered. She shivered as the delicious wickedness of what she *had* imagined came to her mind. Refusing to grant him her friendship—and more—was becoming increasingly hard.

'Good morning. I wasn't sure when I should wake you. Robbie and I have been amusing ourselves as you can see.'

Robbie let go of the cat and hurled himself, squealing, at Lucy's legs. She picked him up and kissed his soft cheek. Roger was watching over the top of Robbie's head and Lucy was struck with the odd urge to bestow the same greeting on him.

'Why did you take him last night?'

'Hearing you speak of your circumstances made me consider what I had done.' He looked abashed. 'I can do nothing now for Kitty, but I can help you.'

Of all the reasons he might have given, this was the least expected.

'It was only to salve your conscience?'

'No!' Roger exclaimed. 'You made me wish I had acted better, but also I wanted to help you. That was genuine.'

A mix of emotions assailed her. Disappointment that he had been motivated by his guilt over another woman vied with satisfaction that he appeared to regret what he had done.

'I did appreciate the sleep,' Lucy admitted, giving him a smile.

'Well, I wasn't going to sleep while he was crying.' Roger smiled back. 'I've trained any number of horses to do my bidding. A little firmness is all that is needed. A boy who was already tired was much easier by far than my roan destrier was to master.'

'My son is not a horse!' Lucy giggled, then pressed her lips together at the unaccustomed sound.

'True enough.' Roger's eyes danced as he glanced at Robbie, then back to Lucy. 'His teeth are less painful when they bite down.'

Lucy watched him in curiosity. Last night she had been appalled to learn he had left a woman in the same situation Lord Harpur had left her in, so to see him appearing so fond of her son was unexpected. If he truly felt shame for what he had done, it would be surprising.

'Thank you, Roger,' she mumbled, feeling suddenly shy.

Though she had begun thinking of him without the honorific, to speak it out loud felt strange. The way his eyes lit with pleasure at the use of his name alone made her resolve to become more practised at using it.

'My pleasure, Lucy.'

Roger inclined his head in the manner he had when he had asked her to dance. He rested a hand on Robbie's head before dropping it to Lucy's arm, fingers tracing a light path from elbow to wrist. Lucy's stomach tensed. She lowered Robbie to the ground. He toddled to the counter and began pulling down the bowls, scattering them across the floor.

'Now you're awake I should dress.' Roger gestured to his shirt. Lucy's eyes followed his movement, coming to rest on his chest, visible where the garment hung loose in a deep V at the neck. The hair she glimpsed was dark, fanning out across his chest save for the place Lucy had singed it off with the poker. The blister was healing, but the area still hairless. Lucy wondered if it would ever grow back or if the mark would be permanent. The stirring she felt inside took her by surprise: unexpected and unwelcome. She looked away, disconcerted by the desire she felt which was becoming increasingly harder to deny.

'What is it?' Roger asked.

She lifted a finger and pressed the tip gently against the spot, just to the right of the small mark. Roger's muscles tensed as she touched him. The steady rhythm of his heart pulsed beneath her fingertips. Hers felt twice as fast in comparison.

'I'm sorry for this,' Lucy murmured.

'I'm sorry I gave you cause to inflict it!'

He covered Lucy's hand with his, trapping her fingers against his chest. He stepped closer to Lucy in one fluid movement until they were close enough for Lucy to see the honey flecks smattering his horse-chestnut-coloured eyes.

'Do you realise how magnificent you were that night?' Roger whispered. 'You tell me you were terrified, but I can't think of a woman in a hundred who would have been as capable and quick-thinking as you were. I only wish I had been fully conscious to appreciate it.'

Roger's lips were slightly parted, the neatly trimmed beard and moustache framing lips that were full and tempting. Lucy licked her own lips and noticed how Roger's mouth curved into a smile in response. He tilted his head slightly to one side.

Excitement boiled in Lucy's belly, rising up to meet the lurching anticipation that squeezed her heart in a clash that either could win. She looked into Roger's eyes and found them asking a question. She wondered what answer he would see in hers.

A crash cut the silent anticipation that had arisen between them, breaking the spell that had cast itself over Lucy. Both she and Roger jerked their heads to the source of the sound.

Robbie had tipped over the flask of lamp oil Lucy had stored away now the nights were growing lighter. The oil had spilled all over the rushes in a wide puddle between the counter and hearth. Lucy gave an exclamation of annoyance and rushed to retrieve the empty flask before Robbie covered himself, too. She watched in dismay as the oil soaked into the rushes, beyond saving.

When she looked up again Roger had left the room.

Neither Lucy nor Roger spoke of what had almost passed between them when he returned, fully clothed. He had smiled warmly, but when she greeted him with arms firmly folded and the smallest smile politeness would allow, he frowned and asked what she wished him to do. Lucy set Roger to work emptying out the straw from the chicken run while she strained the wort from the batch of ale she had brewing. Robbie followed his new friend to see the chickens, the temptation of this double treat being irresistible. Lucy shook her head ruefully whenever she thought of how close she had come to kissing Roger—which was more frequently than she would have liked. How foolish to have ever revealed the fascination he held for her.

'No more,' she muttered beneath her breath as she tipped the remaining liquid into the fresh bucket. She resolved that she would be polite, but there would be no more nights sitting together by the fire, no more dancing, and however much Robbie cried, her bedroom door would remain firmly shut.

She dragged the heavy tub of waste grain to the door of the brewing shed, intending to store it for Mary Barton to collect. What she saw as she looked outside made her stop in astonishment.

Roger had finished his task and, with nothing better to occupy him, was using the broom as a sword. Lucy leaned against the door frame and watched the spectacle in fascination as Roger drilled himself in exercises, changing seamlessly between positions, feet dancing and shifting back and forth with a lightness that surprised her given his broad frame and height. He made a series of sharp thrusts towards an invisible opponent with skill that took Lucy's breath away and made her want to cheer aloud. Robbie, equally captivated, had stopped his game and drawn close, his expression rapt.

Lucy's pulse began to race in astonishment at Roger's prowess. She had long admitted his appearance caught her fancy, but that had been easy enough to ignore when his arrogance and the assumption it was enough to command her had overshadowed it. It had not been Roger's attractiveness that had brought her to the brink of giving in to him that morning, but his kindness the night before, his gentleness towards her and the sincerity with which he had thanked her for what she had done. Watching him as he parried, back straight and head erect, he became the knight she had not seen before.

He had more sides to him than a honeycomb and at times proved just as sweet.

Perhaps she had been too rash. She need not exile herself from his presence as long as she was careful to keep a safe distance and did not find herself looking into those eyes that captivated her and made her lose all sense of propriety. Then her heart and what remained of her virtue would be safe.

Roger was starting to tire. The arm that held the makeshift sword wavered ever so slightly as he held it aloft and advanced step by step towards the chicken coop. So much vigorous exercise with a wound still fresh seemed unwise, but Lucy could see no fresh blood appearing on his shirt, no matter how closely she studied his broad shoulders.

Roger made another series of manoeuvres, but Lucy could see he was aware of his diminishing capabilities. He dropped the broom abruptly to the ground and threw his head back as he stretched his limbs, then unexpectedly sagged. He rested his hands on the fence, shaking his head gently and muttering under his breath. His entire body spoke of despondency that tore Lucy's heart to see. She stepped towards him.

'That was wonderful!'

Roger stiffened. 'How much did you see?' His face was guarded. Tendrils of hair clung to his cheeks and forehead where he had worked up a sweat. Lucy's fingers itched to brush them back.

'Enough to know you spoke the truth when you said you were a great knight.' Lucy smiled.

Roger snorted, though he looked pleased at

her compliment, giving her a wide smile. Embarrassed at her unguarded enthusiasm Lucy gestured to the brewing shed.

'I'd better…'

'Let me help,' Roger offered. 'I'm fascinated by what you do.'

Lucy stepped back. Her pulse had begun to slow and sense was taking over.

'There's no need. I can manage by myself.'

Roger looked hurt.

There were a dozen jobs she could assign him, but Lucy cocked her head towards him. Roger fell in beside her, taking hold of the bucket handle so they carried it between them. He asked eager questions about what she was doing and what was still to come. Lucy found herself explaining in further and further detail to an unexpectedly interested listener. Perhaps Roger himself regretted the kiss that had almost happened and this was his way of avoiding the issue. But if he had wanted to do that he could have left her alone rather than accompanying her.

'Why are you making more?' Roger asked. 'You don't appear very busy.'

Lucy ground her teeth. As if she needed reminding of how quiet the inn was! She crumbled the yeast into the wort and stirred the pan vigorously, as if doing so could hurry the process.

Head bent, she dragged the wooden lid across, not wanting Roger to see in her expression how important this batch was. The urgency of ensuring she sold enough to pay off Risby twisted her innards, anxious nausea making her feel faint. Time was passing too quickly and as yet she had no sign of meeting her obligations. She blinked back sudden tears before continuing.

'It's the St Barnabas Fair in Mattonfield two days from now. The current batch won't keep that long. Even if I waste it I can't afford not to brew more. I can't miss the opportunity to sell there. I have to pay…some debts.'

She trailed off, sensing Roger's attention was elsewhere. His eyes were faraway and his smile eager.

'A fair? It's too long since I've visited one. I'll look forward to it.'

Lucy looked at him in surprise. 'Isn't it better for you to stay here? What if you're seen?'

'Then the men who have hunted me will have to answer for what they did. I'm not hiding, Lucy. Besides,' he said wistfully, 'I miss the excitement and liveliness that a fair brings. The games, the dancing, the food…'

He trailed off, his eyes softening as he was lost in thoughts of pleasures to come. For her a fair meant whispers behind hands and judgemental eyes on her and Robbie as they walked among the people who knew her shame. She didn't want Roger to witness the level of contempt she was held in.

'I'm sure you'd be disappointed if you went. It won't be like one of your grand tournaments,' she cautioned. 'Mattonfield is a small town. The jousting isn't even on horseback. You'd hate it.'

'Jousting!'

She knew at once that she had said the wrong thing because Roger leaned towards her over the edge of the pan, almost upending it in his enthusiasm. Excitement was etched into every line of his face, giving him a boyish air.

'Not on horses,' Lucy cautioned.

'Just as well, considering I don't have one.' Roger laughed. 'Which variation is it?'

'I don't know what it's called. Running on foot at rings or hitting a target on a wooden arm.' Lucy waved her hands vaguely to illustrate her meaning.

'That's called a quintain. The rings are a tilt. Of course I won't hate it, I used to practise both when I was a squire. It's been so long since I had the chance to compete in anything.'

'What about France?'

'War is nothing like a tournament.' His voice became gruff. 'I wish I had known that before I went there.'

He half turned away with a shake of his head. Lucy walked around the boiling pan and rested a hand on his shoulder. He met her eyes and blinked, ridding himself of whatever memories haunted him.

'It will do me good to remember what I loved. I'll be strong enough to walk that far by then.' He clasped her hand suddenly. 'You'll be there to watch me, of course!'

Lucy hid a sigh. It was not her place to prevent Roger doing as he wished. Even if it had been within her power, seeing the delight on his face was enough to banish all thoughts of trying. If he was intent on competing in the fun, he might not notice the way she was shunned by the people in the town.

'Of course I'll watch you. Robbie, too.'

His smile set her heart glowing.

For the next two days Lucy brewed and, when Roger was not watching the process or carrying out the tasks she assigned, he practiced his swordplay. Travellers to Mattonfield passed by and some stopped to laugh at the sight of the tall man swinging a broom as a sword. Lucy noticed that when others were present Roger's strokes became clumsier, more like a novice with none of the skill she had previously witnessed. She smiled her best and joked with them and succeeded in selling ale to two of the men, though not as much as she would have liked.

She bade them farewell and took their cups inside. Roger joined her. Lucy cracked eggs into a bowl, conscious that Roger was still standing there.

'What's wrong?' she asked.

'I've watched you with the travellers passing through,' he said, leaning against the table. 'You smile and jest and play the coquette.'

'I don't do it because I like them!' Lucy exclaimed. She had not been aware how closely Roger must have been observing. She took a knife and beat the eggs furiously. 'They put bread on my table. If a smile and the possibility of a kiss makes them feel more inclined to spend, then I'll do it.'

Roger folded his arms. 'That's very calculating.'

'I'm too poor to be anything else,' Lucy said. A knot began to tie itself in her throat as she thought of the essential purchases she needed to make and the debts she had. Risby's face loomed in her mind, knowing how she would have to pay him.

'You never smile on me as you smile on them,' Roger remarked.

Lucy had smiled on him plenty, and each had been genuine and more freely given. The injustice of his words stung.

'You have nothing to spend and you owe me enough already.'

'And if I did, would you grant me a smile like that too, dove?'

His tone held no mockery. Lucy met his eyes, intending to flash them in the manner he had criticised her for, but his expression was so sincere her heart leapt.

'I might.'

He bowed his head. 'Then I had better win at the games tomorrow.'

Lucy poured the eggs into the pan of pottage and carried it to the fire. For the first time since Risby's visit her stomach was not filled with lead. Roger had as good as said he would pay her if he won. In turn she might be able to pay Risby and not be forced to resort again to means she preferred not to dwell on.

That night as they sat by the fire Roger told tales of tournaments in which he was invariably triumphant in the lists. He found a willing audience in Robbie as he galloped the child's toy horse across the floor to illustrate his stories.

Lucy sat at Roger's side, drawn in by his enthusiasm and glad she could put Risby from her thoughts. Her mind was filled with images of brightly streaming pennants, gleaming armour and roaring crowds, and she tried not to imagine the ladies vying for the attention of the knights at the feasts and dances he had described. Why had she not danced with him while she had the chance? She imagined the sort of woman a young knight must most likely encounter. Simpering, modest girls like Katherine Harpur, who spent their days idly waiting to be found a husband while others tended to them. Women who had never needed to raise their voice and most likely would not dare to. No doubt Sir Roger would marry such a woman one day. Until then, of course, he would amuse himself by seducing women like Lucy. All the more reason to resist her heart dragging her towards him.

Robbie tired of the tales long before Lucy and began to yawn and screw his fists into his eyes. Lucy drew her son on to her lap and rocked him gently. Roger watched with a serious expression. Robbie had trailed after him persistently for days, but the knight did not seem to mind.

'I should put him to bed,' Lucy murmured when she felt Robbie growing limp and heavy in her arms. 'I think I'll stay there myself. We have an early start. If you intend to win tomorrow, you had better get some sleep.'

Roger smiled. In an unexpected gesture he leaned over and stroked Robbie's hair.

'He's a good child.' He studied Robbie intently, then raised his eyes to meet Lucy's. 'His father missed something wonderful by not acknowledging him.'

Lucy frowned. 'I don't think he would have cared whether or not the child was biddable or a devil as long as he did not have to provide for him.' The lie she had told sprang to mind. Why had she not told Roger of Robbie's true parentage? Harpur was surely nothing to him, just as she had been nothing to Harpur. She eased herself from the stool and gripped Robbie tightly.

'I don't think he would have cared if Robbie had lived or died,' she said bitterly. 'A stillborn would have been more convenient to him. He said he hoped as much when he cast me out.'

Roger spat a curse so violently it made Lucy jump in alarm. His face was thunderous, half-hidden by shadows.

'Men say stupid things when provoked and the heat takes them. Cruel things they later regret.' His lip twisted as he saw Lucy's alarmed expression. 'A man might discover he wishes he had the means to make amends yet not have the capacity to act on that urge.'

'I doubt *he* regretted it,' Lucy muttered.

'Then he's all the more a fool than he was for leaving you.'

Lucy stared at him blankly, the intensity of his tone unanswerable and the look in his eye unmistakably one of intense desire. Perhaps it was not Harpur he was thinking of, but himself and the child he had denied. She bowed her head and rushed past him, up the stairs and into her bedchamber.

She carried Robbie to bed and laid him down. His cheeks were cool now the tooth had come. There would be no more night waking. Lucy would be able to sleep peacefully and Roger would have no call to invade her room tonight. She stared at the wall, picturing Roger lying on the other side.

Loneliness consumed her and she sagged wearily on to her bed. For four nights she had shared Roger's company and the evenings had been happier than any she could remember. He had been an initially unwelcome presence in her home, but she had grown used to him. Now she became aware that he would not be there forever. She would miss his presence more than expected and could not dismiss the sadness she felt at the thought of never seeing Roger again. When she heard his footfall on the stair she wrapped her hands around her chest, doing her best to ignore the aching craving that consumed her.

If she went to his room she knew he would

admit her. Perhaps, unlike John Harpur, he would not dismiss her as soon as he had sated himself, but they could lie together until morning. For that she would risk what remained of her reputation, but to give him such power over her without assurance of anything in return would be foolhardy. Instead she faced the wall and when she did sleep it was restlessly with half-remembered dreams of passionate words she had never heard, nor ever hoped to hear.

Roger was already waiting when Lucy came downstairs the next morning. He was wearing his leather jerkin and had thrown his cloak across his shoulders.

'Are you ready, dove?'

Lucy bound Robbie to her chest, winding him in a long cloth. She pulled her grey cloak around them both.

'Why do you call me dove?' she asked as they set out on the long climb towards Mattonfield, taking turns to pull Lucy's small cart containing the ale barrel.

'You remind me of one. Small, mild and grey.' Roger looked her up and down. 'You should wear colours.'

She twisted the end of the deep green ribbon she wore in her braid, the one concession to colour

she allowed herself. 'Some in town would doubtless have me parade my shame in a yellow hood.'

'Why do you care what they think?'

Lucy stared at the ground. She redoubled her
efforts, yanking at the cart handle. Roger caught
her by the elbow. Lucy slowed once more and he
fell in beside her. She kept her eyes fixed ahead
and arms rigidly by her side. He prised her fingers
from the handle and took over pulling.

Lucy gave him a sidelong glance. He was wearing the serious expression that was in contrast to
the vigour she knew possessed him most of the
time, but his eyes burned.

'Why do you care?' he repeated.

'However much I hate it, I have to live here. If
I thought I could kick my heels up and bid them
all farewell I would.'

'Why don't you?' Roger asked. He dropped
the handle and took Lucy by the hand. He swept
the other wide, taking in the whole of the vale
before them.

Lucy's heart tugged. She'd dreamed of such a
thing, but to be asked so blatantly made escape
seem beyond impossible. She freed her hand from
Roger's and turned in a slow circle, drinking in
the sight of the plain that spread out in one direction until the horizon blurred in the mist.

'I tried that once. I took myself to the hiring

fair against my father's wishes. Not in Matton-field, but the other direction to Bukestone.'

'What happened?'

She stroked Robbie's hand, astonished he had to ask. She turned to gaze at the hills over which Roger had come and her expression darkened.

'I got with child and had to return.'

'Ah. I should have realised.' He sounded contrite.

'How could you understand what it meant? You never had to live with the scandal, even if Kitty's child was yours. You were untouched.'

'Perhaps I should have been.' Roger spoke quietly. 'The man who left you should have been shamed, just as I should have been.'

Lucy stared at him in surprise at the admission of culpability. She gave a deep sigh. 'But he wasn't and you weren't, but Kitty and I were.'

She stalked ahead, not stopping until they reached the brow of the hill. Mattonfield lay before her and with it Risby and whatever awaited her. She'd never wanted to run from Cheshire more than she did at that moment.

Chapter Fourteen

Lucy was withdrawn the rest of the way to the town. His suggestion that she leave Mattonfield and the people she so clearly disliked should not have provoked such a response. Perhaps it was tiredness, or maybe the burden of carrying Robbie who drowsed against his mother's chest. She wore the pinched expression he had not seen on her face for days and which upset him to see.

Every attempt to make conversation was met with distracted answers aside from one exchange. Roger was musing aloud on the possibility of recruiting men to join the Northern Company when Lucy whipped her head round to glare at him.

'You make money by persuading men to be killed?'

'I make no money from recruiting them and no one has to join, but for men with no prospects it's a way to make their fortune with a share of the spoils,' Roger pointed out. Something about men of the north made his brain itch. He shook his head, dismissing it. 'When Thomas and I left France we each had a share of the prize from the last campaign. Not much, but an encouraging amount.' He kicked at a stone in the path. 'It's a shame mine was on the horse when Thomas took it. It gives me hope that if I went back there would be more to win.'

'You'd go back?' Lucy's voice was low. 'How much does a man need?'

'Enough to hold his head high,' Roger said. 'I don't intend to return to my father's house empty-handed.'

Lucy was tight-lipped.

'Would you refuse riches if they came your way?'

'Of course not,' she answered. 'But I wouldn't kill to get them, or send others to be killed.'

'No, you just flirt with men you dislike,' he retorted.

Lucy drew a sharp breath, turning red. 'Men have their way, women have ours. I doubt either sex would understand or condone the methods of the other.'

Once again she stalked ahead, dragging her cart. Roger stared after her thoughtfully. Her meaning was clear. Women made their wealth through marriage. Some men succeeded in increasing theirs in the same way. Many women had tried to catch Roger over the years and he in turn had aimed high and fallen short of winning Jane de Monsort.

With a baseborn child, how was Lucy ever to catch a husband? No wonder she continually wore an expression of worry and talk of money made her so agitated. He vowed to repay her everything he owed, if not today then at some point in the future when he had received his reward from King Edward.

They walked in silence until they reached the outskirts of the town, where Lucy handed Robbie to an older woman almost as broad as she was tall who smothered him with kisses and glared suspiciously at Roger, who lingered with the cart.

'Bring him to the games if you can,' Lucy cajoled. 'Our friend here will be competing.'

'You didn't pretend our relationship,' Roger pointed out as they walked away.

'No need. Widow Barton knows who Robbie's father is.'

Mattonfield was small but bustling and on the top of a hill. A road wound upward to the market square faced on one side by a church and open on the other to the hills where they had come from. Roger would once have scorned the town as too small for his notice, but after days of seclusion it filled him with excitement.

He followed Lucy around as she completed her errands: a new length of linen for Robbie's shift, a small pot of linseed to patch holes in the window strips, the smallest bowl on sale to replace one that was cracked. Each purchase saw the leather pouch at her waist grow emptier and her expression more bleak. She was met everywhere with coolness that made Roger seethe, but she kept her head high and affected a manner of unconcern. Finally she stopped.

'I'm finished. I'm going to set up on the corner one street over and see what I can sell.'

'You aren't coming to watch?' Roger asked. He failed to keep the disappointment from his voice, but he had been looking forward to demonstrating his skill to Lucy. She looked as disappointed as he felt.

'I'm sorry. I can't pass up this opportunity.'

Roger nodded in understanding, thinking back to Lucy's purchases. Everything had been essential and the minimum she could buy. She had bought nothing for herself, though her eyes had lingered on the honey-glazed pastries and lengths of braid. He helped her drag the cart to the street.

'Good luck,' he said gravely.

'You also.'

She smiled and reached out a hand to straighten his collar. Her fingers brushing against his neck drove him wild. Roger made his way to the square where the games were taking place, skin still feeling warm where Lucy had touched him. Farm lads and apprentices dressed in thickly padded jerkins and ill-fitting helmets swiped at each other with wooden swords. Others entered the quintain, running at targets on spinning arms or tilting at rings suspended by ropes. The melee had never held attraction for him, but tilting made his blood race with excitement.

Roger walked towards the grandly dressed guildsman in charge of proceedings. He gave his name, not bothering to think of a pseudonym. If he was being trailed, his prowess in the games would draw enough attention to himself.

With a swagger Roger walked into the square and took the lance from the squire, enjoying the mutter of interest that rippled round the square. This should be easy. With his eye on the target all he had to do was hit the centre and dodge the weight as it came round behind. He had done it a hundred times on foot and on horseback.

He pulled the lance to his chest, tucking it beneath his arm for balance. A throb of pain shot through his shoulder and he grunted aloud as the lance dropped a touch. He gritted his teeth and pulled it tighter to his body, lifting it back into position. He faced the course and broke into a run.

By the time he reached the wooden target the dull throb had become a brand of fire coursing through his upper body. The tip wavered as he ran. By the end of the course, sweat was pooling in his lower back and beneath his arms. The impact of the lance on the wooden target sent a pain through his shoulder almost as great as the arrow itself. The tip glanced off the outer edge. Stunned, Roger did not move quick enough. The weighted bag swung round, catching him in the back and knocking the remaining breath from him.

Roger shoved the lance towards the waiting boy. He wouldn't have been able to hold it much longer in any case. His hand trembled as he stared at it in disbelief. One or two laughs broke out around the square. Roger swept his head from side to side, hoping to find the culprit, but there were too many people pushing close. He knew what they would see: not a knight in polished armour with a retinue to serve him, but a man standing alone in a mended cloak and ill-fitting shirt. He was nobody to them. The flames that had lapped his arm and shoulder spread to his face. Roger lowered his head and stormed from the square. Halfway across he heard his name being called.

He spun on his heel to see Lucy dodging through the crowd towards him.

'I saw what happened. What went wrong?'

'What do you think? I wasn't strong enough. I failed!' Roger snarled. Knowing Lucy had witnessed his shameful failure was too much to bear. 'I thought you wouldn't be here!'

She recoiled, her face twisting in dismay at his outburst. The sight was a slap to his face, making his innards writhe with shame. Once before, Roger's angry words after defeat had pushed Joanna away from him and into the arms of his brother. He could not drive Lucy away now by making the same mistake.

'You didn't deserve that. It isn't you I'm angry with,' he said, summoning all his self-control to master his disappointment. 'Come with me now.'

She stood with hands on hips, glaring. 'What do you want of me, Roger?'

His gentleness transformed her shock to anger. He held his hands out. When she did not take them he reached out and unwrapped her hands from her waist. He slid his hands up her arms and tugged her gently towards him. She came reluctantly, but came nevertheless until she was standing before him.

'Your company,' he said. 'I need a drink and I don't want to be alone.'

Her chin came up and she scowled. Roger gave her a smile. 'I want to drink with *you*.'

Lucy's face softened. She glanced over her shoulder to the street where she had planned to sell her ale. 'We may as well drink some of mine as neither of us have any money.'

Roger followed her. The cart was pushed against a wall and the barrel was almost empty.

'There was more than this before!' Lucy cried. 'I was only gone a short time.'

'A pair of villains helped themselves,' called an old man who sat on a low wall tending a dozen brown geese. Lucy covered her face with her hands, her shoulders sagging. Roger reached a hand to her shoulder, but she pulled away with a sob that tore at his heart. He sat on the edge of the cart, waiting patiently for her to gather her feelings.

When she faced him her eyes were too bright in a face that was pale. She filled two cups of ale and passed one to Roger. He noticed despite his own turmoil that her hand was shaking. Losing her ale had hit her hard.

'You can make fresh,' he said, hoping to comfort her a little. Her smile was sad and slight.

'I know. But not for today.'

'Today was important to me, too.' Roger sighed. 'The first chance I had to prove I could still hold a lance.'

He drained his cup. Lucy refilled it. 'You're probably not going back to France. Why do you need to fight?'

'This isn't about fighting, but if I can't hold a lance at the tilt my career is ended just as surely as if I was unable to wield it on the battlefield. If I can't hold a lance I can't joust and if I can't do that—'

He broke off as the enormity of it consumed him. He stared at the ground, examining the dirt between his feet so he felt rather than saw Lucy sit beside him, the wakening of every sense in his body alerting him to her nearness. The cart was short so she had to squeeze close and her arm brushed against Roger's. It sent prickles of excitement racing up and down his arm and for the second time that day his hand trembled, though for an entirely different reason now.

'If I can't joust I don't know what I will do. It's all I ever wanted. The only life I've known. From the age of seven when I was sent to train as a squire I watched my master ride and vowed that one day I would be the best in Yorkshire. The best in England.'

'Which you were,' Lucy said warmly. 'You can be again.'

She meant it kindly, but Roger was caught in the exaggeration he had spun her. He leaned back against the wall and turned his face to the sun. He closed his eyes to block out the glare and found himself in the past, young and fresh, ambitious and determined to make his name. Momentarily he grieved for the boy of seventeen who never became the man he hoped to.

'I was never that good. I practised and rode enough to convince myself I was making the effort, but never enough to make the effort worthwhile. I enjoyed the glory and the thrill of competing, and the attention that taking part brought me, but I lacked the resilience to see it through when things didn't go my way.'

He shook his head. 'I wanted a simple life— glory and riches at the tilt, good wine and merry women to share my bed. I thought the war would be exciting, that it would be like the tournaments, but I've seen men and horses drowning in their own blood, towns burned and women scream- ing for mercy. I don't think I can ever be simple again.'

'Do you know what I think?'

Roger looked at Lucy eagerly.

'You need to stop being so self-pitying.' She put her hands on her hips. 'You have freedoms that are denied so many people, but you sit here wallowing in misery! All you have to do is decide what you want and do it!'

Her words came like a slap to the face.

'You have no idea what you're saying!' he growled.

'You have your life and your wealth and your name.' Lucy stared into the distance. Roger realised she was facing the direction of the inn. 'You have a home to return to and people who love you.'

'Love? Perhaps. I'm my father's younger son, but I am his heir nonetheless. Can you explain that puzzle?'

Lucy furrowed her brow.

'My father sired a child on his mistress only months before I was conceived. He brought the boy—Hal—into our house and raised him alongside me. He preferred his bastard to me and made no secret of the fact.'

Years of resentment boiled to the surface, souring Roger's stomach.

'Hal was my idol growing up as only an older brother can be. He was destined to be my squire, but he wanted no part of the life that was marked out for us both. It doesn't matter that I carried on down the path assigned to me. However much I tried to earn my father's approval I fell short.'

Lucy's face showed nothing.

'I last saw my father two weeks before I left England,' Roger continued. 'I'd had a series of failures at tournaments around England in the summer of fifty-eight. Hal and I had quarrelled— my doing entirely, though I was innocent of the greater wrongs he believed I had committed. I went to the tournament in York and returned to Wharram without the bride my father was expecting me to bring. Her father decided I was not a worthy suitor after I failed to win any significant prize. My father was disappointed, though tried to hide it. So I swapped the gaiety of the pageants for the battlefield. Becoming a mercenary was a step lower still. I'm not sure what will redeem me in my family's eyes for the harm I've caused and the lives I might have ruined. How can I return even more of a failure?'

Lucy raised her face, which looked as sorrowful as Roger felt. 'My father was furious when I left for the hiring fair. He was even more so when I returned home in disgrace. He never tried to hide it. I think if he was not already ailing he would have cast me out to starve as the priest told him to.' Her lip trembled. 'Every time he looked at me in the months before he died I could see in his eyes that I had disappointed him. I had to weather that every day, but I did it.'

Roger bunched his fists. 'I escaped that humiliation at least. My father is blind. His eyes revealed nothing to me.'

His jaw clenched and he had to force his admission out.

'It was my doing. Just one in a long line of ways I disgraced myself in my family's eyes.'

Lucy stared at him with the serious grey eyes that bored into the depths of Roger's soul. He did not want to tell her about the dark day in Yorkshire, where the determination to prove himself had ended with irreparable tragedy, but he had gone too far in his story to stop now. When she knew what he had done she would look on him with contempt, but the need to spill out his tale to the woman who had proven to be so understanding compelled him on.

'When I was first knighted I did drive myself hard and others with me, sparring with any man I could challenge, until…'

His throat constricted as he remembered what his ambition had led to. A young knight full of jealousy towards the brother his father had loved best, determined to prove himself worthy of regard. A shadow crossed the sun, stealing the heat and light from Roger's heart. He bowed his head.

'It was November, almost a decade ago. I'd been riding for hours and was angry at failing. My father told me to give up. The light was fading and the weather was closing in so he spoke sense, but I saw him as judging me to be lacking. I was furious and determined to prove him wrong so I insisted we rode again.'

He blinked to clear his eyes and felt Lucy's hand slip into his. Admitting what had happened to the quiet woman at his side, in this moment of stillness, was suddenly not so terrible.

'My lance hit him full in the face. He was blinded by a shard and lost the use of his arm when he fell.'

Roger bent his right arm at the elbow, raising it in front of his face, feeling the muscles in his forearm flex and tighten. 'Some might say this is retribution at work. Perhaps it is.'

'Would your father think that?'

Lucy's voice was soft. Her fingers laced their way between his. When he craved sympathy she gave him a tongue-lashing, but when he expected scorn she astounded him with her understanding.

'When I was insensible in your inn, I thought he had come to tell me that, but it was only my dreams. While others were angry, he accepted it was an accident. He has never blamed me. Perhaps he expected nothing more of me.' He gave a curt laugh. 'That makes my failures all the harder to bear. If I could vanish into the night and leave Hal to take my place, perhaps everyone would be happier, me included.'

'Do you mean that?'

'Baseborn or not, Hal is a better man than I ever could be. He even married the girl I had dallied with—and she's happier with him than I would ever have made her.'

Roger sighed, remembering his last, angry quarrel with Joanna and how he had not been able to resist hurting her with spiteful words and casting doubt on his brother's love for her. 'I behaved badly towards her and what little I did to make amends was poor in comparison to the hurt I caused.

'Doesn't it appeal to you, to begin again without past reckonings hanging over you?' he asked. 'Just because it didn't work last time does that mean it never can?'

Lucy pushed herself from her seat. The hardness filled her eyes again.

'Where would I go? I've lived with my mistakes. I've weathered the gossip and the condemnation. I have my path to tread and I will walk it however much I hate what I have become. To run is the coward's way.'

'Do you call me a coward?' Roger sprang to his feet.

Lucy faced him down. 'Do you give the title to yourself?'

'I've faced and defeated men in battle. I'm no coward.'

His blood raced, expecting more argument, but Lucy's answering smile was sweet, with only a hint of triumph in it. 'Then go home without a fortune and without a bride and see if your father accepts you as you are.'

Roger closed his eyes. To return home a failure...

Perhaps Lucy was right and he was a coward after all. He'd stayed at the inn longer than he had expected—or intended. He gazed towards the hills that were visible in the distance. Somewhere out there Thomas was travelling or hiding. Somewhere were the men who had made an attempt on Roger's life. There were men to be recruited to the Northern Company and King Edward's message to deliver. The walk to Mattonfield had put no strain on him and Lord de Legh's home was now within easy reach. He had nothing at the inn to collect. He need not even return there.

But Lucy was here and Roger found himself reluctant to leave her. All the excuses he had made had been just that, a pretext to stay close to this woman who fascinated him so.

'Maybe when I return to Yorkshire I'll take the recipes for your ale with me and make my name as a brewer,' he jested.

'You'd never brew it so well!' She was indignant, but beneath there was a teasing note in her voice and her eyes shone with humour, not outrage.

'Maybe I'll take you with me to teach me.' Roger laughed. He stopped abruptly as the idea hit him like a punch to the gut and slid Lucy a glance. 'Would you come if I asked?'

She snorted and looked away, but hadn't been quick enough to disguise the brief look of yearning that had flashed across her face. Yearning to escape, or yearning for Roger himself? He burned to find out.

'Once I have completed my commission and dealt with the men who did this to me I'll go there. Now I'm going back to the games. I want to try again.'

Lucy's eyes flickered with approval.

'Will you watch?' Roger asked.

Lucy glanced at the ale barrel and a change came over her face, anxiety creasing her brow. 'I can't. I have one more matter I must attend to.'

She looked so careworn it twisted Roger's heart to see. He put his hands on her shoulders and tugged her closer. When she came with no resistance he slipped his arms around her back.

'Can I help?'

Her mouth twisted into a wry smile and Roger was left with the distinct impression he was missing something significant.

'Not with this. It's only business.'

She dropped her head on to his shoulder with a small sigh. Roger tightened his arms, feeling the movement of her slender frame beneath his hands. He glanced back towards the marketplace, the shouts from the tournament pulling his heart in one direction, the desire to discover the cause of Lucy's distress tugging it another. She raised her head and prodded him gently in the chest with a finger.

'Go! You don't want to miss your chance.'

'Will you give me a favour to wear, my lady?'

Lucy raised her brows. She reached behind her head, pulled the green ribbon from her hair and pressed it into his hand. Before he could thank her, Lucy reached on her tiptoes and brushed her lips against his, pressing so lightly Roger half-believed he was imagining it, and so quickly that he did not have the presence of mind to reach out and hold her there to prolong the experience.

'For luck.'

Lucy ducked her head away and slipped free of his hold. Roger walked away with his heart singing, fingers pressed to the spot she had touched. He'd received favours of silk tippets and gold-threaded ribbons from titled ladies and daughters of wealthy merchants, but nothing had made his heart sing as loudly as Lucy's kiss.

'Back again!' The guildsman looked down his beaked nose at Roger as if inspecting a weevil-filled loaf.

Roger indicated the rings. He needed to spear each one. The knots would come loose and each ring would slide down the shaft of the lance. It required a better eye, but less force than the quintain.

'Every one to win?'

This time Roger was anticipating the pain. He braced his feet, bending his knees to take the weight of the lance and drawing deep breaths as it was placed into his arm. He wriggled his fist against the guard and ignored the way streaks of heat flickered through his shoulder until he was satisfied he had found the balancing point. He stepped forward, one foot at a time, and began a march. It would be slower and prolong his discomfort, but would result in a more accurate strike.

He approached the first ring and grunted as he shifted his torso to adjust the aim. The tip slipped through and the ring was caught. The second, too, then the third. Dimly Roger could hear the bubbling of astonishment through the crowd and this spurred him on. When he speared the fourth the noise surged and he blinked before refocusing on the final ring. Eight more steps and he was there. With one great roar, Roger pulled his shoulder round, centring the lance and spearing the centre of the ring with an aim that was true.

Applause thundered in his ears, something he hadn't heard in far too long. He barely noticed as he handed the lance to the squire and the small purse was pressed into his hand. The one face he craved to see wasn't there. Brushing off the congratulations of the guild master, he left the square and made his way back to where he had left Lucy. He pictured the look on her face when he returned bearing hands full of coins. She would have a new ribbon, Robbie one of the jointed wooden dolls and they would all eat honey cake. He would pay her what he owed, too, and then...

A grin spread across his face. The idea that had been forming at the back of his mind since his earlier jest about taking Lucy to Wharram with him now seemed less outlandish. When he had spoken of Joanna he had not been entirely truthful. He had not loved her at first, but by the time the feeling had come over him it had been too late. He recognised that same feeling when he thought of Lucy and was determined not to make the same error.

What if she did go with him? He would be happy with her in his life. Whether he could be content if she was not was something he didn't want to consider. There was no inn in Wharram

Danby, only a house or two where the alewives served from their doors and served the folk of the village. Roger's father would be overjoyed at the idea of good ale and would surely provide a dwelling.

If he didn't, Roger himself would build an inn where Lucy and Robbie could live and he could visit. He pictured Lucy welcoming him with a kiss and taking him in her arms. Evenings sitting with her beside the hearth while Robbie played, such as those they had shared, and not a mean fire with each log eked out, but a great one with enough warmth to fill the house. After that, long nights in bed, limbs entwined, bodies cleaving together. Somewhere he could come home to.

A home. He stopped walking and ran his fingers through his hair, a wide smile spreading across his face. He was starting to think like his brother, something Roger had long scorned, but which now burrowed into his brain enticingly.

The corner where Lucy had stationed herself was empty and her cart was gone. 'Do you know where Mistress Carew is?' he called to the goose man.

The man hacked up a mouthful of spittle. He pointed towards the river. 'Try Risby's mill. They were talking earlier.'

Lucy had not said she needed bread or malt, but

her cart stood beside a door at the mill. The door was closed, but Roger lifted the latch and went in.

What he saw stopped him short, nailing him to the spot in disgust and dismay.

Two figures occupied the dimly lit, dusty room. The man stood with legs spread and half-closed eyes. Roger recognised him as the miller. It took Roger a moment to fully understand that the woman with her back to the door, one hand on the miller's waist, was Lucy.

Chapter Fifteen

A knife stabbed Roger's chest, knocking the wind from him harder than if the blow had been real. He gripped the door frame. He must have made a sound because the miller's eyes focused on him.

'Wait your turn,' the miller barked. 'She hasn't yet started on me.'

Lucy whipped her head round. Her face twisted with horror. She pointed a trembling hand at the door.

'Get out!'

The miller jerked Lucy round to face him once more.

'You've not even begun yet,' he said harshly, putting his hands on her shoulders and attempting to force her to her knees.

Lucy looked over her shoulder at Roger.

'I told you to leave.' Her words turned to a sob.

Roger stepped forward and tugged her hand from the miller's belt.

'You're leaving with me.'

She wrenched free and ran from the room with her head down.

'Where are you going?' demanded the miller.

Roger bared his teeth in a warning growl to silence the man, then followed. Lucy was running at full tilt towards the river and the road skirting round the town. She ignored Roger's cry. He broke into a run and seized her by the arm. She fought him, but Roger was not to be deterred.

He took her by the waist and held her tight, hands spread in the hollow of her spine. She wriggled in his arms like a dove trying to escape a hawk. He'd dreamed of holding her this close, the tantalising moments when they had come close to kissing had driven him wild, but this was not what he had imagined.

'What are you doing here?' Lucy asked through gritted teeth. 'How did you find me?'

'I won the game and the purse. I wanted to tell you, but you weren't where I had left you,' Roger said. Remembering the plans he had been making on his way there, he felt his temper surge.

'Is that Robbie's father?'

'No!' She stiffened in his arms.

'Is he your lover?'

Was this the reason she had refused him? The miller already had a claim on her affections. Roger's pride revolted at the idea that she would give herself to a repellent figure like Risby while refusing Roger. She refused to meet his eye, twisting her torso away from him. Roger took his hands from her waist and stepped back, his heart splitting in two.

'I take it that means he is.'

Lucy made a sound of disgust. She fixed him with eyes full of contempt.

'Is that what you think love looks like? That says more about you than it does about me! Do you really think I could love a man like him? Don't you know anything of me?' Her lip trembled and her voice dropped to a whisper. Her eyes filled with tears that made Roger's heart break. 'I owe him money I haven't got. He suggested another way I could pay the debt.'

Understanding flashed through Roger, followed by revulsion. Lucy was not doing this through love, or even desire. It was a cold-hearted transaction. Roger wasn't sure if this was worse or better than believing her in love.

'You were going to give yourself to him?'

'Not completely,' Lucy protested. 'There are other ways to satisfy a man, as I'm sure you know!' She covered her face with her hands.

'All the time I've lived under your roof I believed you a virtuous woman. Now I discover I could have bought an hour's tumble if I'd had the money.'

'The commodity is mine to do with as I please.' Lucy's eyes were now free of the tears he had seen threatening to spill and were full of icy fury.

'Is that how you view your body?' Roger asked in disgust.

'Isn't it how men see it?' She drew herself up to her full height, shoulders back, causing her breasts to jut forward in a way that Roger could not ignore.

'You'd have paid if you thought that might allow you to wet your staff, you just admitted it. How many women like me have you swived in your time? How many do you think wanted to be doing it? Did you ever stop to wonder why they took your money?'

'I rarely had to pay them.'

'Not in coins, perhaps,' Lucy muttered.

Roger thought of the women in his past. Kitty, the maid at Lord Harpur's house, even Joanna who he had never persuaded to do more than kiss and fumble, to say nothing of the handful of women he could barely even remember. A pang of loneliness shot through Roger.

'Are you suggesting they only accepted my attentions for what I gave them? I always assumed they had loved me.'

'That's my point!' Lucy shouted. 'Perhaps they cared for you, perhaps they felt forced, but you never asked. It never occurred to you that you had to. At least I'm honest enough not to pretend I care for Risby and I know he cares nothing for me. Tell me, what should I have done instead? How should I survive with no money and no one to help me?' Lucy flung an arm out violently towards the miller's house. 'It doesn't matter who you are, poor men like him…rich men like you… like Robbie's father…'

She swept closer to him, trembling with anger, her cheeks scarlet.

'You use women like me until you've had enough, then you leave us to mend our lives and reputations as best we can.' She wrapped her arms around herself, trembling violently. 'You have no idea what it costs me to do this. How I die inside each time, wishing it would be over. You dare to sit in judgement over me? How dare you!'

In the face of her bile, Roger recoiled. How had this changed from his abhorrence at what she had done to her attacking him?

'If the woman you fathered a bastard on hadn't died in childbirth, would she be doing anything different to me now? How many of those others did she lie with willingly and how many so she didn't starve?'

Her words knocked the strength from Roger. He shook his head, unable to defend himself against her accusations.

'You have nothing to say? From the moment you met me you did your best to talk me into your bed.'

'I tried to get you into bed, but I wanted you to come willingly,' Roger protested. 'I wanted it to mean something.'

'Mean something? To you or to me?' She laughed. She actually laughed, loud and shrill, until Roger understood it was no laugh at all, but pain escaping in an alarming flood of emotion. 'I know you want me and you know I want you, too. I've resisted you and tried to ignore the feelings and desires I know will only lead to misery but it hasn't been easy.'

She reached out and put her hands on Roger's face, fingers spreading to caress his cheeks. The gesture was so unexpected after her venomous outburst that Roger accepted her touch without thinking. She looked into his eyes, piercing his soul with her intensity.

'Now you know what sort of woman I am, do you still want me?'

He did. Despite what he had seen, the thought

of touching her ran like molten iron through his blood. She was in his arms, her breasts pushing against his chest, sending a surge of longing through him. His lips craved hers...

'You have money now. Will you spend your winnings on rutting in my bed?' She ran a hand slowly from his cheek down his chest to settle at his waist. He gasped as lust riddled his body, instantly hardening him. Her eyes flitted down and she looked into his eyes triumphantly.

'Should I do that for you instead and use your money to pay *him*?' she breathed.

Roger growled in revulsion as the blood that had raced hot became ice. He clenched his jaw, only realising as she whipped her hands away that Lucy would have felt the tension through her fingers.

She gave one distraught sob before she turned on her heel and ran.

The sound ripped Roger's heart from his chest, leaving him hollow and the strength that had been ebbing since his exertions at the tilt failed him.

This time he let her go.

Lucy had abandoned her cart in her haste to escape from Roger. He slumped on the edge and stared at the contents. The meagre amount of food, the essentials she needed to live. The almost-empty ale barrel. His conscience pricked him. Lucy had left her position and missed valuable selling time to console him after his failure. Other men had stolen her wares. Perhaps if she had left him to his own devices she might have made what she owed. Instead she had listened to Roger's self-pitying woes, while all the time she must have been in turmoil, thinking about what lay before her. She had pushed him back towards the marketplace rather than explain the snare she was tangled in and he had ignored the suspicions he felt and had gone. Selfish and self-serving as always!

The resentment that had settled on his chest as heavy as a mail shirt lifted to be replaced by guilt that weighed double. He had told her the worst of his misdeeds this afternoon and she had said not a word of censure. Not even the worst, now he thought of it, because he had told her nothing of his attempted seduction of his brother's wife where he had been so forceful she had recoiled in horror. He couldn't ignore the sickening voice whispering that he was, as Lucy had accused him, no better than the miller. He was not fit to judge her.

He counted the coins he had won—now tarnished, in his eyes. He walked back to the miller's house and pushed the door open. The miller was sitting in a chair. He looked up when Roger entered, his face alert and beginning to form a leer.

When he realised Lucy had not returned he pushed out his lower lip petulantly and glared at Roger.

'Have you frightened her off or is she waiting outside?'

'She's gone,' Roger said in a calmer voice than he felt. 'She won't be back.'

'I know your face, don't I?' The miller scowled. 'You were on the path to the inn a few days back.'

'I was, and as you can see I arrived safely.' He stepped closer, looming over the seated man. 'Mistress Carew is under my protection now.'

'Who are you?'

'I'm someone who cares for her,' Roger answered. 'If a word of this gets out you'll answer to me. I'll let it be known in the village. What will the other men think of you?'

'D'you think they don't know already? Do you think I'm the first, or the only? She's got to put more than bread on the table. She'll be back or I'll see her in the assizes for failure to pay.'

Roger swung, balling his fist as his arm came round. The impact on the miller's jaw sent waves of pain up his arm into the still-raw nerves of his shoulder, but the retching whimper from the miller as he slid to the floor more than made up for the discomfort.

'How much does Mistress Carew owe? I will settle her debt.'

The miller wheezed out a figure. Roger drew his fist back again and the price was halved. Roger drew out a coin and pressed it into the man's hand. He closed the fat fingers around it, pressing tightly until the miller winced as the edge bit into his palm.

'Now, get out,' Roger said grimly. The miller stumbled from the room, even though it was his own.

Roger slumped into the chair the man had vacated, trying his best not to think how many times Risby might have sat in that place and received Lucy's attentions. He rested his head back against the wall and closed his eyes.

In the darkening room, Roger Danby looked inside himself and disliked what he saw. He winced as if a blow had struck him. Lucy had hit him, not with fists but with truths and they left a blow that stung harder by far and for long after. The disgust he had poured on her was nothing compared to that with which he scourged himself. He deserved every word she had said and more. Lucy had asked if he was a coward and he had denied it. Now he wondered if he had the courage or the ability to become the man he should always have been.

He still had money. He could buy fresh clothes smart enough to gain him admittance to Lord de

Legh's presence. He could hire the use of a mule to get him there and spare his legs. He knew he would do neither of those things. His heart belonged in the inn. More than ever he was determined that Lucy would play a part in his life and he a part in hers. He wanted her to be his, and his alone. She had asked if he wanted her in his bed and he did, but more than that he wanted to hold her and keep her safe from men like Risby... and himself.

Even though it pained him to think of the reception he would receive, he would return Lucy's cart and for the first time in his life he would do something he should have done many times in the past. He would beg her forgiveness for his deeds.

Lucy ran. There was no voice demanding she stay, no arms about her waist. Roger was not following her. She resisted looking back, the cold revulsion on his face lashing her mind. When she neared Mary Barton's home she knelt by the river and splashed water over her hands to rid herself of the scent and feel of Risby's flesh, though she had been interrupted before beginning what she had bargained to do. Somehow she managed to remain calm while she collected Robbie and listened to Mary Barton's account of the day, including the news that the stranger who had been with

Lucy had succeeded in spearing all five rings. She smiled through clenched teeth. He had won his long-sought-after money and would no doubt be leaving as soon as he could.

The ugly, angry words they had thrown at each other loomed large in her mind. Did she regret them? Not in the slightest. Roger's condemnation of her behaviour was far too hypocritical considering what she knew of his past. Even so, she wished she could have prevented him discovering her secret. Seeing the light of disappointment in his eyes was worse than when she had returned home to admit to her father why Lord Harpur had cast her out.

She started on the path to the inn with a heavy heart. The road was littered with travellers leaving the fair, but none of them was the familiar figure she wanted to see. She barely noticed when someone fell in beside her until she felt a hand at her elbow. Her heart soared as she stopped dead. However, it was not Roger, but a hooded figure close to her height.

'Keep walking, Sister.'

She gasped in surprise.

'Say nothing that will attract attention. Even now we might be watched.'

'Thomas, where have you been?'

If he had returned one day earlier things would

have been so different. Thomas would have taken Roger away and he would never have discovered her shame. Thomas might even have brought money so she could have repaid her debt honestly.

His eyes darted from side to side. 'Has anyone come looking for me?'

'The men who came before? No. Nor anyone Roger recognised.'

'Have you been in the brewing shed?'

Lucy wrinkled her nose, confused at this change of subject. 'Of course, I go every day. Why?'

Thomas glanced around. 'No matter. Sir Roger will be able to help me when I speak to him.'

Lucy caught hold of his wrist. 'What trouble are you in? What can he do?' She bowed her head, barely able to speak his name. 'Roger isn't at the inn.'

Thomas clutched her skirt. 'Did he survive the arrow wound? I must speak with him urgently. Where is he?'

'He survived. I helped him. I don't know where he is now. He may come back to the inn.' Lucy swallowed a sob. 'But perhaps not. If you wait—'

'Not the inn!' Thomas interrupted. 'They're searching for me. I know it now.' He paced around. 'Remember the old well where we used to play? I'll hide there. Tell Sir Roger to come when he can.'

'What if he doesn't come back?' Lucy asked. The idea she might never see him again was unbearable, but she would have to bury that feeling deep inside.

'Then I am lost,' Thomas growled. They were walking fast and nearing the small group that walked ahead of them. Thomas dropped Lucy's arm. 'I have to go now.'

He peeled away and headed from the road into the hills. Lucy watched him go, until she became aware that standing staring at the forest was a sure way to draw attention to his presence. If Thomas was lost, that was nothing to how Lucy felt. She shifted Robbie into a more comfortable position and returned home.

The inn was dark and cold. Lucy lit a single taper for Robbie's comfort. She didn't mind the cold and there was no reason to sit in the light when there was no one to sit with. When they had argued before and she had thrown Roger out, her feelings had been of overwhelming relief. Now his absence filled the room.

She soaked bread in milk for Robbie. He ate sleepily, leaving more than Lucy was prepared to throw away. She felt too despondent to eat, but scraped the bowl anyhow, remembering how Roger had insisted she eat the whole portion while he shared with Robbie. She smiled at the memory even though it caused fresh tears to fill her eyes. Such a foolish reason to fall in love with someone, but that along with other small kindnesses had worked into her heart more surely than any silver-tongued words or poetry might have.

She carried Robbie to bed and went back downstairs to sit by the hearth. She had spent more evenings than she could count sitting alone and had no expectation of a future where she did otherwise, but until Roger arrived she had not seen what pleasure the company of an amusing companion could bring. She rested her head against the wall and let the tears fall.

A soft tap at the door roused her from her misery. She tensed, hardly able to move. The tap came again and Lucy ran to the door, lifting the latch with trembling hands.

Roger stood framed in the doorway, silhouetted in the dusk. Lucy's heart leapt to her throat and she almost flung herself into his arms until she remembered the cold disgust in his eyes and the way he had frozen under her touch.

'What do you want?'

'We have unfinished business. May I come in?'

Lucy stepped back. Roger did not move at first, but then ducked his head and stepped inside. His face was unreadable in the darkness of the solitary taper.

'Why are you sitting in the dark? You haven't even lit the fire.' Roger's voice was disapproving. Lucy shrugged. It was a small criticism compared to his earlier words. He crossed the room and knelt, striking the flint until the sparks caught the straw. He lit two more tapers and came to stand in front of Lucy, holding one up so he could see her. Her eyes felt swollen and sore. She hated him to know she had been crying.

'I wasn't sure if you would come back now you have your money.'

'I wasn't sure either.'

'You could leave Mattonfield.'

'I considered it.' His body was rigid as he towered over her.

'Before or after you discovered what I am?'

'After. But as you can see I am here.' Roger reached out a hand. 'You've been crying.'

Lucy crossed her arms. 'Yes, I have. But I'm not now. If you've come to condemn me further you can leave.'

'I haven't.' Roger's voice betrayed no emotion. 'He said he wasn't the first. Was he speaking the truth?'

She could have lied, pretended virtue she didn't deserve, but she was done with deception. 'The physician was. My father needed medicine I could not afford. What else could I have done?'

He smiled sadly. 'I've brought back your cart.'

It was no answer, but until then it had not occurred to Lucy that she had even left it behind. His small kindness swept her feet from under her and, angry as she was, she felt her face soften into a smile. She forced herself to hide it.

'Thank you, but there was no need. I could have collected it tomorrow.'

'I don't want you returning to the mill.' A shadow passed over Roger's face. 'For any reason.'

'I don't want to,' she admitted. She began forming an explanation, then stopped and walked away from him. The fire was beginning to catch and she stared into the flickering depths.

'I told you before, I made my choices and I've lived with my mistakes. I won't justify myself to you.'

'You have no need to justify yourself. Truly. I don't like it, but I can understand why you were going to do it.'

He came behind her, close enough that she was aware of every small movement. Lucy kept her back to him, uncertain what was happening. She had expected a further tirade against her morality or recriminations about what she had said to him, but Roger sounded nervous.

'I didn't come here to quarrel with you.' Roger's voice was earnest.

'Then why did you come?'

'I never got the chance to tell you why I was looking for you,' Roger said.

'To tell me you had won?'

'More than that,' Roger said. 'To thank you for sending me back to try again. I won because of you, dove.'

He moved closer to her. Lucy lifted her head to look at him, her heartbeat thumping in her ears. He took her by the hand, then ran his fingers slowly up her arms, across her shoulders and finally put his hands to her cheeks, burying his fingers in her hair. The gesture was so intimate that it caused the breath to catch in Lucy's throat.

His eyes were soft and his lips slightly parted. He stroked her cheek with his thumb as his fingers slipped behind her head, drawing her towards him. He was going to kiss her. And she intended to let him.

Roger's mouth sought hers. Lucy tilted her head until it was within reach. His kiss was eager, his lips hungry for hers. The scent of him flooded her limbs, the taste of him made her grow weak. She gave herself over to the pleasure, allowing him to guide her in pace and pressure until her head spun.

Roger broke away first. He held her gaze in a moment of stillness, the world containing only them.

'After I won I started thinking about my future and yours. You don't have to live the way you do. There is another way.'

He pushed a lock of hair behind Lucy's ear in a gesture that was at once intimate yet proprietary. He smiled.

'I want you to become my mistress.'

Chapter Sixteen

'Oh!'

Lucy pulled her hands free, feeling foolish. The kiss had been like a sensuous dream she hadn't wanted to wake from, obliterating all thoughts and worries. For one moment she had thought Roger was about to ask her to marry him, so his words brought the dream crashing down in flames.

'What's wrong?' Roger wrinkled his forehead.

Lucy's throat tightened and she felt tears prickle her eyes. He clearly didn't think he'd asked anything wrong.

'You scorn me for being a whore one moment, then the next you ask me to perform the same service for you! You're just the same as Risby.'

Roger's mouth fell open.

'I'm not asking you to go on your knees for me to pay a debt. I'm asking you to be my lover.

Surely it's better to belong to one man than to anyone who will pay.'

Lucy lifted her chin haughtily. 'I don't intend to "belong" to anyone. I did what I had to in order to clear my debt—which thanks to your interruption still hangs over my head.'

'No, it doesn't.' His face grew solemn. 'I settled what you owe and left him with a bruise or two to remind him how to behave in future. He won't bother you again and if he tries he'll answer to me.'

That he'd do that for her made her want to weep. 'So you think you've bought me. My debt was for me to clear, not for him to sell on.'

'He didn't sell it on. That's not why I'm asking.'

'And you still want me now you know I'll whore for anybody?' She swallowed a knot of distress that choked her. 'Or perhaps because of that?'

'That's not fair.' Roger's face darkened. 'I was on my way to ask you anyway when I discovered you with the miller. I want you because you drive me wild with desire. When I go back to Yorkshire I want you to come with me. Robbie, too. We can be together, sharing our lives with each other. You cannot deny that we feel something for each other.'

He pulled her to him, wrapping one arm around

her waist. He bent his head, burying his face in her hair. 'Seeing you today doing what you were doing caused me greater pain than any arrow. Knowing why you did it was even more agony. I would spare you that again. I'll protect you. I'll keep you safe. Tell me that kiss did nothing for you. I know you feel what I do.'

Roger's muscles were taut, the strength in them distractingly beguiling. It would be all too easy to give in to what he wanted. What her body cried that she wanted more than ever. Lucy closed her eyes, imagining a future where she did not have to face the people who scorned her. Where Roger was with her and she could give in to the sensations that drove her to distraction. At least until he grew bored, or she fell with child and he denied all responsibility.

'And if it did, what then? You'd keep me until you get tired of me, then you'd leave!' Lucy said, wriggling free.

'I won't do that!' He leaned close, as if he intended to embrace her again. 'I'll never tire of you, Lucy. You're unlike any woman I've ever known.'

She stepped back out of his reach. 'Have you had many mistresses, my lord?'

'A handful,' he admitted.

'And where are they now? Do you think about them?'

'From time to time.'

'But you did not love them enough to stay with them.'

She moved past him to sit on the stool beside the fire. Roger came and knelt at her feet, the picture of loyal affection.

'I have never kept a mistress I did not like. With every other woman I always expected it to end, but I can't imagine a day you aren't in my life until I die. Your wellbeing matters to me. I'm... very fond of you, dove.'

Lucy's heart fluttered. If he had professed love she would have left the room, but his reluctance to name the emotion was oddly more convincing.

She touched his cheek. 'Strange though it may seem, and much against my better judgement, I'm growing fond of you, too. And you know I want you. I always have. But even if my heart did not race when you look at me in that manner, I won't be one of those women. All men leave eventually. It's just a question of time.'

'If that's what you believe, then why not enjoy yourself until it ends?' Roger took hold of her hand once more, resting his thumb on the underside of her wrist and moving it in small circles that made her innards squirm with desire. 'For both of us to share in the pleasure that lovemaking can bring.'

'Because I don't want any more fatherless bastards. It's too easy for men to sire as many as they like and refuse to acknowledge them.'

'That's not true of every man. I wouldn't do that to you!'

'You condemned yourself by that measure already when you admitted what you did to Kitty,' Lucy said sadly. 'I've been the plaything of one nobleman and I'm not going to make the same mistake again.'

Roger raised his head sharply. 'You're talking in riddles. What nobleman?'

Lucy drew her hands away from his. 'I said I met Robbie's father when I worked on Lord Harpur's estate. *He* fathered Robbie, then cast me out when I told him I was with child. Did you ever wonder why I took you in and lied for you? It's because Thomas said Lord Harpur was pursuing you and I hate that man beyond all others.'

'John Harpur? And I thought you took me in because you felt compassion for my pain. Are you certain he is the father?'

She rounded on Roger furiously. 'I told you already I was a virgin when he took me.'

'When he took you?' Roger eyed her sharply. His hand tightened on her arm. 'Was it rape?'

Lucy closed her eyes, reliving the first time with the cold, rough bricks of the brewery wall against her back, remembering her thrill at the way the nobleman was half out of his braies before she had uttered a word.

'He was forceful, but I agreed to what he asked. He flattered me and I wanted him, but he made promises he had no intention of keeping. I won't be so foolish a second time.'

'I apologise for my suggestion,' Roger muttered. 'For everything.'

'You see why I did not press my claim on Lord Harpur,' Lucy said. 'I was not prepared to suffer the humiliation, knowing full well it would prove useless. Unfortunately, unlike Kitty, there was no one to take care of my bastard so I live as I live and do what I do and my son will grow up with the shame of being baseborn.'

She blinked away tears.

'What about when you marry, my lord? Would you take our children to live with yours? Would you keep your mistress while you slept in your wife's arms? How many months would we have together before that happened?'

'I don't want a wife. I want you,' Roger said gruffly.

'I will be no man's mistress, so I thank you, my lord, for the great honour you do me, but I must regretfully decline your request.'

She spoke coldly but with a gentle smile because even now hurting his feelings made her writhe inside. Roger's face fell. His eyes filled with pain. He squeezed her hand tightly and his mouth twisted downward.

'You'd rather go down on your knees for other men than live as my mistress.'

She glared at him. He dropped his gaze, shame-faced. 'I'd rather command my own fate than be at the whim of a man who could leave at any moment. At least when I do what I do it's on my terms.'

'I understand.'

He pushed himself to his feet and walked out of the inn, back erect, shutting the door quietly behind him.

Lucy bent double in her seat, hugging herself tightly, trying to contain the sorrow that threatened to consume her. Thank goodness Roger had walked out when he did because it had taken all her strength not to accept his offer. Would it have been as foolish as she believed? How fortunate that he would be gone before long and temptation would no longer be in her path.

She sat up, realising with a start she had not told him about Thomas's return. That would have to wait until morning now, but when she did, Roger would surely leave, taking her heart with him. Her life would return to normal and gradually she would learn to bury inside her the feelings that could never be satisfied. Perhaps she had been too rash to refuse because besides her there was someone else who could benefit from what Roger had suggested. She glanced at the ceiling, thinking of Robbie who slept there peacefully, unaware of the turmoil that was happening below.

Roger stomped down to the stream, removed his boots and breeches, and waded in wearing only his braies and shirt. The water was bitterly cold, reminding him of the beck at Wharram where he would hurl himself after a bout of swordplay. He needed the cold water to bring him to his senses after the turmoil of the afternoon.

Scrubbing away at his hair and body, he played over in his mind what Lucy had said. He had convinced himself she would not refuse, especially after the kiss that had turned his stomach inside out and left him a quivering shell of lust, but now he saw himself through her eyes: a man guilty of the same offences that had caused her misery.

He had even contemplated repeating his father's mistakes and causing pain to the unknown future wife that he must one day take, because he could not imagine a time when his heart would not belong to Lucy. He had done nothing to give her any reason to believe she could trust him, so it was no wonder she was not prepared to risk herself. She should be someone's wife, to be treasured and kept faith with.

Roger sat on the bank of the river, eyes sliding to the inn, picturing Lucy sitting alone. He loved her, more truly than he had loved anyone before. It was not only the need to possess her that drove him, but the need to be claimed and possessed in return. To be judged and found not lacking. He'd been wrong to suggest his idea today. It was too soon after the hurtful words that had passed between them. Perhaps he had been wrong to suggest it at all, but he could see no other way of sharing Lucy's life.

Perhaps he did not deserve that honour.

For the first time, Roger deeply understood that the unkindness he had inflicted on others with his casual use and dismissal of them was rebounding on him and deservedly so. He beat his hand against the ground. Small darts of pain shot through his arm and shoulder.

He drew his knees up and put his head in his hands, grief and shame and hopelessness overwhelming him, not caring that the sun had dropped from the sky and the evening air caused the wound on his shoulder to ache.

When the cold became too uncomfortable to bear he pulled his shirt back on. Appearing half-naked would do nothing to convince Lucy his feelings were driven by more than lust. He walked back to the inn and let himself in quietly. Lucy was sitting where he had left her. From the tensing of her back and shoulders as he entered he understood she was as aware of his presence as he was conscious of her every movement.

'There's something I have to tell you. I should have told you as soon as you arrived.'

Roger braced himself for further revelations to shatter his heart.

'Thomas is back.'

He instinctively stared around, scalp prickling.

'Not here. He found me on the way back from Mattonfield. He says he knows who is pursuing him. He said you could help him.'

The blood coursed hot through his veins in anticipation of putting an end to the mystery that had plagued him and taking his retribution on the men who had attacked him. He was lost in the thoughts until he noticed Lucy standing very still in front of him, waiting for him to return to the present.

'Tell me everything.'

In a low voice, she repeated everything Thomas had said and gave Roger directions where to find her brother.

'It's too late now. I'll leave at first light.'

'And then you'll be leaving for good,' she said quietly.

'It looks that way.' The thought made him sadder than he thought possible that his time with Lucy was ending. Perhaps when he had done what needed to be done there would be time to prove he was worth risking her heart on, but duty called. He bowed his head, straightening the objects on the counter top, rearranging the oil jar and Lucy's knife rather than face her and let her glimpse the emotions that threatened to overwhelm him.

'When you return to Yorkshire, will you take Robbie with you?'

'What?'

Lucy tilted her head slightly to one side, her profile sharp in the shadows. 'You can give him a life I can't. I know he's younger than is customary, but you could find a place for him in your father's house.'

'What about you?'

'I'll be happy here knowing he's cared for.' She faced him, looking utterly alone. Roger's heart cracked, hearing the lie beneath her words.

'No, you won't.' He wrapped his arms around her until she was enveloped tightly against his chest.

'You would have me take your child and leave you here?'

She nodded, still tightly held in his arms.

'If you care for me at all, do for him what someone did for your child. He is no more at fault than your daughter is. Redeem your past mistakes by helping Robbie.'

Her voice was muffled against his chest and he had to strain to make out the words. His shirt was becoming damp and he realised with a start she must be crying. His own eyes welled up. To take the son she loved so much but to leave her behind was inconceivable. How would that buy him redemption?

'I do care for you. So much more than I thought possible,' Roger whispered. He kissed the top of her head. Her body stiffened, then her chest rose and fell, pushing her breasts hard against him. He left another kiss on her temple, then another beside her eye, tasting the salt tears.

Lucy sighed. Her eyelashes flickered against his lips. Roger risked another kiss, this time on her cheek. Her arms slipped around his waist, meeting in the small of his back. Her breath tickled the soft hollow behind his ear and he felt himself growing harder. Lucy turned her head a little more and Roger found her lips against his for the second time that day.

His first impulse was to grasp the opportunity with as much passion as he had previously, but he reined himself in. He craved so much from Lucy, but what he desired more than the brief release of a moment of ecstasy was this quiet closeness. Instead of eagerly parting Lucy's lips, his tongue delving inside to bring her under his command, he gently brushed them with his.

Roger closed his eyes, surrendering to the emotions engulfing him. Their lips moved in unison as both of them finally acknowledged wordlessly that what they felt for each other went beyond mere lust.

'Stay with me tonight,' he pleaded once he was able to draw breath. 'It's been a horrible day. I've spent too long alone and so have you. Don't let tonight be another night like that.'

'I won't lie with you. I've told you that already,' Lucy answered, drawing away.

'That's not what I'm asking,' Roger said. 'We both need comfort and, whatever happens after tonight, I want the memory of sleeping with you in my arms. Will you do me that honour? Please.'

A subtle change in her stance told Roger she was willing to be persuaded. She rested her head against his shoulder and shifted closer until the gaps between their bodies disappeared. She was already planning her surrender and needed only a gentle nudge.

'I'm scared. I want you so much it terrifies me, but I won't bear another bastard, not for any man.'

'I swear I will not ask that of you,' he whispered.

'If I do this, will you take Robbie?' Her eyes were glinting with tears that remained unshed. 'Is that the price?'

'There is no price. Tonight I'm making no promises, setting no conditions,' Roger ran his thumb across her cheekbone, wiping away the evidence of tears. 'Do this for us alone. Because we both want to. There's nothing to be gained from pretending otherwise.'

She was already loosening her braid as he led her to the stairway.

Chapter Seventeen

A different man awoke where Roger had slept. He'd woken with other women in his arms, but always after a night of entertaining acrobatics that had satisfied him to some degree or other and demonstrated his skills to the woman in question. He had been as good as his word, making no attempt to seduce Lucy. They had done nothing more than hold each other and kiss. Oh, but how they had kissed, with passion so deep and heartfelt it made him quiver to think of it.

She had cried in his arms while he held her and bit back unexpected tears of his own. He had comforted her and relished the feeling of being needed and wanted. Whereas he would once have scorned such behaviour as hours wasted, he did not consider them anything of the sort.

True, he had not satisfied his craving to discover what sort of lover Lucy might be—and he carried so much pent-up desire that he was certain he would explode if her hand so much as brushed against him—but he had never before woken already counting the hours until the next night where he could repeat the experience. He knew instinctively that he would never again be satisfied to pass a night with a woman he cared nothing for. He would be satisfied by no one but Lucy.

He should be leaving to meet Thomas, but Lucy was asleep, lying in the crook of his good arm with her foot hooked over his, and he had no inclination to move. At rest, her face was untroubled by any of the cares she had spilled out to him lying in the blackness. She, too, was fully dressed, but Roger was aware of every limb, soft swelling and beguiling curve of her body where it touched his. He pulled the blanket higher, cocooning them in warmth. He shut his eyes until he felt Lucy beginning to stir, then craned his head and watched her eyelids flicker as she woke. Her hands moved beneath the covers as she checked her clothing.

'You're wearing everything and behaved perfectly modestly.' Roger tried to ignore the stinging implication that he could not be trusted. 'Do you think you sleep so soundly that you wouldn't notice me doing anything? I gave you my word and I kept it.'

She relaxed. Roger wrapped an arm around

her back, rolling to face her until their eyes met. He began to kiss her, at the same time sliding his hand down to rest in the small of her back. Instead of the eager warmth she had shown the night before, she twisted her head to escape his lips and drew back.

'Don't pull away from me,' he entreated, her withdrawal cutting into him like a knife.

'I told you last night that I would stay with you for one night only. It's morning now.'

Roger pulled her closer until her head rested against his chest. 'I know. I was only thinking that we are here in the warm, Robbie appears to be sleeping and once you leave this room you won't return. Can you look me in the eye and tell me that spending the night in my arms meant nothing to you?'

'What does it matter what it meant? It can't happen again. I won't risk having a baby.'

Roger laughed softly. 'Oh, dove, there are other ways to please each other. Things lovers can do which won't result in a child.'

'What do you mean?'

'How many men have ever made love to you?'

'You know how many!'

Her eyes narrowed. Roger put a finger to her lips.

'I asked how many had *made love* to you, not

bedded you? Did that oaf who fathered Robbie ever take time for more than a quick grind up against a wall?' He hated to even bring Harpur to mind.

She looked confused, which was all the answer Roger needed.

'I thought not. You have a whole body to experience pleasure with, and I have plenty of ways to give it. Hands, lips…' He paused and slipped his hand down to her waist. She gazed back with an expression of curiosity that sent him weak. 'What you were going to do yesterday, for example, has anyone done that for you?'

She shook her head, mouth falling open in astonishment and a pink flush rushing to her cheeks. 'Is that even possible?'

Roger took her hand and kissed the soft mound at the base of her thumb before applying his teeth gently. As he ran his tongue lightly in a circle over her wrist where the pulse thumped she moaned softly. A throb of lust pounded through Roger. It was so acute, bordering on painful, that he could barely breathe.

'Your heart is racing,' he murmured, moving his lips higher up her arm, sliding the sleeve of her dress aside to allow him access to the smooth, cool skin beneath. He guided her hand to his heart and held it there. 'So is mine.'

Lucy slipped her hand under the open neck

of his shirt and pressed the cool tip of her finger over the scar she had left him with the poker. Her nails grazed his chest, tipping him to the brink of control.

'You made me yours when you branded me,' he murmured.

Why had he not recognised earlier that they belonged with each other? He had squandered his efforts on trying to seduce her for a quick moment of pleasure rather than trying to win her heart. Oh, the hours that could have been spent showing her he was worthy of her love beyond a casual tumble between the sheets! He knew deep in his heart that Lucy was the last and only woman he would love.

'Those things you mentioned, have you done them with your other lovers?' Lucy asked. He heard the undisguised curiosity in her voice and a touch of jealousy, too. The mention of previous women was enough to bring his body back under his mind's control.

'Most,' he admitted. 'But last night when I held you in my arms it meant more than all those times combined.' He laced his fingers between hers. 'I wish you could have seen the man I was before I met you.'

'I don't know that I would have liked you,' Lucy said cautiously.

Roger's jaw tensed. 'You'd have hated me. But you would understand how much knowing you has changed me. Made me better. I remember scorning your brother for...' He shut his mouth, remembering that in Lucy's mind it had been he who had seduced and bedded Katherine Harpur.

'Marry me.'

His words astonished him as much as they did Lucy. Her eyes hardened.

'Don't toy with me, Roger.'

She threw back the bedclothes and climbed out. She began to run her fingers through the knots of her hair, pulling at them with an aggression that must have stung. 'How could a woman like me possibly be the wife of a knight?'

An outrageous idea struck him; that he could stay with her here and the pretence that she was his wife need not be a falsehood. Would he trade his name and rank to become an innkeeper's husband? Perhaps that would convince Lucy that his devotion was as true as he claimed.

'If I could stay here...' he suggested, sitting up.

'You can't and you won't.' Lucy smiled sadly. 'You won't abandon your responsibilities or your family, not even for me.'

Roger threw himself back on the mattress. Once he might have done something so rash and irresponsible, but he was no longer that man. He dismissed the idea with painful regret. As much as he dreamed of leaving Hal to inherit their father's title and lands, such a thing was not possible. He could not be the cause of any more disappointment and misery to his father than he had already been. He didn't know the answer, but now the idea was in his head there had to be one. Was it beyond the bounds of respectability that he could take Lucy with him as a wife rather than a mistress?

'Go find Thomas and finish what you need to do,' Lucy commanded. 'I'll put Robbie out to play with the chickens and empty the cart. I want to oil the window linens while the weather is fine.'

She left the room. Reluctantly Roger pulled on his boots and cloak and went downstairs. Lucy was sweeping the ashes from the hearth. She paused when she heard his footstep.

'Be careful. I don't want you to get hurt. Either of you.'

'You'd care if I died. That's something at least,' Roger said with a grimace. He knelt at her side by the fire with the pretext of striking the flint. 'But not enough to be my mistress?'

'You know the answer to that.'

Roger pressed the flint into Lucy's hand and left, pondering the misfortune of falling in love with a woman who knew her own mind so well.

* * *

Fine rain hung in the air. Roger followed the directions Lucy had given him along the line of the stream, feeling vaguely guilty that Thomas had spent the night in the damp while he had been warm and comfortable with Lucy.

With each step he found his mood becoming more serious. If fortune was on his side—which he had no reason to believe it was—Thomas would have brought his horse and belongings. The saddlebag containing his clothes and his share of the prize from his time in the Northern Company would be his once more. He would pay Lucy what he owed her and more besides to ensure that she would never struggle to survive.

The clearing was deserted, but a bundle of clothing piled beside a crumbling well and the remains of a small fire indicated someone had been sleeping there. Roger approached cautiously. Sweat broke out across his body as he realised the clothing was in fact a figure.

Thomas was face down, one arm twisted below his head, the other at an angle to one side. A hefty branch beside the boy's head revealed the weapon that had been used to strike him.

Roger gave a soft moan of despair, thinking of the sorrow Lucy would feel at this discovery. He sat back on his haunches, looking at the place Thomas had met his lonely end. He was so absorbed in regretting the destruction of such a young life he was unaware he was not alone until he felt breath on his neck and the kiss of a knife against his throat.

'I knew you weren't far away, Mister Danby.'

The voice was slow, the accent thick, from even further north than Roger. No one who had heard the slow, lumbering tones could ever forget Gilbert Seaton. If it had been this man on the hilltop that day, the mystery would have been solved in a stroke.

Roger turned his head as far as he dared with the cold blade pressed beneath his ear. He looked at the giant Northumbrian he had not seen since he had left the Northern Company after the division of spoils. Now Roger knew what matter the business related to.

'You're a long way from the Northern Company, Gilbert. I take it you are responsible for Thomas's death.'

Roger felt pain as the knife twisted slightly in Gilbert's hand and nicked his ear. Not more than a scratch, but enough to warn him to keep his tongue still.

'He ain't dead yet. Where is it?'

'Where is what?'

Another flick and more pain, this time stinging Roger's cheek.

'Don't try fooling me. He tried to keep it from us,' Gilbert growled. 'He'll wake soon and then I'll be askin' him again.'

'I have no idea what you mean,' Roger said. The reference to more than one assailant was a worry he would have to deal with later. 'Whatever you think I have—or Thomas has—you're mistaken.'

'Your friend cheated us,' Gilbert said, his voice harsh. 'The contract was simple—equal shares for all who fought. We want what is ours.'

Roger held his hands to the side to show he was unarmed. His legs were starting to ache from maintaining his position and if he did not move soon he would find himself unable to take action if the chance arose. He edged his head away, but the knife followed, the tip of the blade pressing deeper against his windpipe.

'Is it at the inn? Perhaps the woman knows.'

Roger's stomach constricted at the mention of Lucy. His skin grew clammy with terror.

'What woman? What inn?'

The bluff was pitiful and Roger knew it. Gilbert sneered. He flicked his wrist and for the third time Roger felt the blade. Another sting on his cheek followed by a trickle of blood. He flexed his hands, feeling the inequality between his left and right. If he had a weapon he might meet Gilbert as an equal, might even prevail, but he had not worn even a dagger since arriving at the inn. Without anything he had no hope.

Gilbert cocked a thumb at Thomas. 'His sister. Wilmott's keeping her company. Shall we leave them alone a while longer?'

Roger bit down the nausea that rose within him at the name. Gilbert was seldom without his associate Wilmott: a man who thought a beating with his fists was legitimate foreplay and resistance made the act so much sweeter. It must have been Wilmott who had asked after him on the road. Imagining Lucy alone with the brute made Roger sick to the guts with fear for her. What of Robbie? Was the boy also at Wilmott's mercy? He closed his eyes, bringing Lucy's face to mind.

'I'm going to stand now,' he said, keeping his voice calm. 'Then we're going to return to the inn. I truly don't know what Thomas took, but I'll help you discover it.'

Anything to keep Lucy safe.

'Bring him,' Gilbert said, indicating Thomas with a jerk of his head.

Roger stooped and hefted the boy over his good shoulder. Thomas sighed and slumped against Roger, only half-succeeding in standing. Carrying him back would take all Roger's strength. Strength he would dearly need if he hoped to prevent harm befalling Lucy. As he staggered through the forest, Gilbert's sword in the small of his back, he fervently hoped he was not already too late.

Lucy carried the pot of linseed oil to the table and spread the strips of linen beside it. She methodically brushed the foul-smelling liquid across the window panels, glad that the monotonous task meant she could give free rein to her thoughts of Roger and indulge in fantasies involving the acts he had hinted at. It was just as well he hadn't mentioned *those* the night before or she would never have dared to share his bed. She rested the brush on top of the jar, the fumes causing her head to spin. At least, she tried to blame the oil, but she knew full well it was the memory of Roger's arms about her that addled her senses.

For the first night in her life she had felt cherished and protected and desired. It would never be enough, but she would cling on to the memories long after Roger had left. Part of her yearned to surrender to him, to experience those pleasures in the arms of the man who had captivated her so completely, to take whatever time they had together whatever the consequences.

Could he really remain faithful to her? No, he must marry sooner or later and however he jested, it would never be to a penniless woman who whored herself out to pay her debts.

She stabbed angrily at the linen strips, splashing droplets of her precious linseed oil on the table. She wiped them hastily, knowing how easily they could catch fire if a spark ever came close.

A crash came from upstairs and Lucy frowned. Robbie had refused to play outside in the rain so she had carried his toys upstairs to the bedroom where he seemed happy enough. Perhaps she should bring him downstairs to play by the fire, but while she was using the linseed she preferred him to be elsewhere.

Lucy smiled wistfully, picturing a future where he grew up to be a squire or something equally promising. Whatever else she doubted, she believed Roger when he said he cared for her, so had no fears that he would find a place for her boy.

She had just picked up the brush when there was a soft tap at the door. Hating the way her heart leapt into her throat, she counted a dozen heartbeats before opening it, hoping to see Roger.

'Good morning.'

The swarthy man was one she had last seen on the night Roger had barged into her life. Lucy gasped in alarm. She tried to shut the door, but the man was through before she could react.

'I did not introduce myself last time we met. I'm Wilmott.'

He pushed her roughly and as she fell with a grunt, he shut the door behind him. Lucy opened her mouth to scream, but closed it again. There was no one to help her and it might scare Robbie into coming downstairs.

'I know you're alone. I watched him leave this morning.' He pulled Lucy to her feet, bringing her face close to his until his stench filled her nostrils.

'Was it Roger Danby in your bed that night?'

'Yes!' Lucy smirked defiantly. 'And you never guessed. I saw to that!'

He slapped her, open-handed. She gasped in pain.

'Lying slut! We've been half over the country trying to track them.'

'He's gone now. He won't be back.' It hurt worse than the slap to admit it.

Wilmott grinned. 'He'll be back. My friend Gilbert will make sure of that. Remember him?'

He raised his hand high above his head. The giant. Icy fingers clutched Lucy's chest. Wilmott drew a knife and held it to her breast as he backed Lucy up against the wall beside the hearth. She whimpered as the tip pricked the skin through her dress. Her eyes slid to the poker lying beside the hearth almost within her reach.

'I don't think so.' Wilmott grinned, following her gaze. He drove the poker deep into the flames. 'I'm going to start searching and you're going to stay very still. Every time you move I'm going to cut you. First on the arms, then the face. After that we'll see where else I can find. You don't want that, do you?'

Lucy shook her head, more terrified than she had ever been in her life. She sat where he instructed, hands on the table before her, and watched in hopeless fury as Wilmott ransacked her home, tipping over jars and pots, hurling boxes across the room, even pulling the newly laid rushes from the floor. The precious linseed oil pooled on the table, dripping on to the rushes below. The sparse furniture was overturned and kitchenware strewn about the room. Bowls were broken and the cooking pot tipped to one side on the hearth. The destruction made her want to weep, but Lucy kept her gaze down, barely breathing in case he took it as a cue to begin his torture, wishing Roger would return and dreading the moment he did.

A low whistle came from outside. Wilmott paused in the middle of his search and grinned nastily at Lucy.

'I told you he'd be back.'

Chapter Eighteen

The door opened and Roger entered, supporting Thomas in a dreadful recreation of the first time they had arrived. The hulking figure of Gilbert followed. Lucy had never needed more self-control than it took not to hurl herself into Roger's arms.

'Thomas! Is he hurt?'

'He'll survive.' Roger looked in poor condition himself. Blood welled from cuts on his cheek and trickled from his ear down his neck.

'Good day, Master Danby. Master Carew. You've both caused us a lot of trouble,' Wilmott said.

Roger helped Thomas on to a stool at the table. Thomas groaned. Now Roger was here, Lucy no longer feared Wilmott's threats. She slipped from her stool and knelt beside her brother, examining his head anxiously.

'Wilmott, it's been a long time,' Roger said. 'Your friend tells me you're searching for something.'

'We came here before. This slut said you weren't here,' Wilmott growled.

'Perhaps I wasn't when you came.'

'She had a man in her bed she swore was her husband.' Wilmott stepped beside Roger. 'She took some persuasion today to admit it had been you.'

An expression of cold fury filled Roger's eyes. 'Has he hurt you, dove?'

'Not yet,' Wilmott growled.

'Well, now you know she was lying there's no need. What can I say? She was happy to welcome me there. I can also be persuasive, though admittedly with a little more refinement.' Roger leered at Lucy, an action so unexpected she gasped in surprise.

'How did you find us?' Roger asked. 'Has this fool been leaving a trail all over Cheshire?'

'We lost him,' Gilbert snarled. 'But fortunately we heard Lord Harpur was full of anger at some innkeeper's son who had tried to bed his daughter. He was happy to give me the name of Carew. Seems it isn't a popular one in his household.'

'You told me it was Roger who did that!' Lucy exclaimed.

'I blamed him.' Thomas looked shamefaced. 'I was scared.'

'Why did you let me think that of you?' Lucy asked.

Roger shrugged, looking more ashamed than if he'd truly done the deed.

'It seemed easier to continue the fiction and spare your brother's reputation, seeing as you thought so little of me. What else would a man like me do?'

He sauntered to the counter and righted a cup, pouring a measure of ale, which he knocked back in one go.

'Now my reputation has been restored and the lad's blackened there's nothing more to do here. Let's have a drink and be on our way.' He filled two more cups.

'You're coming with us?' Gilbert rumbled.

Roger gave a charming smile, the sort that he must have given to a hundred women before Lucy. It looked out of place and it struck Lucy that she hadn't seen an insincere expression on his face for days.

'I don't know what you're searching for, but whatever Thomas cheated you out of, he cheated me also. I want my share.'

He sauntered along the counter towards the hearth. 'You've torn this place apart thoroughly.

Whatever you're looking for clearly isn't here so we'll have to search elsewhere. We'll take the lad to show us where to look and what we're looking for.'

Wilmott eyed Lucy. 'What about her?'

Roger shrugged. 'What of her?'

Lucy's eyes filled, blurring the room. She glared at Roger. He met her gaze and held it with the intensity he had shown when he promised unending affection.

'Do you think I'd want to stay somewhere like this?' he asked Wilmott. 'Why, there isn't even a decent fire to warm me on a cold morning.'

He moved closer to the fire, prodding the poker deep.

'Did you think I cared for her because she took me into her bed? Don't you know my reputation?' He regarded the room, slicking his hair back from his face. 'I'm Sir Roger Danby, the man who has swived his way round half of France and most of England. I break hearts and ruin reputations. Can you imagine me falling in love?'

He looked at Lucy, unblinking.

'Can you imagine me lying awake, burning to be in the arms of a woman such as this one? My thoughts filled with nothing but her, hoping, wishing, praying that she might love me in return but knowing that I was undeserving of such a treasure?'

His tone was mocking, but his eyes never left hers. Lucy nodded slowly, answering a question that had not been asked aloud. Roger dropped his hands to his side.

'Could you imagine what I would do for a woman I loved, if I found such a woman? A woman worth dying for if necessary.' He whipped his head round to face Wilmott, his eyes blazing. 'And could you imagine what I would do to the man who hurt her?'

He reached behind in one fluid movement, grasped the poker and spun it around. Before Lucy could cry out in warning he lunged towards Wilmott. Embers tumbled across the hearth. The rushes were still greasy from when Robbie had spilled the lamp oil and small flames began to flicker along the dry stalks. Wilmott hurled himself across the table, lunging at Lucy as the poker came down beside him, sending sparks flying. The linseed oil ignited, streaming across the table in a river of flame. Wilmott shrieked as his sleeve caught.

Chaos erupted. Roger hurled himself on to Wilmott, reaching for the knife that had dropped from his hand. Foul smoke began to fill the room, seeping into lungs and eyes. Lucy ran towards the stairs, but was seized from behind by Gilbert who pinned her arms by her side. She squirmed wildly, beside herself with desperation to get to Robbie. The flames that had taken hold of the rushes grew higher, deadly fingers stroking Lucy's skirts as she flailed. She screamed.

'Thomas, get her out of here,' Roger cried.

Her brother roused himself and began to attack Gilbert with the leg of the stool. The large man dropped Lucy and raised his arms over his head, running for the doorway. Lucy beat at her skirts, ignoring the pain in her hands. Through watering eyes she saw Roger and Wilmott locked in a deadly wrestling match, raining blows on each other. The table tipped. Lucy watched, horrified, as both men lunged for the knife that had fallen to the floor. They scrabbled among the rushes, which ignited as the linen strips fell to the ground. Roger yelled in pain as one flapped against his hand and he shook it away. She thought she saw him gain possession of the weapon, but could not be sure because at that moment Thomas seized her by the waist and dragged her out of the building. He dropped her on the damp ground and turned on Gilbert, who was coughing and retching, and began kicking him in the stomach. Instantly Lucy ran back to the building. Roger met her coming out, colliding with her and knocking her sideways.

Blood ran down his cheek and his eye was swollen. The knife in his hand was red to the hilt. Lucy pushed herself to her feet and ran for the door.

'The flames are too fierce,' Roger cried, grabbing her tightly by the arm. 'We need to get water if we're to save anything.'

'Robbie's upstairs,' Lucy screamed, scrabbling to push past Roger.

Without another word Roger spun and vanished inside, the door slamming behind him.

'Help me over here,' Thomas cried. Lucy tore her attention from the door to where her brother was still pummelling Gilbert.

'Let him go,' she cried. 'Help Roger. He went back after my son. We have to put the fire out.'

Thomas looked from the giant to the building.

'There's no sense in us dying, too.'

Lucy dropped to her knees, his words gutting her. Smoke billowed from the window where she had removed the linen shutters. Thomas spoke sense. Following Roger inside would do no good, but she could not lose them. Either of them.

'I don't care. Go to the stream or you'll live to regret it.'

Roger stumbled towards the stairs, eyes streaming. He had to pick his way through the rushes that were burning fiercely in clumps, growing larger as he watched. If only he had known Robbie was upstairs and that his makeshift weapon would lead to such catastrophic consequences. The fire was the result of his ill-conceived attempt to overpower Wilmott. What else could he have done though, with Lucy at risk?

He leaned one-handed against the wall, clutching his aching ribs. Each lungful of the greasy smoke made the next breath harder to draw. He took the stairs two at a time.

Robbie was absorbed in his game and squealed in alarm when Roger entered the room. The cat streaked out between Roger's legs, causing him to swear in surprise. Robbie backed into the corner.

'Robbie, your mama wants you to come with me,' Roger called.

Robbie blew a spit bubble and picked up his toy. 'Hoss!'

'I know. It's a lovely horse.' Roger held his hand out. 'Let's go play with it outside. Would you like me to teach you to ride a real horse one day?'

Robbie stuck his bottom lip out, looking obstinate. Roger's chest tightened, with panic as much as from the smoke. If he failed to get Lucy's son to safety, he would not be able to live with the guilt. He was prepared to grab the boy forcibly if necessary, but there was no need. Holding his precious toy horse, Robbie toddled to Roger who knelt and held his arms out. With a trust that would leave Roger overwhelmed whenever he thought back to it, Robbie climbed on to his lap and put his arms around Roger's neck.

'It's very hot downstairs. Take a deep breath,' he whispered in Robbie's ear.

As an afterthought he pulled the blanket from the bed, wrapping it around Robbie, and headed downstairs into the ever-thicker smoke. The heat hit him like a fist and he reeled, head spinning. Robbie began to wail in fear, scuffling against Roger. Roger pulled Robbie's head closer on to his chest. There was nothing to be gained by delaying. The cat clawed at the door, yowling in terror. Lucy waited on the other side, relying on him to carry Robbie to safety.

Ignoring the pain as fire licked his legs, Roger thundered across the room and pushed his entire body weight against the door. It refused to open and it took Roger stomach-churning moments of panic to recall it opened inwards. He dragged it back. The cat vanished outside and Roger was faced with Thomas and Gilbert bearing buckets of water that they flung into the room.

He pushed past them, hurling himself outside to draw fresh air into his aching lungs. Through eyes that could barely focus he held Robbie out to Lucy. He felt the child taken from his arms. Relieved of his burden, he dropped to his knees and fell forward. Face down in the dirt, Roger allowed himself to slip from consciousness, no longer caring if he lived or died.

When Roger next became aware of anything it was that he was no longer lying face down. He opened his eyes, but saw only grey and began to panic as he imagined a life condemned to darkness. He tried to speak, but his throat was dry and the only sound that came out was a rasping, heaving retch. For some reason this resulted in cool hands seizing his face and pulling his head upward. He blinked and understood that the greyness filling his vision was Lucy's lap. He felt himself lifted, clutched to a warm bosom. With difficulty he reached his hands out, fumbling for Lucy with a need that was too great to articulate. He heard a sob and something wet splashed his cheek, stinging the cut.

'Is it me you're weeping over, dove?' he asked gruffly. His eyes finally began to obey his demands. Lucy's face was twisted, her eyes swollen from crying.

'Of course it is! I thought you were dead!'

'Does that matter to you?'

Lucy sagged down beside him, her hair brushing his cheek. In one arm she clutched Robbie as if she would never let go, but the other found room to pull Roger to her.

'How could you even ask that? If you had died so would I.'

The cuts on his face and ear stung, his shoulder ached and his hand was ablaze with agony, but Roger smiled through the pain. His throat was parched and he licked his dry lips. He craved water, but instead Lucy's lips were pressing themselves against his as she kissed him with a frenzy that took Roger's remaining breath away.

He was vaguely aware of Thomas and Gilbert rushing back and forth with buckets, but could not summon the strength to aid them. He reached his arms around Lucy and Robbie, holding them both within his embrace, and they lay sprawled on the earth, three together, as he wanted it to be for the rest of his life.

Some time later a voice demanded to know what Lucy thought she was doing, dragging Roger away from paradise. Thomas was red-faced with outrage.

'You have some explaining to do first, lad,' Roger growled. 'I've guessed most, but I want to hear it from you. Get on with it before I tan your arse.'

Thomas looked rebellious, but a sharp word

from his sister had him confessing to theft from the profits of the Northern Company.

'You always were a thief!' Lucy exclaimed. 'What did you do with it?'

'I hid it in the brewing shed, on the rafters.'

'You ruined my batch!' Lucy exclaimed. 'It was full of dust!'

Roger laughed weakly at her indignation over such a minor matter. He had even noticed the difference in the two ends of the beams, one freshly dusted and the other encased in cobwebs, but had not understood the significance.

'Better show us what you've got.'

Thomas rushed off. Roger pulled Lucy closer.

'Marry me. I asked you before and I'm asking again. I won't accept a "no".'

'I'm not rich enough to be your wife.'

'I don't care about that. I'll take you in the clothes you stand up in and nothing more. It's you I want. Come with me to Yorkshire as my wife.'

Lucy looked sceptical. 'We barely know each other. Is such a short time enough to decide we'd suit each other?'

Roger took her hand, circling his thumb in the palm. He knew her well enough to recognise the slight shiver she gave as evidence of the same desire he felt for her.

'We'll have a lifetime to get to know each other. I know this now—my life is better for having you in it. *I'm* better for having you in it.'

Lucy clutched his hand tightly. Roger never discovered if she would have accepted because at that moment Thomas returned. He knelt beside Roger and revealed a small box. Gilbert joined them as Thomas opened the box. Roger and Gilbert swore. Lucy gasped.

'What are they?'

Roger tipped the contents into his hand. Three gold rings and the broken links of a heavy bracelet, all studded with matching blue stones, glinted in his palm.

'Sapphires, I think!'

'Those are mine,' Gilbert growled. 'They belong to the Company. They should have been divided along with the other spoils.'

Roger closed his fist. He wondered who the original owners had been before they had died at the hands of the Company. He'd gladly hurl them into the sea rather than dwell on the fate he might have been party to, but that would not bring back their previous owners.

'Your friend is dead. Your companion who attacked me on the road died also. This is your compensation.' Roger flipped the smallest ring towards Gilbert who caught it. He lowered his voice. 'Take it and don't come back unless you want me to send you to join them.'

With a snarl at Thomas, Gilbert lumbered off.

'What about my share?' Thomas asked, his eyes never leaving Roger's hand.

'You have your life!' Roger snapped. 'And Lucy's inn.'

He reached for Lucy's hand and put the remaining rings and bracelet into it.

'These are for you. They should more than pay what I owe you for my board and lodging, though nothing I have can repay the debt for saving my life. And for making me the sort of man I should be.'

Lucy stared at the jewels, open-mouthed.

'I can't take these!'

'Yes, you can. They belong to no one else.'

Thomas began to protest, but Roger cut him off. 'For the trouble you've caused, you're lucky I'm not going to horsewhip you from here to London.'

'Roger, he helped save your life. Does he deserve nothing for that?' Lucy admonished.

'And I still have the message for Hugh Calveley,' Thomas added. 'I kept it safe.'

'You didn't even manage to deliver it!' Roger exclaimed. 'I still have to traipse all over Cheshire after everything else I've endured! Why do you deserve anything?'

Lucy put a hand on his arm and looked at him reproachfully with the cool eyes that made his pulse quicken. She held her palm out before him. Left to him alone the boy would get nothing, but when faced with such entreaty...

Roger sighed inwardly, wondering if Lucy would always be able to raise his conscience with a single glance. He tugged one of the links free from the broken bracelet and held the stone out to Thomas.

'Here. It's yours. You can return to the Northern Company if you choose, or stay here and learn to brew. Perhaps your sister can give you some ideas if you ask her nicely.'

Lucy was still staring at the remaining jewels.

'They should buy you whatever sort of life you want. Respectability is easily come by when you're rich.'

He watched her eyes drift to plans he could only imagine and which he did not like to contemplate for fear they did not include him. When she straightened her back and glanced towards the inn, Roger threw caution to the wind.

'It would be a handsome dowry. No husband could ask for more.'

'You mean you, I suppose!' Lucy put her hands

on her hips and stared at Roger indignantly. 'A fine suitor to give me such a gift, then demand it back!'

Roger gazed at her in rapture. What other woman would accept a gift in such a manner? The forthright, belligerent Lucy he loved. Life with her would never be serene and he wanted nothing less. He grinned, then grew serious.

'With any man you choose. Or none if you'd prefer. You could walk away now and no one would prevent you.'

'No one would prevent me.' She ran a finger across the sapphires, eyes taking on a faraway look again. Roger bit his lip. The choice had to be hers to make, but waiting was agony. Determination filled him and he could bear it no longer. He pulled her into his arms and brought her face close to his.

'I wouldn't presume to prevent you going, but if you leave me the sun will go out of my world, my heart will beat for nothing. I'll spend my days and nights thinking only of you and regretting not telling you now that I love you. You're richer than I am now. There's nothing I have that you need…but perhaps there is something you want.'

She raised her head and he saw in her eyes that the desire she had tried to hide was now fully visible for anyone who cared to look. And Roger cared very much. He put his lips close to her ear, speaking only for her to hear.

'It would make a good heirloom, too, to pass on to any children we had. Any more besides Robbie, I mean.'

Lucy glanced at her son, who was lost in the world of his toy horse.

'I'll treat him as my own,' Roger promised. 'He'll never want for anything. He can be a squire, or a knight, or whatever he chooses to be.'

'And what of me?' Lucy asked. 'How do I know you will stay true to me? That I'm not just a passing whim? That you won't do to me what you did to others and what John Harpur did to me?'

Roger had no answer, no proof beyond the sensation of his heart being bound to Lucy's by the all-consuming love he felt for her.

'I'm nothing like the men who have hurt you! Or at least, I don't want to be any longer.' He pulled Lucy's hands back into his. 'You said some harsh things to me yesterday. Now I think of it, you've said harsh things to me from the moment we met, and every one of them was deserved.'

'Yes, they were!'

Roger gave a soft laugh, the skin at the corner of his eyes crinkling in amusement.

'That's why I need you, Lucy. I am not good, or selfless, and I've done so many things that shame me deeply, but I'm a better man for knowing you and I can be better still. I want you in my life.'

'You need me! You want me to marry you in order to make you a better person?'

Roger lifted Lucy's hands and held them to his lips, bowing his head over them. He looked into her eyes.

'No. I want you to marry me because I love you.' He drew her close. 'I told you I did not regret what happened with Joanna, but it was not entirely true. I did not realise I cared for her. I didn't value what I had until it was too late. I've regretted that mistake ever since.'

She looked like she was about to cry. 'Why are you telling me this?'

'Because by the time I realised what she was worth I had lost her. When I think of her now, she's eclipsed every time I look at you. I won't make that mistake a second time. I care for you, Lucy. I love you more truly and more deeply than any woman I have known or wanted. I mean to have you and to keep you. Each day with you will be one day more than I could hope for and one less than I crave. On my deathbed I know that my greatest regret will be our time together being at an end.'

Lucy rolled her eyes, though her mouth twitched at the corner. 'That sounds like poetry! Not what I would expect of you.'

'Do I disappoint? Very well, no more fine words. Let me ask you a question—did you come to my bed last night only so I would help Robbie or because you wanted to be with me?'

'Both.' She looked at him. 'I'm scared of how I feel when I'm around you. How you make me feel. If I let myself trust you and you betrayed that, I don't know if I would survive that pain. I know my heart isn't at risk if I stay here.'

'Is your heart at risk with me?' Roger asked.

She bit her lip and looked away. Roger's heart soared. She cared for him as deeply as he did for her.

'Then I believe we're on an equal footing because the thought that you might leave me is more terrifying than any army I've faced, any arrow I've dodged. Come with me.'

'You've burned my house down. I have precious few options!' Lucy said, though her eyes smiled.

'The building is sound. You could repair it and work with Thomas if that's what you choose,' Roger replied. He took a deep breath to quell his rising fear that she would do so. 'If you don't want me, say the word and I'll walk away now. I'll go back to the Northern Company and you'll never have to see me again.'

He pulled himself to his knees, but was almost bowled over as Lucy flung herself into his arms with a cry, burying her head against his good shoulder.

'Don't leave!'

He steadied himself, wrapping his arms around her and tilting her back so he could see her face.

'Is that a yes?'

'It's a yes,' she agreed, reaching up to kiss him.

It was some time later before Roger's lips were unoccupied and he could speak.

'I'm staying in England for good. Once I've delivered the message to Hugh Calveley I'm going back to Yorkshire. I can't promise you what kind of welcome we'll receive. My father may cast me out or spit in my face, but I intend to start my life again and I'd like you by my side.'

'We both have pasts that we regret,' Lucy pointed out. 'But we can have a fresh start together. Let's build a future worth having.'

There were still uncertainties in Roger's life. Perhaps it was not too late to repair the damage he had done to his family. He did not know, but he no longer thought about it with such dread. As he bent his face to Lucy's and began kissing her again, one thing was absolutely certain in his mind. Whatever happened he would not do it alone, but with the woman who was returning his kiss with mounting passion.

He'd do it with the woman he loved.

Epilogue

It was a month before they arrived in Wharram.

With no desire to stay in the inn until it was repaired, Lucy, Robbie and Thomas accompanied Roger to Lord Calveley's house. The message from King Edward was delivered and the requested troops agreed upon. Calveley promised he would himself ensure payment was sent to the two messengers: wealth enough for one man to begin repairing an inn and for another who was adding a wife and child to his household.

They parted ways at Lord Calveley's house: Thomas to Mattonfield and Roger and Lucy to Yorkshire.

Hal's face was stony as he greeted Roger at his house in York, his infant daughter in his arms.

'It's been a long time. We thought you might be dead.'

'Thought or hoped?' Roger asked.

'Never believe that,' Hal said with more warmth than Roger felt he deserved.

It was Robbie who proved to be the unwitting diplomat. He walked to Hal and Joanna's son who played with an enviable collection of wooden animals before the hearth and threw himself down to play. The two mothers followed.

'Is the boy yours?' Hal asked.

'Not by birth, but he's mine to raise,' Roger answered. 'There's another child I need to visit, too, isn't there?'

Hal raised his eyebrows, then nodded, surprised approval showing in his eyes.

And that was the first battle won.

Despite Roger's entreaty, Lucy refused to marry without the blessing of Lord Danby. As the two families travelled to Wharram, Roger reflected on the vexation of loving a strong-minded woman.

'It's frustrating indeed to love someone who refuses to commit to a date, isn't it?' Joanna said archly.

Roger grinned. Joanna regarded him thoughtfully. Unsurprisingly, she had proven less willing to forgive than Hal.

'You nearly tore us apart, but Hal says you also pushed him back towards me. I don't trust you, but I'm willing to be proven wrong.'

She gave him a slight smile and took herself

off to sit in the cart with Lucy and their children. Roger could only hope they were talking of the three children and Joanna's swelling belly, and that by the time they reached Wharram Lucy had not heard enough to put her off marrying him entirely!

They arrived at the red stone manor house in Wharram around mid-afternoon. Roger paused at the door in trepidation. He felt Lucy's hand slip into his and squeeze tightly. At his other side Hal put a reassuring hand on his shoulder. Roger gave each a smile, then entered alone.

Lord Danby was sitting beside the fire with his wife. Lady Danby gave a cry of astonishment, rising from her chair at the sight of her son.

'Is that Hal?' Lord Danby asked.

Roger knelt before his father. Lord Danby was greyer and thinner than before, but exuding the vitality he always had.

'I'm Roger.'

'My son!'

His father's sightless eyes filled with tears. Roger's own grew moist. Lord Danby reached a hand to Roger's cheek, before raising him to his feet. Any lingering doubts Roger entertained that he would be welcomed home vanished in his father's fervent embrace.

Lucy was introduced and approved of, the marriage blessing was given and the family feasted that night in a peaceful atmosphere. Some matters were discussed, others alluded to and dropped by common consent. Roger gave a selective account of his time in France, preferring to emphasise his accomplishment at delivering the King's message and the subsequent reward.

'So you found your fortune, my son,' Lord Danby remarked as the three men sat at the table, a bottle of good wine to hand.

Roger glanced towards Lucy, who was sitting by the fire, Robbie drowsing against her breast. His heart swelled with love for her and hopes for their future together.

Lord Danby could not see where he looked, but Hal did. A look of understanding passed between the brothers and Roger knew that all was going to be well.

'Yes, Father,' he said. 'Yes, I did.'

* * * * *

If you enjoyed this story, you won't want to miss these other great reads from Elisabeth Hobbes

*FALLING FOR HER CAPTOR
A WAGER FOR THE WIDOW
THE BLACKSMITH'S WIFE
THE SAXON OUTLAW'S REVENGE*

MILLS & BOON®

& HISTORICAL

AWAKEN THE ROMANCE OF THE PAST

A sneak peek at next month's titles...

In stores from 5th October 2017:

- **Courting Danger with Mr Dyer** – Georgie Lee
- **His Mistletoe Wager** – Virginia Heath
- **An Innocent Maid for the Duke** – Ann Lethbridge
- **The Viking Warrior's Bride** – Harper St. George
- **Scandal and Miss Markham** – Janice Preston
- **Western Christmas Brides** – Lauri Robinson, Lynna Banning *and* Carol Arens

---

Just can't wait?
Buy our books online before they hit the shops!
www.millsandboon.co.uk

Also available as eBooks.

MILLS & BOON®

EXCLUSIVE EXTRACT

Spy Bartholomew Dyer is forced to enlist the help of
Moira, Lady Rexford, who jilted him five years ago.
He's determined not to succumb to her charms *again*,
because Bart suspects it's not just their lives at risk—
it's their hearts…

Read on for a sneak preview of
COURTING DANGER WITH MR DYER

Bart longed to slide across the squabs and sit beside
Moira, to slip his hands around her waist and claim her
lips, but he remained where he was. If he could give
her all the things the far-off look in her eyes said she
wanted, he would, but he wasn't a man for marriage and
children. To take her into his arms would be to lead her
into a lie. Deception was too much a part of his life
already and he refused to deceive her. 'I'm sure you'll
find a man worthy of your heart.'

'I hope so, but sometimes it's difficult to imagine,
especially when I see all the other young ladies.' She
picked at the embroidery on her dress. 'I don't have
their daring, or their ability to flirt and make a spectacle
out of myself to catch a man's eye.'

'You may not make a spectacle of yourself, but you
certainly have their daring and a courage worthy of any
soldier on the battlefield.'

This brought a smile to her face, but it was one of
embarrassment. She tilted her head down and looked up

at him through her eyelashes, innocent and alluring all at the same time. 'Now I see why they only allow male judges on the bench. No female judge could withstand your flattery.'

'Perhaps, but a man is as easy to flatter as a woman, one just has to do it a little differently.'

She leaned forward, her green eyes sparkling with a wit he wished to see more of. 'And how does one flatter you, Bart?'

He leaned forward, resting his elbow on his thigh and bringing his face achingly close to hers. He could wipe the playful smirk off her lips with a kiss, taste again her sensual mouth and the heady excitement of desire he'd experienced with her five years ago. Except he was no longer young and thoughtless and neither was she. He'd experienced the consequences of forgetting himself with her once before. He had no desire to repeat the mistake again, no matter how tempting it might be. There was a great deal more at stake this time than his heart.

Don't miss
COURTING DANGER WITH MR DYER
By Georgie Lee

Available October 2017
www.millsandboon.co.uk

MILLS & BOON®

Why shop at millsandboon.co.uk?

Each year, thousands of romance readers
find their perfect read at millsandboon.co.uk.
That's because we're passionate about
bringing you the very best romantic fiction.
Here are some of the advantages of
shopping at www.millsandboon.co.uk:

* **Get new books first**—you'll be able to buy
  your favourite books one month before they
  hit the shops

* **Get exclusive discounts**—you'll also be
  able to buy our specially created monthly
  collections, with up to 50% off the RRP

* **Find your favourite authors**—latest news,
  interviews and new releases for all your
  favourite authors and series on our website,
  plus ideas for what to try next

* **Join in**—once you've bought your favourite
  books, don't forget to register with us to rate,
  review and join in the discussions

Visit **www.millsandboon.co.uk**
for all this and more today!

Join Britain's BIGGEST Romance Book Club

50% OFF your first parcel

- **EXCLUSIVE offers every month**
- **FREE delivery direct to your door**
- **NEVER MISS a title**
- **EARN Bonus Book points**

Call Customer Services
0844 844 1358*

or visit
millsandboon.co.uk/subscriptions

* This call will cost you 7 pence per minute plus your phone company's price per minute access charge.

BKCB3